D1523864

A Corpse in the Condo

M.K. Dean

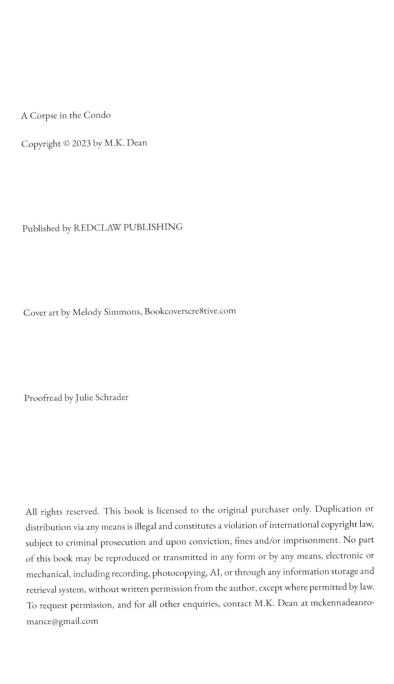

A Corpse in the Condo

Copyright © 2023 by M.K. Dean

Published by REDCLAW PUBLISHING

Cover art by Melody Simmons, Bookcoverscre8tive.com

Proofread by Julie Schrader

Contents

Chapter One

I SWEAR, IF OUR road trip had lasted just thirty minutes longer, I would have been forced to commit sororicide. That's the act of murdering your sister if you didn't know, and if you knew my sister, you'd hand me a hammer.

Older than me by three years, Liz was everything my mother had hoped for in her daughters—and everything I was not. I'd never seen Liz less than impeccably turned out, transitioning from corporate businesswoman to soccer mom with astonishing ease. Always the right outfit for every occasion, with matching lipstick and appropriate, tasteful accessories. Case in point: she sat in the passenger seat looking like an ad for a fun-filled week at the beach, wearing a fluttering white cotton blouse over canary-yellow capri shorts and powder-blue espadrilles that showcased her perfectly tanned legs.

The chunky blonde highlights expertly added to her cinnamon-brown hair brought out the blue in her eyes; coloring she'd inherited from our father. Motherhood had added generous curves to her petite frame. For the trip, she'd tied an expensive scarf over her hair and wore cat's eye sunglasses that probably cost as much as my car payment. Like always, she'd turned heads when we stopped for gas.

Next to her, I felt like the giant from *Jack and the Beanstalk*. I'd inherited my mother's bright red hair, currently cut in a pixie, freckles that coalesced to mimic a tan, and muddy green eyes the color of the local duckpond back home. I'd gotten my height from my dad, standing a good six inches taller than my mother and four over Liz. My basic uniform was a T-shirt and jeans. I had an absolute gift for picking the wrong shade of lipstick and usually skipped makeup altogether. I put on sunscreen every morning because otherwise I'd burn to a crisp. Since I work with animals, my jewelry tends to be minimal and plain. The last thing I want is for some puppy to catch hold of a dangling earring.

The odd man out in the Reese family, the hulking Amazon, the tomboy who'd chosen horseback riding lessons over dance class, I'd gone into veterinary medicine instead of becoming a "real" doctor. I'd also chosen my profession over raising a family, having grown up with parents who tried to do both—with us kids losing out. I wondered how successfully Liz balanced her job as a graphic artist for an ad company with her demands as a parent. Not a question I'd ever ask because Liz would never admit that her life wasn't perfect, even if she was on the verge of a nervous breakdown. Perfect was Liz Grant's brand.

I'd recently inherited a large sum of money through no merit of my own, so although I could now match Liz's square footage house-wise, it wasn't without baggage—namely, guilt that I was now well-off and living in a small town where most people struggle to make ends meet. The unexpected legacy from my friend, Amanda Kelly, meant I didn't have to work another day in my life. I wasn't so sure how I felt about that.

It took Amanda dying for me to realize that I didn't have many friends, and it took my house burning down to realize I needed to work harder at the fractured relationships in my life. Inviting Liz to join me on this trip was meant to be a step in that direction.

What had I been thinking?

Liz jumped at my invitation with an alacrity that had surprised me, but who turns down a free week's trip to the beach? Yet from the time I pulled into her driveway, I knew my offer was a mistake, starting with her obvious dismay over the fact that my dog, Remington, was in the backseat of my car. It went downhill from there. My car was dirty and hairy (thanks to said dog). My taste in music leaned toward "angry screaming women" instead of the country music she preferred. There wasn't enough room for her five-piece matching luggage set in hot pink.

And so on.

"You look like a movie star," I told her with a tight smile, rolling the windows back up again once the worst of the dog hair had blown out of the car. German Shepherds shed a lot.

"You look like you're going to a sci-fi convention." She pulled her shades down with one finger to give me an assessing stare. "Aren't you a little old to be wearing graphic T-shirts?"

"If I'd wanted snarky comments about my appearance or general self-worth in life, I could have invited Mother to come with me instead."

Well, *that* shut Liz up. She pulled a tablet out of her voluminous bag and began reading with a simmering silence that was all too familiar. I let that ride for a bit, but then put on my peacemaker hat and asked how her kids, Lindsay and Olivia, were doing in school.

Liz accepted the olive branch and thawed enough to tell me about Livy's performance as a fairy in the school play and Lindsay's science fair project. She warmed to her theme and spoke at length about the desire to get both girls enrolled in an exclusive private school, where they would receive an outstanding education. Not to mention, opening social doors that would benefit them later in life.

"I dunno. We didn't go to private schools and turned out okay."

"It's a wonder we got into college at all, coming out of that Podunk school in Greenbrier." Liz's voice was darkly prophetic, as though it weren't too late for disaster to befall us. "Say what you will, but Mom was the best thing that ever happened to her students. She made sure they got the strongest education possible under the circumstances."

I internally bristled at the dig at our hometown, a burg on the Virginia-Carolina border so small that it barely qualified as a township, but kept my mouth shut. What I remembered about my mother's tutoring was the late-night flashcards and an impatient parent who couldn't understand why her daughter struggled with math. But I said nothing and let Liz chatter on about her hopes for my nieces.

Catching up on her family news ate up a good dozen miles. Some families gab on the phone together at least once a week. Not the Reeses. Holidays, birth announcements, and funerals were more our speed. We're just not that close a family, you know?

On my side, the topic of conversation was somewhat juicer. Not unexpectedly, the murders in Greenbrier this past spring and summer both horrified and fascinated Liz.

"I'm surprised someone hasn't made a documentary yet."

"Or at the very least, changed the town name from Greenbrier to Murderville," I agreed.

"What's this I hear about Joe Donegan coming back to town? According to Mom, he nearly railroaded the two of you off to jail."

"He did no such thing," I said stiffly, concentrating on the road in front of us instead of turning a burning glare on my sister. "He was doing his job as sheriff, which meant he had to rule us out as suspects. Regardless of what Mom told you, she didn't help matters one bit. If anything, he had to be harder on us so no one would think he was giving me special treatment."

Which had been challenging, given the two of us had dated in high school.

"Uh-huh." Liz's noise of agreement was anything but. "Then why did you end up poking your nose in things? And almost getting killed in the process, I might add."

"You had to have been there," I said shortly, increasing my speed a little so that I could get out of this car as soon as possible before I brained her.

"So how much money did you inherit, anyway?" She spoke with an archness that made my teeth ache.

Oh, now we were getting down to it.

I hedged, giving her the answer I'd given everyone else who had asked. "To be honest, I don't know the exact amount."

"Don't be ridiculous." Her tone was such a close match for our mother's that had we been talking on the phone, I'd have been hard-pressed to tell the two apart. "You must know how much money that artist friend of yours was worth."

I'd learned the hard way to avoid using the word *estate* when referring to Amanda's bequest. For friends and neighbors who lived paycheck to paycheck, the term was like waving a red flag in front of a bull. The less I said about this inheritance, the better. "In addition to the house in Greenbrier, there's the condo we're checking out, which she listed as a vacation rental property to pay the mortgage when she wasn't using it. I'm paper rich, but cash poor."

Naturally, I would have loaned Liz money if her family needed it, but I wanted to open a vet practice in Greenbrier. Every time I tried to formulate a business plan, the cost of opening a clinic was enough to give me a heart attack. I'd also inherited Amanda's stock in her father's company, but it was in deep financial trouble. With one breath, my new financial advisor cautioned me to hold on to the stocks because someone might buy the company, and then the stock will be worth something again. With the next breath, he said that it was very likely that if they couldn't find a buyer, my stock would be worthless. Amanda's artwork and merch from her shop were currently bringing in money, but at some point, that resource would dry up without new inventory.

"You're keeping the house in Greenbrier, I take it."

If only she knew how much she sounded like our mother. I would *not* grind my teeth. "Since my old place burned down, it only makes sense."

"I thought Mom said some developer wanted to buy it. Offered a ridiculous amount of money, too."

I hunched forward behind the wheel, conscious of the press of traffic all around us. "That's not what Amanda wanted."

"Well, it seems silly to me for you to stay in a big house all by yourself when you could find a nice little place in town."

Her implication being that as a single woman without children, an apartment would be plenty of room for little ol' me. I couldn't let that slide. "As for my being in that big house, I'm not alone. I have Remy and Ming. Not to mention there's room to keep the horses there and a place to ride them."

I'd inherited Ming the Merciless from Amanda as well. The senior Siamese had attacked Amanda's killer in an attempt to defend his mistress. No one in their right mind would mess with a pissed-off Siamese. Sadly, even a ferocious cat had been no match for Amanda's murderer.

Liz huffed a little, unhappy she failed to get a reaction she wanted. Then she shot me a sly smile. "What's this about Joe sleeping over at the new place?"

Gah. I knew the rumor mill had been working overtime on that one. If I chewed the inside of my cheek any harder, I'd make it bleed. "One night. He stayed in the guest room one night. It was a temporary situation while tying up the most recent murders. He's building a house out near Potter's Mountain, but it's not finished. It was easier for him to stay over that evening than to drive out to his homestead."

Especially when he hadn't even laid the foundation for the house yet. Joe lived in a camper on his property while he tried to build his house. When he got home from his day job of being the new sheriff, that is.

"And you're telling me nothing's going on between you?"

Oh, there was something, all right. Something that occasionally sparked like a current leaping from a faulty outlet to the nearest metallic surface, threatening to electrocute anyone in its path. But so far it consisted mostly of memories of the heat between us when we were teenagers and flickers from my current imagination.

"I hate to disappoint you." I let the dryness of a martini infuse my voice. Maybe she would take the hint.

"I hear he's as hot as ever." Liz fanned herself playfully.

For the briefest of moments, I could picture him in a series of mental snapshots. Joe, dressed in a blue-checked shirt and leather chaps, removing his Stetson to wipe the sweat from his brow as he led his horse into the barn. Joe, wearing his sheriff's uniform, the dark brown material molding itself to his body like an Armani suit. Joe, in jeans and a tight T-shirt, oozing charm as he leaned in the doorway as though his bones had been removed and the jamb was the only thing holding him up. Joe, smiling as he ruffled his young cattle dog's ears.

"Well?" Liz asked with a cloying sweetness that set my teeth on edge. "Is he?"

"I suppose so." I refused to be baited by her.

My relationship with Joe ended the day he drove out of town, brushing the dust of Greenbrier off his boots along the way. That had cut deep, even though I'd known intellectually we'd go our separate ways after high school. When you receive an injury that hamstrings your heart, you make darn sure to protect that organ again in the future. I would never open myself up to that kind of hurt again.

I changed the subject. "Thank goodness it's not too much farther from here. I'm not sure this drive is worth it."

Liz turned her face toward me, dark lenses blacking out her eyes and hiding her expression. "What do you mean?"

"I mean making this drive for a week at the beach. One of the reasons I'm coming down here is to decide if I should keep the place or sell it."

"Sell it?" Liz's voice rose an octave. "You're kidding me, right?"

"Liz, I've been on the road since six-thirty this morning. What was supposed to be a six-hour drive has been closer to eight because of the traffic delays. How often will I make this trip? I doubt I'll come down here more than once every couple of years."

"It might be six hours for you, but it's only three for me. Do you have any idea how much a week at Hilton Head costs for a family of four?"

"No, but I have a feeling you're about to tell me." It was hard to tell whether my grip on the steering wheel was due to the increased flow of traffic or the expectation of what was about to come out of my sister's mouth.

"Over seventy-five hundred dollars during the height of the tourist season. Of course, now that it's after Labor Day, the rates won't be as high, but there are lots of people who enjoy going to the beach in the off season."

I couldn't help it. I gasped. "For a *week*? Are you kidding me?"

Liz shook her head. "Nope. I priced it when you invited me to come. I thought seriously about bringing the girls with me, but they're back in school, and you said this was going to be business trip of sorts."

It became obvious now why Liz had been annoyed that I'd brought Remy. My dog got to go on our vacation when her kids had to stay home.

"That's crazy. Why on earth would it cost so much?" Weird to think I now owned a place I couldn't have afforded to rent this time last year.

"It's a small island with a reputation for exclusivity. It has its own airport and plenty of golf courses. Most of the properties are inside gated communities, even the tourist places."

"By all means, let's keep the riffraff out," I murmured.

Liz had heard me, despite the quiet voice. Must be a mother thing. "It's fine for you to take that sort of stance, but you hate Myrtle Beach because it's such a tourist trap, right?"

"I hate Myrtle Beach because beaches and someone with my complexion aren't a good combination in general. I have to put on sunblock with SPF 2000 just to go to the grocery store."

"I keep telling you, try going to a tanning booth." Liz gave the perfectly golden skin on her arm a pat. "That would give you a nice base to start."

"There's a reason tanning beds look like coffins, you know."

Liz ignored me and continued to crunch her imaginary numbers. "So, let's say you can get a decent condo in Hilton Head for around 250 K. If you put down 20 percent, you'll need a thirty-year mortgage for two hundred thousand. Leaving off taxes and homeowner's fees for the moment, your monthly payments would be around fifteen hundred a month. If you rented out the condo, just during the tourist season, at five thousand a week to keep it simple..." She paused while she did the math, and then turned to me with her mouth hanging open. "Ginny, that's eighty thousand dollars for just four months of renting the place. It pays for itself and more. Extend your rental season, and you can pay off the mortgage early. It's making you money while you still get to enjoy a nice vacation whenever you want it. You'd be *crazy* to let it go."

"Oh heck. Some things are starting to make more sense now." A sinking feeling lodged itself squarely in my gut.

"What do you mean?"

Taking both hands off the wheel to rub my face would be a mistake. I kept my gaze firmly fixed on the road ahead. "I've been having problems with the property manager who's in charge of the condo. We've been going back and forth for weeks now, first by email and then on the phone—that is until he simply stopped responding to my messages."

"What kind of problems?"

"He's been extremely uncooperative in general. I tried to avoid coming down here at all, but Laney Driver—she's the agent in charge of Amanda's collection—wanted me to confirm the presence of some of Amanda's paintings for her inventory and catalog assessment. I asked the manager, Jeff Brinkman, to do that for me, but he made a big deal about not disturbing the renters. Then I had to tell him to cancel all the remaining rentals until the probate was sorted, which he didn't like by half. He kept saying these people wouldn't have a place to stay and the rent money could just go into escrow until I took possession."

"Well, he has a point. For a lot of these places, people book their stays a year in advance."

"So he said. But with everything in limbo, I couldn't see continuing to rent the place out. Anyway, our interactions became more contentious, and he stopped returning my calls."

The possibility that Brinkman had never canceled the rentals and was pocketing the fees had occurred to me, which would explain why he'd been so adamant about my not coming down. That was exactly why I'd chosen to drive down on short notice.

At last, the sign on the side of the interstate ahead listed the mileage to our actual destination. Farther than I'd hoped, but the end was in sight. Relief made me add, "Besides, why hang onto a place that I'll probably never use? Especially when I could put the money into building a nice vet clinic?"

"In Greenbrier?" Disbelief and scorn raised the pitch of Liz's voice another notch. "Is that the best use of your money? Anyway, I thought that chain bought Doc's old clinic. Do you really think Greenbrier needs two vet hospitals?"

"The people of Greenbrier need a choice between spending top dollar for vet care they can't afford or going without." I had the same argument with our mother at least once a week. "If anyone's going to lose business in Greenbrier, it will be Champion Veterinary Corporation, not me."

Liz made an audible sniff. "You mark my words. They'll be grateful at first, but then when you don't slash prices to the bone or give away your services for free because you have 'all that money,' your clients will end up resenting you."

"Mom said pretty much the same thing. She thinks I should relocate where no one knows I inherited anything."

Liz shot me a wry grin. "Don't you hate it when she's right? Anyway, hedge funds are buying up all the housing properties, just like chains are buying up all the vet clinics. You'll never be able to afford to buy something like this condo again. You should hang on to it."

"Not to mention, it would make a nice vacation spot for your family."

"Something like that."

"Well, I hate to break it to you, but the condo isn't on Hilton Head."

"What?" Liz's head snapped around so quickly I expected to hear vertebrae crack. "Then why tell me that's where we were going?"

I shrugged, keeping an eye on a sporty red car zooming up on my left. "Because everyone knows about Hilton Head. The condo is actually on a little island I've never heard of. Berry something. I've got it. Hartberry Isle. I remember now because it reminded me of blackberries. Apparently, there are hundreds of these barrier islands."

Liz already had her phone out and was doing a search. "I'm not even seeing it listed...oh!"

"Oh, what?" I asked, sparing a glance at her.

"Oh, it looks like it's a *very* exclusive community." She continued scanning her screen, flicking through the information with a flick of her finger.

"Exclusive?" That made keeping a condo there sound even less attractive. "I didn't realize that. All I know is that it's just beyond Hilton Head."

Liz kept reading aloud. "Hartberry Isle is about six miles long, with over fifty miles of bicycle and hiking trails. There's a ferry that can take you to Hilton Head for day trips—"

"Yes? And?" I added when Liz broke off.

"There's no land bridge to the island. There's a small airport and helipad on the island, but otherwise, the only way across is by ferry."

"What?" I had visions of schlepping Liz's luggage behind me in the ninety-degree heat and it wasn't pretty. Remy and I would both melt. "That can't be right."

"It says right here." Liz tapped the screen and then hissed when doing so changed pages. She hurriedly went back to the previous image.

"No direct road to the island. We're supposed to drive to Hartberry Station—that's a small town on the coast—and take the ferry across."

"Huh. I see why Amanda wanted a place out there now. She was a wildlife artist, and she loved peace and quiet."

"She's not the only one." Excitement sharpened the pitch of Liz's voice, and she fluttered a hand in front of her face. "Hartberry Isle is a secret getaway of the rich and famous!"

"Not so secret if it's on the internet," I muttered as our exit came up.

Liz looked up from her phone when we left the interstate. "The rich probably have themselves flown in. Hey, there's the sign for the marina!"

We followed the road over a long bridge spanning a marshy body of water, down to a moderately sized marina filled with a variety of boats of all sizes parked at slips.

"There."

Liz pointed through the windshield at a weather-beaten sign that read, "Hartberry Isle Ferry."

After I dropped a shocking amount of money on tickets, we killed time in the shade, eating ice cream and waiting for the ferry to return. At long last, the ship chugged into sight and slowly maneuvered up to the dock. Few people got off and even fewer waited to board. I handed over my keys to the attendant to park my car, and then Liz and I took Remy to the passenger deck. He panted in the humid heat, despite getting his own cup of soft-serve ice cream, so instead of going to the rail, we opted to take seats inside the cabin.

When we approached Hartberry Isle, I realized with shock that I'd seen this very view before. The red-and-white lighthouse on the point, the choppy waves, the wheeling of seagulls overhead, the colorful display of boats on the water. Amanda must have sat on this ferry and painted this view at one point. When the ferry drew closer to the island, it became apparent the island marina was quite significant in size.

"I guess if you don't fly in, you come by boat," Liz said, echoing my thoughts as the ferry lumbered into the harbor and up to the wide dock that would allow the cars to disembark.

It took almost another thirty minutes before my car was brought forward. I put Liz in charge of navigation, and she entered the address into her phone's GPS. We drove down the main thoroughfare running the length of the island. Instead of stoplights, the roads had traffic circles, which took a little getting used to managing.

"Sand Dollar Cove is that way." Liz pointed to the sign I'd just seen, and I swerved into the lane that would allow me to exit the circle. The person behind me laid on his horn in a prolonged expression of annoyance.

Liz scrabbled at the dashboard as I whipped through the traffic circle. "Don't you know how to drive?"

"Hah-hah," I said, mentally wincing at the other driver's fury. "We don't have roundabouts in Greenbrier."

"You should. Dave says—"

I expected Liz to finish her sentence, but she abandoned the conversation suddenly. On our left, we got glimpses of the ocean between the hotels and private communities. They all had cute "beachy" names like Prickly Crab Hideaway and Snowy Egret Dunes.

"There," Liz said with satisfaction, at the same time the GPS announced our destination was on the right. The entrance to Sand Dollar Cove took us through a wooden privacy fence into a lot marked with signs saying, "FOR RESIDENTS ONLY." The development proved to be a small collection of condominiums within easy walking distance of the beach. The property itself looked as though it was well-maintained, save for the giant pots of wilting flowers at the entrances to each building. You'd think for the amount of money people spent there, the least the management could do was water the plants. Or choose something more heat resistant.

I parked the car at the first building and turned off the ignition with a sigh of relief. "The website description said there were four units on each level and three floors altogether. Amanda's condo should be in this building on the third floor. Number 1301."

"Oooh, I bet it has an ocean view. You can charge more for that." Liz craned her head to peer up at the building from her side of the car. "I hope there's an elevator."

"At this point, I'll settle for indoor plumbing." Remy tried to barrel out of the car when I opened the driver's door, but I told him in no uncertain terms to stay put until I could open the back and clip his leash on. Being sable, rather than the usual black and tan, he often was mistaken for a coyote or a wolf by those not familiar with the range of German Shepherd coloring. He sprang out at my command and gave himself a full body shake before dragging me over to the nearest scrubby bush to relieve himself. I could sympathize. My legs are long, but as soon as Remy was done, I did a short little shuffle toward the first building with embarrassing haste.

"You should have gone on the ferry," Liz admonished as she hefted one of her suitcases out of the back of the car.

"Thanks, Mother. Next time I will."

I hadn't thought about using the restroom on the boat, having spent the entire ferry ride admiring the view. Now the need was impending. I hurried up to the building's main doors.

"Hey!" Liz called out after me. "Aren't you going to bring up anything from the car?"

"Later," I said over my shoulder. "I need to find a bathroom *now*."

"I'm not carrying your bags in!"

Had I been one of her children, I'd probably have turned around and stomped my way back to the car. Instead, I rushed into the building and made straight for the elevator. Normally I'd take the stairs, especially with a big dog like Remy, but the last leg of our trip had pushed my bladder to the bursting point. I leaned heavily on the UP button, pressing it several times for good measure. When it arrived, I bundled Remy into the elevator.

The doors opened onto the third floor. As we came out of the elevator, a door farther down the hall swung wide and a couple exited one of the units. The woman dragged a suitcase on wheels, arguing with the man following her. As we got closer, I heard her say, "I don't care how much we paid for this trip. I won't stay here another minute longer!"

I kept Remy in a heel position as she flounced past, while her partner gave me an apologetic glance when he trailed behind carrying his luggage.

Unit 1301 was ahead on the left. As we approached, Remy lifted his head and scented the air. A second later, I became aware of a nasty, fetid odor. Worse than anal glands. Worse than fish lying out in the sun all day. The reek grew stronger the closer we got to the condo.

It came from Amanda's unit.

"Oh, no." I took a firmer grip on Remy's leash as I turned the key in the lock.

It had to be a wild animal of some sort. A possum or a raccoon. I needed to check it out before Liz made it upstairs. She'd freak out if she knew something had died in our unit. I'd identify the source of the smell, take a quick run to the bathroom, and we'd call maintenance for cleanup.

Still holding tight to Remy, I turned the handle and pushed open the door. Gagging convulsively, I stumbled back out of the unit with my arm covering my nose and mouth, dragging Remy with me when he would have dashed in to investigate. I pulled the door shut just as Liz stepped out of the elevator, hauling two of her five bags behind her, her hair hanging in damp locks around her scowling face.

"Why are you still standing out here?" She demanded as she walked up. Screwing up her face, she added, "What's that horrible smell?"

"Call 9-1-1. There's a corpse in the condo."

Chapter Two

"I CAN'T *BELIEVE* THERE's a dead body in our unit," Liz wailed as we went back downstairs. She rolled her luggage into the elevator behind us, thumping it over the threshold to the lift.

The nearly eight-hour road trip had fried my last nerve even before we'd stumbled upon a reeking corpse. An ice cream cone at the marina hardly made up for missing lunch, and it looked like we were going to miss dinner as well. I might have been a little short with Liz as a result. "The odor alone should have been proof enough."

"Maybe the rest of us aren't all that used to finding dead bodies. What's this, your third since the beginning of the year?" Liz snapped as the elevator doors opened.

"Don't remind me. Where do you think the manager's office is?" I glanced around the lobby. "You'd think it would be here someplace."

"Down there." Tucking her sunglasses into the neckline of her blouse, Liz pointed toward a sign that hung over a door on the other side of the foyer.

We marched into the small office, where a pimply-faced guy in his twenties with limp brown hair sat behind a counter watching television. His slumped shoulders and caved-in chest, combined with the unfortunate soul patch on his chin, reminded me of Shaggy from

Scooby-Doo. He glanced up when we came in, only to leap to his feet as we approached the desk.

"Hey!" He pointed to a sign over his head before glowering at us. "No pets in the office."

"Oh yeah?" This day had just about pushed me to my limits. "I'm guessing no dead bodies in the units, either."

"*What*?" What little color he had leached from his pale skin. "What are you talking about?"

I slapped my key down on the counter. "Unit 1301. We just arrived. Dead body on the living room floor."

He snatched the key up to peer at the number. "That's impossible. Unit 1301 isn't available right now. The owner is dead." He looked up and stammered. "I mean, not dead as in dead *today*, but dead as in murdered this spring." He muttered an abortive curse and added, "Not here. She wasn't murdered here! She was an absentee owner. Anyway, all renters have to come to the office to be checked in and given keys for their stay. You shouldn't have this key."

He glared at us with suspicion as he clutched the key in his fist. "And no dogs in the office!"

"Let me handle this." Liz shoved her suitcases against the counter and put a restraining hand on my arm when I tried to grab the key back. "Young man, we're aware that the former owner of unit 1301 is dead. You're looking at the *new* owner of that condo."

"The new owner?"

If I'd thought he was pale before, he went bleach-white now.

"Yes." Liz shot me a smirk as if to say, *see how easy that was?* "So, we have every right to be here."

"Unlike the dead body in our unit upstairs." When he jerked his attention back to me, I added, "I need to use your restroom."

He opened and closed his mouth several times, making a glugging noise. The resemblance to a guppy was remarkable. It took him a few seconds to process my request. Finally, he pointed to another sign on the wall and repeated the words on it. "No public restrooms. You'll have to go to one of the restaurants down the street."

That tore it.

I reached across the counter and grabbed a fistful of his T-shirt, hauling him forward until we were nose-to-nose. "I have been on the road since six-thirty this morning. I'm hot, hungry, and tired. The dead body in my condo has obviously been there for quite some time. I don't know what kind of place you're running here, and at the moment, I don't care. I can't leave because the police are on their way. I need to pee right *now*."

"Ma'am." Wide-eyed, the clerk risked a gentle tap on the back of my hand and pointed to a closed door when I continued to glare. "Bathroom's over there."

I let go of his shirt. He sagged back to his former position. I gave Remy a "down/stay" command. My dog dropped to the floor on his stomach with a flattering speed. We'd been working on his obedience training and it was paying off. I hurried into the bathroom and slammed the door behind me.

When I came out, Remy started to rise, but then remembered he was supposed to stay put until I released him and slowly sank back to the floor. I walked over to Remy, patted him on the shoulder, and said, "Okay."

He leaped up as if on springs and bounced in a circle around me. I asked him to settle, and he let out a long-suffering sigh and laid back down on the cool tiled floor.

"Better?" Liz asked in that arch tone of hers.

"You have no idea." I faced the clerk, who'd taken his seat behind the counter again, looking a little green around the gills. Immediately, remorse for being a jerk washed over me. "I'm sorry I was so rude just now. We'd come all this way to check out the unit, and then to find a body..."

"And you *had* to pee," Liz said out of the corner of her mouth.

"Can we drop that now?" I hissed at her, before turning back to the clerk. "I'm sorry I lost my temper. Finding the dead person was really upsetting."

"I know you." His tone held a faintly accusatory note. "You're that lady who's been giving Uncle Jeff a hard time."

I winced at that. "Look, I'm sorry we got off on the wrong foot—"

"No, I'm right, aren't I? I heard him tell you there was no need for you to come down. He had everything under control."

"Hardly," Liz interjected with a grimace. "If the body in 1301 is anything to go by."

The young man had been building a head of righteous steam, which deflated at the mention of the corpse.

"Do you—" The clerk broke off and swallowed hard. "Could you—"

I guessed what he was trying to ask. "Er, decomposition was pretty advanced. I couldn't tell much from the quick glance at the body before I locked the unit again."

"What I want to know is how someone didn't pick up on this before?" The accusatory note in Liz's voice suggested management should have been aware of the problem. "Didn't you get complaints?"

The clerk passed a hand over his mouth. "No. I mean, yes. I mean, someone complained about a smell on the third floor, but the beach is right across the street, and stuff washes up there all the time. There's also an inlet that runs behind the development. Someone saw a gator there last week. It's not unusual for a kill to raise a stink for a few days around here."

"You get alligators on the third floor often?"

My sister's drawl had just the perfect amount of sarcasm, but our little clerk didn't pick up on it.

"No, they don't come in the building. You do have to be careful outside, though." He nodded in Remy's general direction. "Don't go around the canals or lagoons with a dog. There're gators, rattlers, copperheads, moccasins..."

Hartberry was sounding better and better all the time.

"Those people on the third floor left just now." I pointed overhead to bring us all back to the subject at hand. "They didn't care how much money they were losing by leaving. Surely, they said something to you before this morning?"

"What people?" Liz frowned for a second before her expression cleared. "You mean the couple getting out of the elevator as I was going up? I thought they were steamed about something."

"The Lewises left?" The clerk glanced out the window behind him at the lot and then shrugged as if it were no big deal. "Well, they were paid through the end of the week, so that's okay."

"I imagine the police will want to talk to them. As well as anyone else who might have mentioned something."

"The police?" The clerk looked around wildly, as though the law might already be there. He lifted the edge of his regrettably grubby T-shirt to blot the sweat from his face, despite the air conditioning in the office.

Liz glanced over at me with lifted eyebrows. When she spoke to the clerk again, it was in a gentler tone. "What's your name?"

"Timmy." The young man blushed and cleared his throat. "Tim Brinkman."

"Are you the manager here, Tim?" I spoke calmly, the way one might to a fear-biting dog.

He turned beet red and shook his head. "Yes. I mean no. I mean, I help out. My uncle Jeff is the manager."

"So, you would be the assistant manager," Liz said in a soothing manner.

Tim brightened and straightened up from his slumped position. "Yeah. Assistant manager. That's me."

"Could we speak to your uncle?" I asked.

"Er, uh, that might be a bit of a problem." Tim grimaced and tugged at an earlobe. "He hasn't been around this week. He sometimes takes off and leaves me in charge for a few days. It's no big deal," he hastened to add. "It's not like there's ever an emergency or anything. This place is usually as quiet as a tomb."

Tim's belated wince indicated exactly when he realized his unfortunate choice of words.

Through the window behind him, I saw a white Dodge Charger pull into the lot with the word SHERIFF emblazoned on the side. I thought briefly of Joe and wished he was the one entering the development.

"Do you have a way to get in touch with your uncle?" I watched as a heavy-set man in a dark brown uniform got out of the lead vehicle and hitched up his pants.

Tim looked doubtful. "I dunno. I have his number, but I'm only supposed to use it in case of an emergency."

Liz closed her eyes and pinched the bridge of her nose. From the way her lips moved, I guessed she was counting to ten.

As gently as possible, I said, "Tim, this counts as an emergency."

"Oh. Right." Tim blinked for a second, then switched off the television and pulled a cellphone out of his back pocket. The ringing of the phone could be heard through its speaker. Tim's forehead furrowed when the phone rolled over to voice mail. Shooting us an apprehensive glance, he stepped back from the counter and turned his shoulder to us to talk. "Hey, Uncle Jeff. It's me, Timmy. Listen, could you call me back? It's kind of urgent."

"Kind of?" Liz was loud enough that no doubt her voice would be recorded as well. "Tim, there's a dead body in our condo and the police are about to walk through the front door."

Tim ended his call and pocketed his phone again.

"When was the last time you spoke with your uncle?" I asked. "How long have you been in charge this time?"

Liz shot me a sharp glance and opened her mouth to speak, but I gave her a slight shake of my head.

Tim put on a thinking face, staring up at the ceiling while he rubbed his chin thoughtfully. "Um, a few days? I mean, a few days in charge, but a bit longer since we talked. He called on Monday and asked me to take over. I've been at the desk since Tuesday."

The door to the office opened, ending any further questioning on my part. The law enforcement officer swaggered into the small area, coming to an abrupt halt when Remy got to his feet. He was a stocky man whose brown hair had been shorn close to his head and his lower jaw jutted out much in the manner of a bulldog. Red stained his cheeks as though he'd been slapped, though I suspected it was merely due to the heat. Remy had taken a tentative step forward, his long tail brushing from side to side, but stopped at the man's tense posture.

"You got a license for that dog, ma'am?" The deputy's hand came to rest on his holstered gun.

"As a matter of fact, I do, Officer." One of the hazards of traveling with a big dog was that you never knew when you were going to run into a stickler for the letter of the law, to put it nicely. I tried not to bare my teeth when I smiled. "License, rabies certificate, and traveling health certificate. My paperwork is in the car. Would you like to see it?"

He seemed taken aback but recovered quickly. "Maybe later. You just be sure you keep him under control. And that's deputy. I'm Deputy Ed Wilson." He fixed a beady eye on Tim. "I thought your uncle had a strict 'no pets in the office' policy, Timmy."

I tapped Remy on the shoulder. When he looked up at me, I gave him the hand signal to sit.

"We had nowhere else to go, Deputy," I said as calmly as possible. "You see, we just drove down for the week, and the body is in our condo. Tim was kind enough to allow us to wait in here in the air conditioning until you arrived."

"Er, that's right," Tim volunteered when both Liz and I gave him a hard stare.

Deputy Wilson hitched at his belt again. "So, you're the ladies who made the call? Think you've found a body, eh?"

The condescension oozing out of his voice, combined with his antagonism toward Remy, put my hackles up. But I knew this type well. He was the salesman who couldn't believe I drove a stick shift and the good ol' boy who didn't think I could handle his pit bull. I tried to temper my response. "I have some medical experience. I know a dead body when I see one. I take it the crime scene team is on its way?"

Wilson snorted. "I'm not going to waste my people's time until we know for sure what we're dealing with. Medical experience, you say? What are you, a nurse or something?"

"She's a veterinarian," my sister huffed.

Wilson got a good belly laugh out of that. "A veterinarian, eh? Well, if I need to have my dog's nails trimmed, I'll certainly call you. As for this nonsense about finding a body, why don't we get Jeff on the phone and sort this whole thing out."

"I tried, Ed—er, Deputy." Tim's face crumpled under the strain of the situation. "I got his voicemail."

"Well, then. You come up with me and we'll take a look around." Wilson nodded at me and Liz. "You ladies can wait here. I'm sure we'll get this sorted in no time."

Tim pushed the key across the desk at Wilson. "Why don't you go without me? I'm not supposed to leave the desk."

Wilson took the key but didn't bother to hide his eye roll as he addressed Tim. "You're the man in charge at the moment. You're coming with me." The deputy tipped his Stetson at me and Liz. "Ladies. This will just take a moment, then I'm sure you can get back to enjoying your holiday."

"What a jerk," Liz said as soon as they'd left the room. She took a seat on one of the orange plastic chairs, her luggage stacked around her as though she were in an airport waiting area.

"Yeah." I smiled despite everything. "Thanks for being offended on my behalf."

"You're my sister. No one can pick on you unless they're family."

I raised my eyebrows at that. To be honest, nothing anyone could say to me was as bad as what I heard growing up, so most insults rolled off my back. Mother would say it was because she'd given me a backbone.

"What was all that fuss about providing papers for Remy?"

"All pets crossing state lines, except for guide dogs, are required by the U.S. Department of Agriculture to have proof of his current rabies vaccination and a valid health certificate issued by a licensed veterinarian within the last thirty days. I keep a folder with Remy's documentation in the glove compartment."

Liz boggled at me. "You're joking, right? How come I've never heard of this?"

"Most of the time, law enforcement isn't such a hardnose about these things. Look, this guy has already shown us he can be a jerk, and he's clearly uncomfortable around Remy. We need to watch our step, or he can make things bad for us."

"I'm not the one who pulled the clerk over the desk by his shirt."

Ugh. She wasn't going to let me forget that lapse in judgment and manners, was she? "Point taken. But seriously, Liz—"

"I'm a PTA mom. I know how to play nice." She pulled out her phone and began scrolling. Without looking up, she added, "Tell me Joe doesn't act like that."

"No, he doesn't." Thank goodness. Come to think of it, though he played the part, Joe was as far from a good ol' boy as you could get here in the South. "As a matter of fact, he's pretty great to work with under bad circumstances." I wished again he was in charge of this investigation, but then shrugged it off. "Fortunately, our part in this little drama won't last much longer."

"Well, I, for one, would like to have a word with Timmy's Uncle Jeff." Liz looked up with the scowl that precedes most requests to speak to the manager. "I'm seriously unimpressed with the way this place is being run."

The notion that the dead body in our unit was somehow the fault of management tickled my funny bone until a sobering thought occurred to me. "You know, it's probably Uncle Jeff in the condo upstairs."

That made Liz abandon her phone to give me her undivided attention. "What makes you so sure of that?"

"Tim's been in charge unsupervised for about four days now. The wilting flowers out front would seem to confirm that. The last time he watered them was probably on Monday. That's also consistent with the—with what I saw upstairs."

I'd started to say "decomp" again but thought better of it. Liz got a strange look on her face just the same.

"What?" I asked, a little bit offended. What had I done to deserve that look? I did my best to avoid triggering subjects ever since a former lover accused me of emptying a Chinese restaurant with my dinnertime discussion of my workday.

"Nothing. It's just odd you would notice the flowers in the first place. Or even think such a little detail mattered. What are you doing?"

I left Remy on a down/stay and went behind the counter. His dark-brown eyes tracked my every move. "Nothing. Just checking to see how full the rest of the complex is right now, being the offseason and all."

I'm not sure what I'd hoped to find as I opened and closed drawers. A mysterious ledger with a second set of numbers? A note from the killer saying, "You're a dead man, Jeff"? The only notebook I found appeared to be a maintenance log. The computer screen showed the complex with available units in green and the rest grayed out. The majority of the units in building one and two were owned outright by private parties, like Amanda's condo, but buildings three through six were predominantly rental units. All of the tenants and residents had to abide by a list of regulations, much like your typical HOA, and the buildings were serviced by the same maintenance crew. Despite being the offseason, most of the complex was booked. Building four looked as though it was currently empty, however, blocked off for renovations. And wasn't that interesting? There'd been occupancy in unit 1301 throughout the summer, despite me asking Brinkman to take it off the books. The last time I checked, there were no listings on the website, so he had to have arranged the rentals himself. Odds were

I wouldn't see a dime of that income because it wasn't supposed to exist.

Remy lifted his head from his paws and tilted it toward the door. I took that as my cue to hustle back to the correct side of the counter and was standing beside him when the door to the office opened.

If Tim had looked a bit greenish before, he was positively the color of pea soup now. Sweat trickled down his face, and he clutched a can of soda with both hands as he staggered over to the plastic chair across from Liz and collapsed into it. He took a careful sip from the can and leaned back against the wall with his eyes closed. Knobby knees poked out from beneath Hawaiian-print board shorts, and his legs ended in red Converse sneakers without socks.

Deputy Wilson came into the office close behind Tim, his presence somehow filling the small space. Instead of pasty white, his face was beet red, and sweat stains showed at his collar and beneath his arms. He spoke into a radio attached to his collar as he entered the room. "Copy that. Scene is secured until the ME gets here. No ID on the vic, yet."

He lifted his brown eyes and met mine in a hard stare. "I'm about to interview the first witness on the scene now."

Chapter Three

DISCOVERING THAT THERE WAS indeed a body in the condo put the deputy in a foul mood and rendered Tim nearly nonfunctional. Wilson wanted to interview Liz and me separately and not in front of Tim, either. The best Tim could offer was the maintenance shed behind the complex, as he couldn't lay hands on the key to the community room. Clearly, from the appalled look on his face, the thought of trying to question us in the sweltering heat of a metal building defeated Wilson.

In the end, he sent Tim out to wait for the crime scene unit and coroner's van to direct them upstairs. Tim was past caring about abandoning his post and walked out of the room with the cold soda can pressed to his forehead.

Wilson reached behind the counter to steal a pen and then took a small notebook out of his pocket and flipped to a blank page. He angled his body so he could lean on the counter while writing and jotted down my name and contact information.

"Sisters, eh?" He flicked a glance between us. "Could have fooled me. And you, Miz Grant. Do you live in Greenbrier too?"

Liz embodied the spirit of our mother as she drew herself up. "No, I'm based in Charlotte, North Carolina."

He took down her information as well. The pen looked awkward in the grip of his meaty fingers, as though holding such an item didn't come naturally to him.

When he'd finished writing, his light brown eyes pinned me as if he'd read my thoughts. The sense of dislike emanating from him nearly made me squirm. Sheesh, it wasn't like I'd put the body in the unit upstairs just to inconvenience him.

"And you came to the island because—"

"I recently inherited the condo. This was the first opportunity I had to drive down and check it out. I invited my sister to join me."

Liz gave a little wave at Wilson, who merely stared back.

"I headed upstairs first—"

"And why was that, exactly?" Wilson broke in with narrowed eyes and a slight smile, as if he knew the interruption would throw me off my stride.

"Er, I was anxious to see the place. I felt the luggage could wait." Even to my own ears, my excuse sounded weak.

"Oh, for heaven's sake, Ginny. Don't be shy. He'll think you have something to hide." Liz rolled her eyes. "She had to pee. Urgently. She didn't wait for me, she just barreled into the building while I started unpacking the car."

"Liz," I growled.

My sister was unfazed. "Ask Tim if you don't believe us. She practically decked him when he refused to let her use the bathroom in here."

"So, you're saying your sister has a violent temper." Wilson nodded as he made notes, the slight smirk growing wider over my sound of protest. "And how exactly did you know the victim, Miz Reese?"

Correcting his form of address wasn't nearly as important as altering his impression I knew the deceased. "I don't have any idea who the dead person is! How could I? This is my first time to Hartberry Isle."

There was a mean little glint of satisfaction in the smile that lingered on his lips now. "Why don't you walk me through what happened when you got here."

"Between driving and taking the ferry, we'd been traveling the better part of the day. As soon as we arrived, I took the elevator to the unit. A couple was leaving with their bags as I reached the third floor. They seemed very unhappy. Before I reached the door to my unit, I was struck by the horrible odor. It occurred to me the smell was why the couple had left."

"And yet you decided to open the door of the unit anyway." Wilson's pen made a sharp staccato sound as he clicked it several times in a row. "Why is that exactly?"

"The odor seemed to be coming from my unit, and I wanted to identify it before my sister came upstairs."

I sensed more than saw Liz's movement out of the corner of my eye. A kind of flinch as the meaning of my words sank in.

"Oh?" Deputy Sergeant Wilson managed to instill volumes of insinuation into a single word. "And why was that?"

I suppressed a sigh. "Because I have a much stronger stomach than she does. I suspected some sort of animal had gotten into the condo and died. You know, like a raccoon. I wanted to see what it was before she came upstairs and freaked out."

"I would *not* have freaked out." Liz was highly indignant.

I turned to her. "You would have insisted on finding another place to stay until the unit could be cleaned. I was just trying to spare you the grossness of it all."

"Well, of *course* I would have insisted on us staying somewhere else. Really, Ginny, it's not like you could throw down a little rug cleaner and be done with it."

"I didn't know there was going to be a dead body in there." Okay, so I'd been afraid that was the case, but I didn't *know*.

Something of my unease must have shown on my face because Wilson latched on like a terrier spotting a rat. "I'm going to need an accounting of your whereabouts for the last...say three or four days."

"You can't be seriously looking at me for this." I gaped at him. "I've never been to this island before today. We just *got* here. You don't even know who the dead person is, let alone when he or she died, or how he died."

"Don't get your panties in a twist, Miz Reese." Amusement twisted Wilson's lips into an unattractive smirk. "This is a purely routine request."

"Didn't you say it had to be the property manager?" Liz frowned as she spoke, as though she wasn't digging a hole for me with every word.

I shot her a look that should have vaporized her on the spot. She had the grace to look sheepish when she realized what she'd said.

"Interesting you came to that conclusion when no one else around here has any idea who the victim might be." Wilson might have smiled at me, but his eyes were as bright and hard as a crow's. "Mighty interesting."

"Just idle speculation on my part, seeing as Tim's uncle seems to be missing." I straightened my spine. "Are you saying this is a suspicious death?"

"All deaths are suspicious until proven otherwise." Wilson clicked the end of his pen again. "Your whereabouts?"

I debated demanding to speak to my lawyer for all of five seconds. But the only lawyer I knew was an estate guy, not a criminal attorney, and then there was the possibility Wilson could decide to hold me for questioning. The thought of leaving Remy in Liz's care—or worse, having animal control come pick him up—made me cooperate. It wasn't like I had anything to hide, anyway.

I pulled up my schedule on my phone for the past three days and read it off to Wilson. Like any person trying to get away for vacation, I'd had to double my workload before leaving town. Honestly, sometimes it doesn't seem worth it to take time off. I rattled off my appointments while Wilson jotted down the names and times. My evenings might have been sadly devoid of anyone able to document my presence, but the distance between Hartberry and Greenbrier was great enough that it was unlikely I could have traveled down and back in time to make the next day's scheduled appointments. I said as much to Deputy Wilson when I finished my recitation.

"Might not have been able to drive down and back, but most folks come to the island by other means." Wilson delivered that statement with a wolfish smile. "What about you, Miz Grant?"

It was eerie just how much Liz looked like our mother when she drew herself up and looked down the bridge of her nose at the deputy, a neat trick since she was still seated and he loomed over her. "You can't be serious."

"Ma'am, I've just pointed out this is what's called a suspicious death. You're a witness, and I need your statement."

"I've already given my statement."

He shut his notebook abruptly. "Are you refusing to answer my questions?"

Liz responded with a perfect replication of my mother's gimlet eye. "Your questions have nothing to do with my witness statement. I'm invoking my right to counsel."

She scrolled through her contacts with haughty precision and poised her finger over the phone when she found the one number she wanted.

Liz had a lawyer in her contacts? Well, I guess I did as well, though I doubted her lawyer was a criminal attorney any more than mine was. She was probably bluffing, which wasn't necessarily a smart move. I had visions of her winding up in the county lockup and our mother sweeping in like the Wrath of God demanding to know why I allowed Liz to be incarcerated.

"Liz—"

"No." She snapped her fingers and pointed at me. "I know my rights. I don't have to talk to the police without a lawyer present. I voluntarily made a statement regarding what I know about finding this dead body—which is *nothing*, as you'd already shut and locked the door by the time I reached the third floor—and this deputy has absolutely no reason to ask about my whereabouts for the last however many days."

Wilson took in a breath so sharp it made his nostrils flare. "I can take you down to holding if you like, Miz Grant."

"On what grounds?" She folded her arms across her bosom and glared.

Seconds ticked by as they locked gazes, but Wilson dropped his glance first. "Have it your way, lady. But we're not done here."

Liz lifted her chin. I knew that look. It was the expression that preceded the summoning of dragons, and I held my breath in nervous anticipation as to what might happen next.

"Are we being detained?"

Deputy Wilson spoke through gritted teeth with a patently false smile. "Detained is such a formal word. The sheriff will likely want to interview you himself when he arrives. Which will take a while, seeing as he's not on the Isle at the moment. Y'all sit tight now."

I wheeled on Liz the moment he left.

"What were you thinking refusing to cooperate like that?"

"Don't you ever watch any television? You *never* give information to the police without a lawyer. You don't let them search your car. Not without a warrant. If they ask you if you know how fast you were going, you say no, you don't. Anything you say can be used against you in a court of law. Or have you forgotten that because your ex-boyfriend is what passes for law enforcement back home?"

"Okay, first of all, I think you're overreacting. Just because I've stumbled onto the occasional murder scene—"

I didn't get a chance to finish before Liz cut in. "Two. You've found two murder victims, which is two more than most people find in their entire lifetimes."

"Fair point." I had to grant her that one. "But for all we know, the person lying dead in my condo died of natural causes. The police *can* toss us in jail for obstructing an investigation, however, and then what would happen to Remy?"

"I'm not going to be railroaded by some local yokel—"

The door opened, and Tim half-stumbled into the room. He went behind the counter without speaking and slumped in his chair.

"What are you doing now?" I asked when Liz began viciously swiping at her screen.

"Looking for another place to stay. Obviously." She rolled her eyes, her finger stabbing through listings as she quickly scanned and dismissed the options.

"Oh, no. We're staying here. We have a perfectly good condo upstairs." I pointed at the ceiling.

"Ginny," Liz screeched. "It's a *crime scene*. Even if the police didn't object to that, I have no intention of crossing the threshold. Ever! Not even after it's been fumigated or whatever they do to clean up after..." She was reduced to waving her hand helplessly.

"I didn't mean the unit where the body is located." Sheesh, Liz must have a low opinion of my sanity. "I mean the unit the Lewises vacated." I smiled triumphantly at her before turning to Tim. "That unit's all paid up, right? So, there shouldn't be a problem with us moving in for the rest of the week."

"The smell—" Liz began.

"Is why no one else will take that rental off your hands." I didn't look at Liz, but instead fixed my gaze on Tim until he gulped.

"I refuse to stay in a condo that *reeks* of death." Liz punctuated her statement by folding her arms across her chest.

"My unit is unavailable for the foreseeable future. The condo next to mine is paid for the week and is currently empty. Remy and I will be fine. If you'd like to arrange accommodations for yourself somewhere else..." I gave a little shrug.

"You were the one who invited me to join you, remember?"

"I'm not dropping—what was it you said? Seven or eight thousand dollars for a room when there's one right here for free."

Tim watched the two of us with such an avid look of interest, I half-expected him to pull a bucket of popcorn out from under his cheap chair and start eating it.

"Fine." Liz all but stamped her foot. "But if the smell is unbearable, I'm out of here."

"Oh, for heaven's sake. It'll be like getting sprayed by a skunk. At first, the odor is awful, but eventually your nose gets used to it."

Liz's brow furrowed and her mouth dropped open as she turned her palms up in disbelief. "Do you even hear yourself right now? No wonder you're still single."

My head snapped up at that, and I started to let her have a piece of my mind when she suddenly shook her head. "I'm sorry. That was uncalled for. I'm just as hot, tired, and upset as you are."

She turned to Tim and held out her hand. "May we have the key to unit 1302?"

Tim reached behind him for the rack of keys hanging on the wall and selected the appropriate key. As he pushed it across the desk toward Liz, he said, "There's a drop box outside for leaving the keys once you're done with them. I'll make sure the Lewises turned theirs in. Wait a sec. I got something for you."

He bent down below the counter, and a metal drawer squeaked as he opened it. After a few seconds, he reappeared, holding out a glass object with a triumphant smile.

"What's this?" Liz said, frowning as she took the familiar item.

"It's one of those plug-in air fresheners," I said helpfully.

Scowling, she snapped at me. "I *know* that. I want to know...oh."

"Yeah." Tim pinched his nose and continued speaking. "You're gonna need it."

"Great," Liz muttered, tugging her luggage behind her as I called Remy to my side and made for the door.

"Hey!" Tim called out. "I thought the deputy wanted you to wait here."

"He won't have to look far." I gave Tim my best smile, the one my mother liked to tell me cost her four thousand dollars to create. "We'll be practically right there on the spot."

He gaped at us, guppy-like, when Liz closed the door behind us.

Chapter Four

DESPITE MY BRAVADO, WE weren't able to get into unit 1302 right away either. The crime scene techs were blocking most of the hallway, and someone in a white hazmat suit, complete with face shield, barred our way.

"Sorry, ma'am. The corridor is off-limits for the moment."

Liz, already annoyed that I hadn't volunteered to haul one of her roller bags myself, lost her cool. "Well, how long is *that* going to take? We want to get to our rooms and unpack."

"It'll take as long as it takes, ma'am." It was impossible to fault the tech's words, but she certainly didn't sound apologetic.

Tail wagging, Remy leaned hard against his collar, eager to try to pull me into the open unit, where all the 'interesting' smells emanated. If nothing else, he wanted to investigate the kits of the evidence collection teams. Their setup reminded me of my on-the-road gear, complete with fishing tackle boxes and utility trunks to store the tools of my trade. I held him back while at the same time fighting a sense of wanting to poke my nose into the process.

Well, not literally. With the open door to unit 1301, the odor was inescapable.

"Several hours, at least," the tech was saying when I yanked my attention back to the conversation at hand.

"What are we supposed to do in the meantime?" Liz raised her head with flared nostrils. "Sit in the office, eating peanut butter crackers and drinking soda? Watch TV with Tim?"

I came to the rescue of the hapless tech. "Is Deputy Wilson around? I'd like to have a word with him."

"No problem."

The tech practically leaped forward to rush into the unit. A moment later, Wilson came out, holding a red bandana over his nose and mouth. He wore booties on his shoes and blue nitrile gloves on both hands. Sweat trickled down the sides of his face and his color was almost as red as the bandana.

"What are you doing up here? Keep that dog out of the evidence. I thought I told you ladies to wait downst—"

I didn't let him finish his tirade. "We're planning to stay next door in unit 1302. Is there any way we can get into that condo now?"

"What part of 'this is a crime scene' do you not understand?" Wilson waved a hand to encompass the entire floor, his eyes bulging slightly with the process.

Sighing wouldn't do any good. "Your technician said you'll be here for hours. You can't really expect us to wait in the manager's office until you're done. You've taken our statements. We'd like to get some dinner. Where's the best place to get calamari around here? Preferably within walking distance but I'm not picky at the moment."

He blinked several times as though he couldn't comprehend what I'd just said.

"Best. Calamari." I enunciated each word in case he didn't understand the question.

"You're interrupting an official investigation into a suspicious death to ask me about *seafood*?" His voice rose on the final note, and though

I hadn't thought it possible for his color to get worse, he turned slightly purple.

I indicated the blocked passageway with my hand. "Since we can't get into our unit, we thought we'd go get something to eat in the meantime. If it's within walking distance, you can rest assured we can't get far because my car will still be in the lot."

"Bennie's Crab Shack is the best around here. I mean, not the best on the island, mind you." The tech's insertion into the conversation was certainly unexpected. "But it's good food at a fair price, and you don't have to dress up to go there."

"Carly." If it was possible to grind up Carly's bones with his teeth and spit them out, I'm sure Wilson would have done so.

"What?" Carly looked blankly at the deputy and then seemed to recall she had work elsewhere. Gathering a couple of sample bags, she hurried back into the open condo.

"Bennie's it is," I said brightly. "Can we pick you up anything, Deputy?"

Wilson made an involuntary grimace at the mention of food and lowered his bandana. "Sheriff Mercer hasn't arrived yet. He's gonna want to talk to you."

"And we'll be available for his questions. We just want to grab a bite to eat." To my ear, the whine in my voice sounded desperate. "You have my cell number. We'll be at Bennie's. Thank you."

From the calculating stare he gave us, I could almost see him weighing the odds of getting a warrant to have us searched before we left and deciding not to place that bet.

I'll never know if it was the "thank you" or the fact he was tired of dealing with us that made him decide to let us go. Perhaps it was because he was out of his depth with this case or that he had more pressing matters at the moment. It didn't matter. Relief washed over me when he finally nodded his head.

"Beat it and leave the car. Don't go far. And be back in less than two hours," he said, dismissing us.

We dropped Liz's suitcases off at the car and walked the five blocks to the bar and grill.

Bennie's proved to be the quintessential crab shack, down to the driftwood-gray siding and ropes joining planks together at the entrance creating a fake pier. It had a worn, sad air about it, though it was doing a brisk business with the dinner crowd. We took a table outside because of Remy, and I immediately had to dissuade him from eating the remnants of crab legs that crunched underfoot. Liz questioned my sudden need for calamari and I explained it was my "test" seafood dish: if the fried squid and tangy dipping sauce was good, odds were I'd enjoy the rest of the menu.

The calamari lived up to its recommendation and the rest of the food was decent as well. The presence of pool tables inside the dark building, where patrons focused on their game with fierce concentration, told me Bennie's catered to the local crowd more than tourists. Although I blended right in, Liz stood out like a hot house plant in the nursery section at the hardware store back home.

I wasn't sure what worried me more, the fact Liz knocked back three glasses of wine while we sat under an umbrella outside or that she didn't seem very much affected by the consumption of so much alcohol.

We'd grown up in a teetotal home, but I knew Liz liked the occasional glass of wine as much as I did. When I expressed concern over needing to keep a clear head to speak to the sheriff, Liz snapped, "Oh for pity's sake. You're not Mom. Besides, I'm on vacation."

I let the subject drop.

The sun started to slant across the buildings as we left Bennie's to walk back to Sand Dollar Cove. Remy's enthusiasm for being in a new place had waned under the damp heat. A nice thing about the island having no direct land access was that car traffic was limited. I caught glimpses of the sea between the businesses on the coastal side of the road and was tempted to skip going back to the unit for a long walk on the beach. Unfortunately, I had neither the right clothes nor shoes for such a venture, and the thought of Sheriff Mercer sending out a team to hunt us down quashed the plan.

The parking lot was still full of law enforcement vehicles as we entered the development.

"You don't think the body is still...you know..." Liz flapped a hand in the general direction of the third floor.

"Lord, I hope not." I shaded my eyes to scan the lot. "I don't see a coroner's van, so if we're lucky, they've come and gone."

Liz drifted toward the car, but I stopped her. "No point in getting the luggage just yet. Not until we know for sure they're going to let us in our rooms."

"Ugh. I hate this." Liz followed me up the short flight of steps and into the lobby.

"It doesn't make my day either," I said.

Two men in brown uniforms stood in the lobby as we entered, and for a split second, I thought one of them was Joe. No such luck. The tousled dark hair and trim physique accounted for the mistaken identity, but a second glance disabused me of that notion.

I needed to stop thinking about him. Joe, that is.

I wasn't the only one. Remy perked up and leaned on his leash, tugging me forward so he could greet the two men, only to hesitate when he realized they weren't friends after all.

One of the deputies stepped forward with an outstretched hand, as though to prevent us from heading to the elevator, but not so close that Remy could get to him. "I'm sorry, ladies. I can't let you go upstairs just now."

"We were here earlier. Ginny Reese and Liz Grant. We found the body. I believe Sheriff Mercer wanted to speak with us?"

The two men exchanged a glance and the dark haired one took a step back to activate the radio on his shoulder. "Sheriff Mercer. The witnesses are back from dinner."

I couldn't quite make out the reply, but it sounded as though he said, "I'll be right down."

The dark-haired man gave a nod to his partner, who said to us, "If you'll wait right here."

Neither deputy seemed inclined to talk as we waited. Remy, bored with the inaction, yawned and sprawled out on the cool tile.

Liz leaned toward me to whisper loudly, "So do you really think it's what's-his-name? The property manager?"

"Brinkman. Jeff Brinkman." I glanced over at the deputies, but they were busy scrolling on their phones and didn't seem to be paying attention to us. "And no, I don't know if it's Brinkman lying in our condo, but it seems awfully suspicious. Who else would have been in the unit?"

Liz nodded as if that made sense to her. "And then what? Had a heart attack? Dropped dead and no one realized?"

"Let's hope so. That would be the best possible outcome, really." I flinched at my own words. "I mean, not for the dead guy, but in terms of our getting access to the condo in the time frame we have here."

"The deputy seemed to jump to the conclusion of foul play pretty quickly."

"Deputy Wilson might have seen something I didn't." It was childish of me, but I laid extra emphasis on the *deputy*. Next time he called me Miz, I'd correct him. All ideas of petty revenge vanished when I finished my thought. "Something that made it clear that it wasn't a natural death."

Liz frowned with great concentration, as though I'd said something silly she couldn't quite make out. "Like what?"

"I don't know. A bullet hole? The back of his head caved in? I didn't get too close."

Liz wrinkled her nose and fanned her face. "You don't have to be gross about it."

That was the problem with lay people. You never knew what their comfort level with a medical discussion might be. Nothing I'd said struck me as particularly gruesome, but there you are. I gave her a wary glance and realized her cheeks had grown quite pink. I hoped it was from the heat.

The light over the elevator finally came on, and the doors slid open. A tall, muscular, blond man in uniform stepped out and strode toward us. His sandy-reddish hair was cut short on the sides, left longer on top, and a darker beard neatly framed his square jaw. Biceps that could only have come from a gym bulged out of the short brown sleeves of his uniform.

"Yowsa. He could lock me up anytime." Liz gave me a pointed nudge with her elbow.

Just what I needed. A slightly tipsy sister about to be interviewed by the law.

"Don't say anything to get the police mad at us, okay?" I leaned to one side to whisper at her.

She mimed putting a key in her mouth, turning it in the lock, and tossing the key over her shoulder.

"Ladies." Mercer's cool gaze swept over us as he joined our party, lingering just a hair longer on Liz than it did me. "I'm Sheriff Mercer. Which one of you is Miss Reese?"

Remy stood up at Mercer's approach. I looped a finger in his collar for insurance and lifted my other hand in a small wave. "I'm Dr. Reese."

Mercer didn't seem to be surprised, which struck me as a little ominous, though I had no idea why. He flicked an assessing glance over me, resting his gaze on Remy for a second before making eye contact with me again. If his intention was to send a chill through me, it worked. Turning smoothly to Liz, he said, "Mrs. Grant, if you would be so kind as to join me in the office for a moment? This won't take long. Dr. Reese, wait here."

Liz shot me a sly look, highly reminiscent of when she'd triumphantly secured a date to prom with the senior I'd been crushing on at the time. My later relationship with Joe had wiped all dreams of Todd Porter from my brain, but back then, it had been a declaration of war between us as sisters.

"I'd be delighted, Sheriff." Liz swept forward to place her hand on his arm and sashayed her way into the office.

A lot of people have given in to the smartwatch craze, but as long as I worked with animals, I preferred the durability of an old-fashioned Timex. Not to mention, counting respiratory and heart rates was easier with an analog device over a digital one. But as I snuck glances at my watch, the second hand seemed to take forever to make a circuit of the dial.

True to his word, however, it wasn't more than five minutes before the door to the office opened, and Liz came out with Mercer behind her. She patted her hair with a satisfied smirk, and I wondered what on earth she'd said.

Mercer didn't follow her back to where I stood. Instead, he motioned me to join him.

Liz giggled as I passed her with Remy.

The hint of amusement on his face seemed to sharpen into a kind of alertness as I approached. He stepped aside to allow me and Remy into the office. Tim was nowhere to be seen. The television was still off, and the room smelled stale coffee and cigarette smoke. An empty cellophane paper lay discarded on the counter like a crumpled leaf, remnants of a vending machine snack.

"Have a seat," Mercer ordered, pointing at one of the hard chairs that had cigarette burns marring the orange plastic. By all accounts, his Southern accent should have made him sound polite. He didn't. As I sat, Remy curled himself around my feet without being asked and watched Mercer with the same unnerving focus he gave bunnies in the yard. Mercer studied him a moment, then patently ignored Remy's intense stare.

Instead of taking a seat himself, Mercer stood looking down at me in a classic power move. "Now, Dr. Reese, if you would tell me what happened."

I recited the events as I recalled them: arriving with a desperate need to go to the bathroom, watching the Lewises leave in a fugue of fury. Picking up on the fetid odor and realizing it had to come from my unit. Opening the door, expecting to find a dead animal, and nearly losing my cookies over finding the corpse.

Mercer popped a mint in his mouth as he listened. He interrupted several times to ask additional questions, most of which were the same question but worded differently. His intent was to hammer me over the details, pushing me into making a mistake or changing my story.

"And you're sure you didn't recognize the victim?" He asked when I'd finally wound down.

My face tightened in a grimace at the thought. "Did you actually see the body before they moved it?"

Mercer nodded.

"I've never set foot on Hartberry Isle before today, Sheriff, so how could I possibly identify the body? Never mind that even the corpse's own mother wouldn't have recognized him or her." I was betting on a "him" though. The size of the shoes alone made me think the victim was male. "Do you know who it is yet?"

The door to the office flew open, causing Remy to lift his head abruptly. The fur on the back of his neck raised—a side effect of the two of us having had so many traumatic encounters lately. I smoothed his hair back in place before he could rise and felt him relax beneath my hand as he settled down to the floor once more.

"It's Uncle Jeff?" Tim pinned Mercer with equal parts despair and disbelief. "Deputy Wilson said so."

Mercer gave a tight-lipped nod. His glower boded ill for either the interruption or Wilson's flapping gums.

"I'm very sorry for your loss." I wasn't just giving lip service. I felt bad for Tim, who seemed ill-equipped to deal with the kind of fallout his uncle's death would create. Drat. I might have suspected the victim was Brinkman, but I'd hoped, for Tim's sake, I was wrong.

I swung back to Mercer. "How can you be sure of the identification?"

He shrugged slightly. "The medical examiner will have to confirm, but we found Brinkman's ID on the victim."

"She's been calling and emailing, hassling Uncle Jeff about the condo. I heard her on the phone with him." Tim gave me a look of betrayal on par with someone having taken his puppy to the pound without telling him. "And now she just *happens* to show up. Without any notice."

"Hold on a minute here. It's my condo." I fixed a firm glare on Tim. "I have legal right to it. And I *did* email Mr. Brinkman notifying him of my arrival."

"And yet, the unit in question is now a crime scene." Mercer spoke quietly, but it had the effect of making both Tim and I face him. Seeing that he had Tim's attention, Mercer added, "Timmy, if you could wait outside? I'd like to speak with Dr. Reese alone."

"You ask her about those calls and emails." Tim did that thing where he made a V with his fingers and pointed first at his own eyes and then at me before wheeling out of the door.

As soon as the door closed behind him, Mercer said, "Now, if you'd like to tell me about your relationship with the deceased? From the beginning."

The atmosphere in the room changed, as though I'd suddenly wandered a little too close to a high-voltage fence.

"We did not have a relationship. As I told you before, I've never been to Hartberry Isle before today, and I've never met Mr. Brinkman." I was determined to remain calm, despite the deliberately provoking line of questioning. "I recently inherited unit 1301. Mr. Brinkman was in charge managing rentals of the unit in the previous owner's absence."

Mercer took out a notebook, flipped it open, and began writing. "The previous owner being..."

"Amanda Kelly."

His head jerked up at that. It was almost as though antenna had come to quivering attention. His eyes fixed on mine, then narrowed. "The wildlife artist?"

I guess I shouldn't be surprised he'd heard of Amanda, given the island's reputation for being a haven for celebrities.

"Yes. She died this past spring." Best not to say how. At least, not yet. "I inherited the condo, but there was a delay to probate the will. In the meantime, I requested that Mr. Brinkman cancel the rentals until I could determine what I wanted to do with the property. I wasn't sure I would keep it."

"But there was a problem with you and Brinkman?"

I sighed. "Initially, he didn't want to cancel the outstanding reservations. He made quite a fuss about it, actually. Gave me a song and dance about obligations to people whose vacations would be spoiled, etcetera. We eventually agreed to honor the existing rentals through the July 4th weekend, but to cancel the rest after that until I knew what my plans were. I wanted the flexibility of being able to come down when I could."

"Rental property around here tends to book far in advance."

"Mr. Brinkman said as much, but I wanted time to check out the unit for myself and remove any of Amanda's personal belongings if I decided to sell. Which would be a lot easier if I wasn't working around renters."

"And that was it? The sum total of your contentious relationship was over the rental of the unit? Seems unlikely to generate multiple phone calls and emails, if Timmy is to be believed. We will be checking on that, by the way."

I frowned, remembering the rest of it. "Well, no, that wasn't all. There was a strong possibility that Amanda had a certain amount of inventory in the condo. Her agent asked me to get a listing of the paintings if I could, so she could compare them to the catalog. I asked Mr. Brinkman if it would be possible for him to photograph any paintings in the unit and send the images to me. There was a lot of foot-dragging about that too. I never got any photos from him."

"So you decided to come down and see for yourself?"

I shrugged. "More or less. My practice typically slows down a bit between the end of the summer when school starts and the beginning of the holiday season, so it was a good time for me to take off work."

"We'll want a list of the inventory in question. I would have thought securing any valuable artwork would have been one of the first priorities after Ms. Kelly's death."

"In all other circumstances, you'd be right. But it seems Amanda liked rotating out paintings in her own properties, and she wasn't always good about keeping her records up to date." Not to mention, there was a lot of art involved. "Her works are on loan to various museums and organizations, in addition to those for sale in galleries. I'm afraid it took a while to realize not every painting was accounted for."

"You seem like a busy lady. We'll be confirming your schedule." His steely blue-eyed stare came to rest on me again. "Been quite a few deaths back home for you, haven't there?"

"Unfortunately, yes." Uh-oh. If he knew that much, he probably knew Amanda had been murdered. My attempt to downplay her cause of death now seemed foolish at best and suspicious at worst. How was I supposed to answer that anyhow? His statement was designed to rattle, nothing else. The frustrating part was that it worked.

"Hmmm." Mercer's text alert signaled. He pocketed his notebook and took out his phone. After typing a brief sentence, he scrolled a couple of times and stared at the screen. He made eye contact with me before holding out the cell toward me. "Paintings like these?"

I leaned forward to look at his phone. The images showed paintings hanging on a gallery wall, but I recognized the style. "Yes. That's Amanda's work."

"An international artist of some renown." Mercer took his phone back and looked at it thoughtfully before taking out a business card to give me. "I'll need a list of the paintings in the condo. Email me. The value of her paintings must have risen considerably since her death."

I shifted uncomfortably in my seat. Remy looked up at me and whined. I stroked his silky ears to soothe us both. "I believe so, though that really isn't my field of expertise."

Mercer hummed again to himself as he scrolled. He pressed a button, and the sound of an all-too-familiar perky song filled the small room. He held the phone out once more. "I believe this is you?"

The bouncy beat of "She's So Bad, She's Good" should have made me tap my toes, but instead I wanted to crawl into a hole and cover myself with leaves. On screen, I'd sprung from my seat at Lucky's Bar and grabbed Derek Ellis by a certain portion of his anatomy. The look on my face was murderous.

I was never, ever going to live that viral video down.

Chapter Five

"FINALLY," LIZ SAID, AS we staggered over the threshold into our borrowed unit.

Not having nearly as much luggage, I still felt the same overwhelming sense of relief. Not the least of which was because the Lewises had left the AC running. I dropped my bags inside the door and unclipped Remy's leash. He dashed through the unit with the enthusiasm of bulls released at Pamplona and almost as much noise.

"Is he going to be like this the entire trip?" Liz set her purse down on the nearest table with a decided thump before tossing her phone and sunglasses beside it. "I swear my children are better behaved."

Because her back was turned, she didn't see me stick my tongue out at her. Instead, I said aloud as I toed off my shoes, "Give him a break. He's only two, and he's been cooped up in the car all day. I'll take him for a run on the beach."

"Now?" Liz infused the single word with all the indignation she could muster.

I glanced at my watch. When I knelt beside my bags, my knees snapped and popped like Rice Krispies. I definitely needed to move around after sitting all day in the car. I fished a pair of cut-offs out of the duffle. "Yes, now. The sun will set soon, and I'd rather introduce him to the ocean in daylight."

"But he'll get all wet and sandy. And track it back here." She spread her hands to encompass our temporary quarters.

She was right about that, but I was hardly going to keep Remy off the beach for the entire week we were here.

"There's this new invention called a vacuum cleaner. Perhaps you've heard of it. Besides, I have some old towels in the car, and I bet there's a hosing station somewhere in the complex."

She still stared at me as though the power of her disapproval would change my mind. She might resemble our mother in many ways, but she didn't have *that* kind of control over me.

"Tell you what. Since I'm headed downstairs, you get first pick of the available bedrooms. Unpack. Unwind. I won't be gone long." I stripped out of my sweaty jeans and slid on the shorts. From the duffle, I pulled out a pair of beach slides and a belt pouch, which contained treats, pickup bags, and a clip for bottled water. Dogs could make themselves sick drinking salt water or swallowing too much sand off their toys, so bringing clean water with us was necessary.

"But we need to go to the store."

"We can go when I get back. Twenty, thirty minutes, tops. Trust me, Remy will be a lot calmer after I run some of his energy off."

Remy and I left before she could protest further. We skirted past the crime scene techs still hard at work through the narrow corridor of tape they'd created for residents after they'd processed the corridor. The heat hit me in the face like a damp trout as we exited the unit, and I almost turned around. But Remy was so happy to be going out again. I took one look at his excited face and committed to the stairs.

We went out of the back of the building into a small social area. There was a decent sized firepit within a circle of chairs and a massive gas grill, the kind that could cook enough food for an entire neighborhood at once. Beyond that lay a grassy stretch that sloped down to a marshy area, complete with weedy rushes. A wooden bridge arched over the sluggishly moving stream and outdoor tables nestled under tall palm trees.

This must be the inlet Tim mentioned. Keeping his warnings about snakes and alligators in mind, we kept to the sandy path that led down to a narrow, paved road between developments. The sky took on a tangerine cast as we crossed the private road heading toward the beach.

Tall grasses rippled in the evening breeze, and Remy lifted his head to scent the salt air as we stepped onto the dunes. I felt the familiar give of the warm, heavy sand beneath my feet and realized it had been far too long since I'd been to the shore. Certainly not in Remy's lifetime. Probably not since the last time I'd gone to a work-related meeting held at Myrtle Beach.

I wasn't a fan of the beach in the summer but adored it in the offseason when most of the tourists left and the temperatures cooled. I loved walking the hardpacked wet sand near the shoreline, listening to the tumble of waves rolling in and the hiss and bubble of the foam as the water receded again. I loved the marshy damp odor of salt and sand, and the cry of seagulls wheeling overhead. On this evening, a pair of dolphins frolicked just beyond the breakers, and I stood for a long moment watching them, shading my eyes with one hand. A sense of peace rolled over me as though it had been carried in on the tide. If only it could be like this all the time.

The shore was nearly empty as far as the eye could see in either direction. A few people presented like tiny stick figures some distance away; but for them, Remy and I were alone. He dragged me closer to the water, only to leap back barking as a larger wave came crashing in. Water swirled around our feet, and he danced excitedly in an attempt to avoid it, as though it were lava. We walked for a time, while I scanned for signs of washed-up jellyfish or broken glass. Normally, Remy had a good recall and he appeared to have a healthy respect for the waves as well. I'd have to make sure he didn't overheat or attempt to drink the salt water, but if I was going to let him off leash this evening, now was as good a time as any.

Taking his favorite cloth frisbee out of the pouch, I let him see it before I unclipped his leash. He dug his toes into the wet sand, his eyes fixated on the treasured toy. I flung it down the beach in front of us, making sure the wind wouldn't send it out over the water.

He took off after it like a bullet, legs driving like pistons into the ground as he covered the shore in a flat-out gallop. He scooped up the frisbee and came running back to me, shaking it with glee. This made the eight-hour trip—even with Liz's complaints—worthwhile. Even finding a body couldn't dampen my pleasure in Remy's happiness just now. The tension from the day oozed out of the muscles in my neck and shoulders, the incipient headache fading away as I tossed the frisbee and admired my dog at play.

Conscious of both the lingering heat and the dipping of the sun toward the horizon, I pulled the plug on playtime before Remy was ready to quit. He brought the sand-covered disc back to me and watched hopefully as I rinsed it off but seemed happy enough to be leashed again. I'd bring him out again first thing in the morning for a longer run. Maybe we could salvage something from this trip after all.

We returned the way we came. I was certain there was a spigot somewhere in the development for rinsing of sandy feet and paws. Probably one for each building. I must have missed it on the way out.

While we were gone, the area around the fire pit had become active. A cluster of people milled about the grill, while others sat around the lit fire pit. The grouping of people had the odd effect of suggesting the opening scene of a play, and I was about to be introduced to a cast of characters. Citronella torches added a festive touch, even as they attempted to keep the mosquitoes at bay. An open cooler filled with ice and beer sat within easy reach of the grill, and the smell of roasting meat made Remy lift his head and sniff the air appreciatively as we approached.

He wasn't the only one. Though I wasn't hungry myself, there was still something compelling about the smell coming off the grill.

I meant to only stop long enough to ask about a rinsing station, but Remy had other ideas. Forgetting his manners, he dragged me into the circle of socializing residents.

"Sorry," I said, as I put the kibosh on Remy licking the nearest person seated by the pit—or stealing the chips from the bowl being passed—I wasn't sure which. "We've been on the road all day and he hasn't eaten dinner yet."

"Gorgeous dog," the man in greatest danger of being slurped said, even as he moved the bowl of chips out of reach. "I'm Troy Doherty, by the way."

Troy was a handsome man in his sixties with hair so white it could have been silver or blond, and gray-green eyes lined by time spent in the sun. He also announced his name as though I should recognize it and part of me vaguely wondered if I'd seen him before.

"Ginny Reese," I said with a nod to the crowd watching our interaction. I indicated the dog. "And Remy. My sister and I just got in today."

"Oh wait, are you the ones then?" A voluptuous redhead with curves like Jessica Rabbit nearly spilled out of her halter top and shorts. She snapped her fingers, a move that showcased her blood-red nails. "You *are*. You must be. You're the one who found Jeff."

She patted the empty chair beside her. "Sit down and tell us about it. We're dying to know. Help yourself to a drink and some food."

This was way beyond my comfort zone, but part of me wanted to know more about Brinkman and speaking with the residents seemed the best way to go.

"There's not that much to say, really," I said as I took the seat. "I just ate a little while ago, thanks. I can't stay long. My sister's waiting for me and I need to feed the dog. It's way past his usual mealtime."

"I'm sure it must have been a terrible experience." The avid gleam in her eye suggested the exact opposite. "I'm Andrea. Jeff is—was—my soon-to-be ex-husband."

By dint of reaching down to corral Remy when he would have barreled up to Andrea where she sat, I was able to hide the worst of my shock. Or so I hoped. "Oh, dear, that's dreadful. I'm so sorry for your loss."

A young blonde at least twenty years younger than Andrea said tartly, "Don't waste your sympathy on her. She was spared the cost of a messy divorce."

Andrea lifted her mojito in a mock toast. "One that I would have won, given that he was sleeping with you, Emily."

I couldn't help but jerk my head in Emily's direction. Her tanned cheeks turned an ugly red, but she shrugged as she continued to sip her own cocktail. She crossed elegantly long legs in an almost deliberately provocative pose, as if to show them off.

What the heck had I gotten myself into?

"Oh, now let's don't bring all that up." An older Black woman with short, curly silver hair came over with a plate of hot dogs and hamburgers in buns. "I'm sure Ginny here would rather forget all about it. I'm Hattie Olsen, my dear. That's my husband, Gordon, manning the grill."

Gordon, a well-preserved Black man in his early seventies, saluted me with a pair of tongs, clacking them open and closed as he did so.

"Now you help yourselves," Hattie said, gesturing to the food. "There's fixin's on the table: relish, onions, tomatoes and so on. Eat up."

She set the platter down on the low table in front of us alongside the bowl of chips. Emily continued to lounge in silence, nursing her drink, but both Troy and Andrea leaned forward and began loading plastic plates.

I had to hold Remy back. I finally persuaded him to sit, but he fixed his gaze intently on the diners, watching every move they made. No doubt hoping they would drop something.

"Poor boy," Hattie cooed, while at the same time keeping her distance from Remy's big paws. "Can't he have a little bite?"

"That's very kind of you to offer, but I'm afraid it might not agree with him. And we're not staying in my condo at the moment. I don't want to risk someone else's carpets."

"At least help yourself to a drink." Gordon joined the group holding a bottle of beer and accepted a plate Hattie had put together for him. "Brinkman was found in your unit, wasn't he?"

On second thought, I could use a drink after all. A small thermos-like cooler sat on the table which contained the makings of mojitos. I scooped a cup of ice out of a nearby bucket and poured myself a glass. Remy sat like a soldier beside me, but a thin strip of drool trickled out of the side of his mouth as he eyed the food being passed around.

"Yes. My sister and I drove down this morning. I recently acquired the unit and this is my first time here." The first sip of my drink was sublime. "We found him when we opened the door. That's really all there is to it. We called the police and the rest you probably know."

"Yikes. Some welcome party." Troy flashed me a quick smile and continued to load a hot dog with relish. I could swear I recognized him from somewhere, but I just couldn't place it.

"It was pretty horrible. He, um, had obviously been there a while. Not really a mealtime subject, as my mother would say."

Hattie grimaced and swallowed, but though Andrea's eyes narrowed, she seemed otherwise unmoved. Emily, however, looked as though she might get sick.

"You acquired the unit? I thought you were renting. I can't believe Amanda sold it. She loves it here." Andrea balanced her plate on her lap and looked up with a frown.

I sucked in a breath and released it slowly. "Amanda died this past spring. She left me the condo in her will."

Gasps and general dismay greeted my announcement, a much greater degree of shock than anyone had shown about Brinkman. But then again, the police presence earlier had been hard to ignore.

"Oh, no! That lovely woman." Hattie reached blindly for Gordon's hand and he took it automatically. "I didn't know she was ill. Or was it an accident?"

"Tell me it wasn't that low-life husband of hers." Andrea sat up straight, baring her teeth like a dog about to attack.

Remy pressed into the side of my leg at her aggressive tone, yet still kept his eye on the precarious balance of her plate.

How on earth to answer? Surely, they could look up the details if they wanted. "She was murdered," I said at last. I tipped my head toward Andrea. "But her husband wasn't involved. I'm surprised she told you about him though. None of us even knew he existed until he showed up at the reading of her will."

"Amanda and I had some common ground." Andrea's eyes flashed, and then she relaxed back into her chair. She picked up her loaded burger and took a vicious bite from it.

"*Murdered*." Shock nearly took Hattie's breath away. She shook her head, and Gordon released her hand to rub her shoulders. "That's so unfair. Amanda was so sweet. So much talent and life to live."

"Yeah." The pang of her loss punched me out of nowhere, as it sometimes did. I studied the ice melting in my drink and blinked back unexpected tears. She'd been the closest thing I'd had to a friend.

Gordon escorted Hattie to an empty seat and assisted her in sitting down. She looked up at him and patted his hand where it rested briefly on her shoulder. He squeezed it back and then took the chair beside her. Their caring gestures struck me as I watched them, and I hoped someday I would have that kind of love to sustain me.

The Reeses weren't exactly a touchy-feely kind of family.

"That explains why the Lewises took off earlier today. They were in 1302, weren't they? Was that before or after the body was discovered?" Andrea asked of the group at large.

No one responded, so I said, "They left just as I was coming out of the elevator. We're actually staying in their unit, since mine is off limits for the foreseeable future."

"You're a resident, not just a renter then. Welcome to Sand Dollar Cove." Troy dabbed a napkin at his mouth before continuing. "During the summer season, there's a mixer on Friday evenings—that's when there's usually turnover with the rentals— where everyone brings drinks and food. Now that it's past Labor Day, it's mostly just those of us who own units. A lot of residents are like Amanda, only here part-time. Are you planning to live here? Or keep renting out the rest of the year, the way Amanda did?"

"That's likely to depend on who they get to run this place now that Jeff's gone." Emily had been silent so long her contribution to the conversation made me jump.

"She does have a point." I chucked my thumb in Emily's direction. I started to tell the truth but then decided a little prevarication might get me more information. "It's doubtful I'll live here, though my sister is trying to talk me into it. I'm not sure how I feel about being an absentee owner. I came down here to try to decide what to do with the place. It's lovely now, but what's it like during the tourist season?"

Each of the residents, with the exception of Emily, gave their opinion. Hartberry was still a small, exclusive island when all was said and done. Tourists tended to be well-off and well-behaved. The island prided itself on its unspoiled reputation and had a slew of legislation to keep it that way. Troy mentioned a turtle sanctuary and the thought of watching baby sea turtles hatch made me look up the website on my phone to see when the observation times occurred. The more the residents spoke, the stronger the appeal of living on the island year-round grew, despite the appalling heat and the potential for devastating hurricanes. The long-term homeowners assured me I would get used to both.

"What is it you do, Ginny?" Hattie asked while Gordon went to check on the food on the grill.

I explained I was a veterinarian and that I was considering building my own clinic back home.

Gordon brought another platter of hot dogs and hamburgers to the table and set it in front of me. "You should think about opening your clinic here."

"He's right." Andrea set aside her plate to refill her glass. "As it stands now, people have to go to either Hilton Head or the mainland, and that's not always easy or practical."

"It's dreadful if your pets are really sick and you can't get in somewhere quickly." Hattie nodded. "I wish we'd had more choices when we moved here with our little Gretchen."

I leaned forward to admire the photo of the elderly Schnauzer, eyes white with cataracts, that Hattie pulled up on her phone. When I asked, I found out the Olsens had lost her two years ago and hadn't replaced her.

"We just weren't ready for another dog at the time." Hattie's voice trembled with loss. "And of course, now—"

"Now, our health isn't what it used to be." Gordon cut in. "I worry Hattie would fall over a dog or it would knock her down."

"Oh, I don't think that would happen, dear."

Remy weaseled his way closer to Hattie and laid his big head in her lap. She stroked his ears and smiled tremulously at him. "They are such great company. Look, he knows I miss Gretchen."

I gently tugged Remy back. "I fear he's more interested in your food, Mrs. Olsen."

Gordon laughed and lifted Hattie's plate of mostly uneaten food out of Remy's reach. "I think you're right about that."

"Oh honey, please call me Hattie." She sent a beaming smile my way.

"My mother would never let me live it down. How about I call you Miz Hattie?"

"That works, my dear."

"Don't be in a hurry to make up your mind about the condo. You said you were down here for a week? Spend some time here before you decide to stay or sell. The fall season on the island is amazing." Troy paused to light a cigarette, holding the matchbook in his palm as he cupped the flame to shield it from the evening breeze. He caught my gaze on him and grimaced. "Filthy habit, I know, but I've given up most of my bad habits and a man has to have a little vice to make life worth living. What was I saying? Oh, right. You can make a decent bit of money subleasing or renting if you don't want to live here."

"Speaking of rentals, my unit was supposed to be empty as of July 4th weekend. Was that not the case?"

It wasn't as though I needed confirmation, after having seen the reservations on the computer. And I'm not sure why I thought anyone here would know of Brinkman's illicit activity. But something prompted me to ask anyway.

Andrea exchanged a glance with Troy, one that seemed to convey a world of meaning I didn't understand. She dropped her gaze back to her lap after a moment and pushed her food around on her plate.

"Can't say as I know for sure." Troy folded one hand over the other in a pose of thoughtfulness, the cigarette balanced between two fingers. It was a studied pose, one of languid grace, that made me think of James Dean or Rock Hudson. Something glamorous and wicked and perhaps not quite to be trusted.

Gordon huffed a little. "Wouldn't surprise me if Brinkman completely ignored your orders regarding the condo. Wouldn't trust him as far as I could throw him."

"Now, honey." Hattie patted him on the arm again. "We shouldn't speak ill of the dead."

"Then we won't be able to talk about him at all." Gordon gave his wife a wicked smile, which made her muffle a snort.

Shifting in my seat uncomfortably, I shot a glance at Andrea. She met my gaze over the brim of her glass.

"Don't mind *me*. I knew exactly what kind of snake Jeff was." She cast a sly look at Emily, whose cheeks were flushed with either anger, embarrassment, or alcohol, it was hard to tell. Emily drained her glass empty in one swallow and set it down on the table with a thump. She made as if to rise, but Troy cut her off mid-movement.

"Aw, now sweetheart. Don't rush off."

Emily's eyes snapped as she addressed the group. "Regardless of how you all felt about Jeff, he was a human being, you know. Is it too much to ask for a little common decency?"

"You're right, my dear. We might have had our issues with him, but no one deserves to die like that." Troy took a drag on his cigarette and pondered the smoke as he released it again. "Alone. Without anyone around to notice or care. That's no way for a man to live or die."

That final sentence rang a bell. More than the vague sensation his face seemed familiar. When he spoke those words, recognition flooded me. I snapped my fingers.

"Troy Doherty. You were in *Logan's Law* back in the '90s, right?"

His grin lit up his face, taking at least thirty years off his age.

"You just couldn't resist, could you?" Emily's anger could no longer be contained. "Face it, Gramps. No one cares that you used to be an actor on a cheesy cop show."

She stormed off, leaving an awkward silence behind.

"Don't pay her any mind, Troy." Andrea didn't seem the slightest bit affected by the unpleasant scene. "I doubt she had any real feelings for Jeff. She just likes being the center of attention."

"I didn't mean to be disrespectful. It never occurred to me I'd used the catch phrase from *Logan's Law*. It just came out." His brow furrowed in what appeared to be sincere distress. He turned to me. "She's right. It was a cheesy TV show no one remembers."

"Are you kidding me? Gruff detective adopts a cute kid whose mom was a homicide victim? I think that was the appeal. It wasn't your standard cop show. My sister had the biggest crush on you. She's going to die when she meets you. Or would you rather not?" I winced as soon as I'd spoken. "I mean, I don't have to say a word."

"That depends." Lightning-fast, Troy's depression vanished in favor of waggling his eyebrows. "Is she pretty?"

"Yes," I spoke without thinking. "In my family, she's considered the pretty one."

"Oh, for heaven's sake." Hattie seemed to have shaken off her dismay at Amanda's death and leaned forward to scold me. "What a thing to say. You've managed to put down you and your sister in the same sentence. Who taught you to think that way about yourself?"

The theme song of the Wicked Witch of the West from *The Wizard of Oz* blared out of my back pocket. I tugged the phone out of my shorts and held up a finger to everyone watching me as I said, "Speak of the devil."

I stood up to move away from the gathering, swiping the screen as I answered the call. "Hello, Mother."

Chapter Six

"WHY ARE THE POLICE calling me to ask about your whereabouts for the past few days?"

My mother's voice was loud enough that I was sure the others could hear her, and sure enough, the expressions of those around me ranged from amusement to pained sympathy. Surprisingly, the wincing look of commiseration came from Andrea, the most cynical—and least emotional—of the bunch. I hadn't expected empathy from that quarter, and even as I noted her glance, it slid away to refocus on her drink again. A bit of a dark horse, Andrea Brinkman.

"Remy, with me," I said softly, patting my leg as I stepped further away from the circle of chairs. With a glance back at my audience, I raised my voice only slightly to speak into the phone. "The police didn't tell you?"

"They said they were investigating a suspicious death but wouldn't give me any details. I told them if they wanted to know what my grown daughter was up to, they should ask her themselves."

My mother's voice somehow managed to wrap steel inside a warm, syrupy Southern accent in a manner that fooled people meeting her for the first time into thinking she was a genteel, soft woman. They seldom remained under that impression for very long.

"Gee, Mom. I'm not sure I should thank you or not. While I appreciate the sentiment, that might be why the sheriff was a little hard on me and Liz."

"That's ridiculous. What possible reason could they have for thinking the two of you had anything to do with this death?"

"I have no idea. I never met the guy. First time I'd ever laid eyes on him, he was lying in the middle of the condo when we arrived."

"What? *Again*? Virginia Anne Reese, I raised you better than that."

At least she couldn't see me roll my eyes. "I hardly see where stumbling upon dead bodies is a moral failing."

"Don't be flip with me, young lady."

I suppressed a sigh. I knew better than to get smart with my mother when she was in this mood. "It wasn't my intention to be flippant. I'm merely pointing out that it's not like I do this on purpose. Believe you me, finding this particular corpse in the condition it was in was the last thing I wanted to do today."

I glanced over my shoulder again, but the others were talking among themselves. The furtive looks shot in my direction suggested they were doing their best to appear uninterested in what I had to say and failing miserably. I took several steps farther away and said, "There's also the fact the victim seems to be the property manager here."

"Wait a minute. That man who was stringing you along and refusing to send you any information about Amanda's inventory? I *told* you it was a mistake to ask him to look into the artwork for you. You should have just gone down there without warning and checked for yourself. I bet you won't find hide nor hair of any art in the place."

"You may be right about that." I shot another glance at the residents and stretched my lips into a smile when I caught Hattie's gaze on me. Through gritted teeth, I said, "Apparently, he didn't cancel any of the rentals either."

"I can't understand you, Ginny. Enunciate. You sound as though you have a mouthful of marbles."

I let go of the fake smile, as it was hurting my face anyway. "He kept renting out the unit, even though I told him to stop."

"So, dishonest to boot. Well, you won't see a dime of that money, either. How long had he been dead when you found him?"

The image of Brinkman's corpse was imprinted on my retinas. I'm pretty sure he would haunt my dreams for some time to come. "Days."

"Well, then. Patently ridiculous. Why on earth would the police be interested in your movements this past week? Not that I told them anything." My mother's sniff came over the phone loud and clear. "As if I could. You're so busy all the time. You barely even remembered to tell me you were going out of town."

Given that the last time I'd planned a major trip, my mother had called me up every day before I left to ask what sort of funeral arrangements I wanted in the event of my death, you can understand why I didn't tell her I was leaving town until the last second.

"Not to worry. We'll sort this out. It may well turn out to be natural causes."

"You mean they think it's a homicide?" Her voice rose on the last word. "*That's* why the police are looking at you?"

I had visions of her getting in the car and driving down, all while hordes of flying monkeys swarmed about her.

"No, no, nothing like that, I'm sure. They just have to cross all the *t*'s and dot the *i*'s. You know."

She made a grumbling sound that might have been a growl. "You've been keeping an eye on the weather, haven't you? There's a tropical storm brewing in the Caribbean. They say it's going to turn into a hurricane. You and Liz need to leave before it hits. You shouldn't have gone down in the hurricane season."

Next to planning our funerals in the event of some tragic accident, my mother's next favorite pastime was monitoring The Weather
Channel. She'd been a schoolteacher, so I could understand where her
penchant for watching the weather reports originated. I confess, as a
house-call vet, I pay attention too.

"Yes, but you know most of these things fail to organize into anything significant. Besides, I'll be home before it's likely to cause any
issues here."

My phone chimed with a text, and I grabbed at the offered life
preserver. "Gotta go, Mother. Getting a text. I'll call you tomorrow."

"You keep me posted," she said, but allowed me to ring off.

I checked the text as I walked back to the fire pit. Remy followed at
my side in perfect heel position, even though I hadn't asked him to do
so. They say three is the magic year for a lot of dogs, the age when they
finally grow out of rambunctious puppyhood, but we still had a way
to go before that milestone and I certainly wasn't counting on it. Still,
he was being a very good boy.

It was getting dark now, and when I read Liz's inquiry, I realized she
was wondering where I was.

"It's my sister. I should probably go back upstairs."

"Oh, don't leave yet." Andrea indicated the food and drinks. "Tell
her to come down."

That didn't seem like the best idea, given how much wine Liz had
drunk already this evening.

"That's right." Hattie smiled brightly as though the realization just
occurred to her. "You're Amanda's friend. Tell her to come join us. It's
been so long since we've seen her."

I was going to say, "What?" when I saw Gordon's face.

"It's been a long day for Ginny, my dear." Gordon squeezed Hattie's
shoulder and gave me a long, pained look. I recognized it, having seen

it in the mirror often enough when taking care of my dad toward the end of his life.

"Your husband's right, Miz Hattie," I said as cheerfully as I could muster. "I've been on the road all day. It was nice meeting y'all, though. I'm sure I'll be seeing you around while I'm here."

"Nicely done," Troy said so quietly. I'm sure I was the only one who heard him. He ground out his cigarette in a container of sand beside his chair and leaned forward, speaking in a more normal tone. "We usually gather here in the evenings about this time, sometimes a bit later. Strictly on a BYOB basis then. But I would be delighted to meet your sister, provided she's interested."

Another text from Liz demanding to know what was taking so long came through on my phone.

"Remember you volunteered when she begins grilling you on details of episode six, or what happened to the girl who played your adoptive daughter, or what Sponenberg was like to work with as a director."

Troy's eyebrows lifted in something that looked very much like alarm before his face went blank.

"I warned you she was a serious fan." I paused in the middle of drafting a text to Liz. "If you'd rather not deal with that, I don't have to tell her of your presence here at the Sand Dollar. On the way down, she went into rhapsodies about Hartberry being a hideaway for the rich and famous."

"Not always so rich or famous," Andrea murmured, watching Troy's reaction.

I have to admit, he was good. His expression flickered only a fraction of a second.

"No, no, that's fine." His smile was back. "Your sister knows actors forget their projects just as soon as they're finished with them, right? We don't remember those kinds of details."

"I'll be sure to remind her." I shot Liz a quick text to say I would be right up.

"Perhaps we should call it a night, too." Gordon touched Hattie on the shoulder.

"So soon? Why it feels like we only just got here." Hattie pointed at Andrea's plate, which was still half-full. "Everyone's still eating."

"I'm drinking my dinner." The ice in Andrea's nearly empty glass tinkled as it shifted when she raised it.

"Come on, love." Gordon put a hand under Hattie's arm to assist her to her feet. "We should be getting back."

"But at the very least we should help clean up." Hattie jerked her arm away, the corners of her mouth pulling down in a pout.

Andrea set her glass and plate aside. "Now, Hattie, you know how it works. The cook doesn't do the cleanup. Gordon ran the grill tonight, so we'll take care of things here."

"We might even have help."

The highly amused tone coming from Troy made me whip my head around in time to see Remy nose deep in the plate of grilled meat. He closed his mouth around three hot dogs and began backing away from the platter.

"Remy!" I cried. "What are you doing?"

Hotdogs stuck out of the side of his mouth like fat cigars, but before I could tell him to "drop it", he took two big gulps and the wieners—complete with buns—disappeared whole.

Hattie let out a peal of laughter as I marched over to take my dog by the collar.

"Oh, don't yell at him. He's such a handsome boy. We used to have a little dog named Gretchen, you know. She was a terrible thief, too."

My gaze slid to her involuntarily for a brief moment before I snagged the miscreant. Remy's ears dropped slightly, but his mouth fell open in a doggy grin, and it was hard to be mad with him.

"I am so sorry. It's my fault for not paying attention. I knew he was hungry and I'm afraid the temptation was too great. Please, let me pay you for the food."

"It was just a couple of dogs." Gordon waved me off with a smile. I wasn't sure if his calm reaction was amusement on his part or pleasure at Hattie's obvious delight. "No harm done."

"Well, it's not exactly like anyone's going to want to eat anything else off that plate now." Andrea stacked plastic plates and cups as she spoke, shooting a glance at the platter and then at me.

Troy reached over and took the last burger with what seemed great deliberation. "There. Problem solved."

I was really starting to like Troy.

The remaining hot dog looked lonely, so I grabbed it. "Guess I was hungry after all."

"Ew." Andrea grimaced and made a gagging noise. "I can't believe the two of you are eating after the dog practically licked the plate."

I met Troy's glance and shrugged. The corner of his mouth quirked upward in a charming smile. No wonder Liz had been crazy about him all those years ago.

"Wait."

I thought Hattie's intent was to stop me from eating the "contaminated" food—even though Remy hadn't gotten anywhere near that side of the platter—so I took a big bite and chewed.

Turns out I was wrong. Hattie watched me eat the plain dog with astonishment. "Don't you want any relish? Mustard?"

It wasn't the first time someone had expressed that reaction to my weird eating habits. I swallowed my mouthful and grinned. "No, I actually prefer them plain. I'll let you in on a little secret, Miz Hattie. I'm not keen on condiments in general."

I paused and took an exaggerated glance in either direction before leaning closer to speak in a stage whisper. "As a matter of fact, I won't eat a tomato sandwich."

"No." Hattie giggled and play-swatted at my arm. "Girl, you must not be from the South."

"What's a tomato sandwich?" Troy raised one eyebrow theatrically.

"White bread, mayo, and slices of fresh tomato. Little bit of salt." Hattie hummed a small noise of appreciation and rubbed her stomach. "We used to pick the tomatoes fresh out of our garden and eat them standing up in the kitchen, didn't we, Gordon?"

He nodded, still poised by her chair as if to move her along.

"Well, I was born and raised in the South, but I can't abide mayonnaise." I pulled a face.

"Can't be a Southern girl, then." Hattie's declaration was amused but firm. "You must be a changeling."

"Something my mother has often told me," I agreed. At one point in time, that notion gave me comfort as the odd duck in my family.

A strange little pall fell over the group. Their faces flickered in the torchlight. Shadows aged Troy before my eyes, turning him from silver fox into a tired, old man. Gordon's face seemed like an expressionless mask; all emotion frozen out of him. Hattie's grin took on a sinister aspect, reminding me of Bette Davis in that psycho-biddy movie, *What Ever Happened to Baby Jane?* Andrea's cheekbones sharpened, making her look hard and coarse.

I don't know these people. And someone around here could be a killer.

My fingers curled into Remy's ruff. My smile felt as though it might crack my skin.

"It was nice meeting y'all. I'm sure I'll be seeing you around."

Remy and I left the gathering. Eager to go back to the building, he tugged at his leash and I let him. I wanted to get back inside as well. The sooner the better. Inside, the bright lights dispelled some of the unease I'd felt with the others.

In the elevator, I shook off the odd feeling. The culmination of a long, stressful day, no doubt. I didn't travel much and I was out of my usual element. Things would look better in the morning. I'd get up early and take Remy to the beach for a nice long walk. Liz and I could explore the island. Maybe we could find that turtle sanctuary. I had a soft, tender spot in my heart for turtles because of Amanda. Since we wouldn't be able to get into my unit for a while, we could focus on the vacation part of this trip. Everything would be fine.

Remy led the way out of the elevator along the corridor. The crime scene techs were still working in the unit; the bright lights mounted on tripods illuminated the interior of the condo like a movie set. As I glanced inside, I saw the section of carpet had been cut away surrounding the area where Brinkman laid, and I was tempted to tell them to pull out all the carpet as I'd have to replace it anyway. I hurried past the door, not wanting to appear nosy or draw any unwanted attention again. Before Remy and I reached the door to 1302, however, the theme song to *The X-Files* burst out of my phone.

Hey, it was Joe's favorite show back in high school, not mine. It seemed appropriate as a ringtone for him, though.

I stopped in the hallway to answer the phone. "Please tell me my mother didn't make you call me."

He laughed, the rich sound settling on me with a kind of warm comfort. Like when Ming climbs on my chest at night and begins to purr.

"No, but I'm guessing you've spoken to her already this evening." He paused and then added. "What the heck have you gotten yourself into this time, Ginge?"

Chapter Seven

"DON'T CALL ME GINGE." The words came out of my mouth on autopilot.

A second laugh, more of a snort really, told me my response had been expected and his intention to provoke was deliberate.

"I'll tell you what I told my mother when she called—finding another body was hardly by choice." My reply was sharp.

Sharper than it had to be, if truth be told. Here I'd been wishing for his presence today and now I was snarling at him like the little demon Chihuahua I once rescued from inside my client's wall.

"You have to admit, it's getting to be a habit." Less amusement now and more sympathy, which had the effect of making my heart do the warm melty thing again. It meant nothing. I'd had a trying day and few people had been nice about it. Even the Sand Dollar residents had only wanted the gory details. At least I'd managed to be vague about those. If I felt a response to Joe's kindness, it was because of that.

"Yeah, well it's a habit I intend to break. Somehow. Seriously, how many dead bodies can one person find before people start to wonder what you had to do with it?"

"That could be why Mercer is being a bit aggressive about establishing your whereabouts."

"Wait, he's contacted you, too?"

There was a slight pause and then Joe continued on in that drawling manner of his that often masked his true reactions. "Purely a matter of form, he assured me."

"Then why am I hearing a big ol' 'but'?"

Remy whined and tugged me toward the door to 1302. I guess three pilfered hotdogs weren't enough to satisfy his appetite. I stroked his shoulder and asked him to lie down, which he did because he's a good boy. The heavy sigh as he placed his head on his forepaws was meant to remind me of that.

"I looked Mercer up. He's got a bit of a reputation for being a glory-hound. Specifically, when it comes to high profile cases." Only a hint of a drawl now. The accent melted into the background when Joe turned serious.

Huh. That made sense. "Mercer seemed to light up when he found out the condo originally belonged to Amanda."

"You need to be careful around him. He's looking to make a name for himself. Word is he ran for sheriff in the county because of the resort clientele and hopes to springboard into bigger and better things."

"What could be bigger than being the sheriff on the Isle of the Rich and Famous?"

"Politics. It's where the money is after all. Solve a case big enough to get into the national news, and his name becomes familiar."

"Is that why you ran for sheriff?" I hoped my light tone let him know I was teasing. "Power and fame in the big city?"

Clearly, I had to be joking because Greenbrier was a "blink and you've missed it" kind of community.

"Oh yes. Definitely. I expect the story of us being called to collect Dwayne Aiken's cow from inside Bucky's store to hit the AP wire any day now."

"Darn it. Leave town for *one* day, and all the exciting things happened. I'm so bummed I missed it." I could picture the havoc Lucinda the Jersey wreaked in Bucky's cramped aisles.

"We could have used you."

I shook my head, even though Joe couldn't see me. "Not my field of expertise. I hope you called Doc Haskell. Large animals are his specialty, not mine."

"Yes, we managed. He came to dart her, and we were able to get her out of the store without proving the bull in a china shop theory."

I laughed at that. I didn't ask how she got in Bucky's in the first place. Lucinda was notorious for busting through or jumping over fences. Still, I would have given anything to have seen the faces of Bucky's shoppers as they found a cow staring back at them from across the zucchini in the produce section.

"I'll take your warning about Mercer under advisement." It was time to wrap up the conversation and go back to Liz. "The victim has a nephew who is determined to paint me as the bad guy, so I'll watch my step. Though that doesn't concern me nearly as much as my belief Brinkman continued to rent out the condo after I told him to cancel the leases."

"I don't like the sound of that. If you need me—"

Need him? Did I need him with his smooth-talking, deceptively country drawl to step in on my behalf with Mercer? I thought not. I'd call Lindsay Carter, the lawyer for Amanda's estate, first. If he couldn't advise me, he'd know someone who would.

"I've got this covered. Why don't you go back to wrangling those dangerous cattle? Don't mess this up—the *steaks* are high." Realizing he couldn't hear the difference in the homonym, I added. "As in the filet mignon kind."

"Hah-hah, very funny. Don't quit your day job." Joe muffled a snort.

"Just be careful. If you give Lucinda any attitude, she'll tan your hide."

"Please stop." Joe groaned, and I could picture him pinching the bridge of his nose. "You're killing me here."

"You mean I'm butchering you." I delivered my last pun with fiendish glee.

"Are you done yet?" He paused only a moment before continuing. "All kidding aside, you know you only need to say the word and I'll be right down, right?"

I hadn't known actually but hearing him state as much made me more determined than ever to deal with this problem without him. "I'm good."

"Now, maybe. But you used to be more adventurous. Remember? Just a little bit bad." His amusement carried through the phone loud and clear.

If I'd been a dog, I would have growled. "Just once I'd like to get through the day without someone bringing up that stupid video."

"Wait, someone down there has asked you about it?"

He still found it funny, darn him.

"Yes. Mercer pulled it up on the phone and asked if it was me. I'm just glad Liz wasn't in the room when he did. If she finds out about it, she'll definitely show Mother."

"Okay, I'm not sure if I should tell you this but..."

"Tell me what." If a voice could be both flat with dread and sharp with panic, mine managed.

"Your mother knows about the vid."

"She what?" I might have screeched, since Remy's ears flattened and one of the crime scene techs popped their head out of the unit to see what was going on.

I gave the tech a weak grin and took a few steps closer to unit 1302 to hiss into the phone. "She's seen it? You're telling me my mother has seen the viral video of me tossing Derek Ellis on his back on a bar table?"

"Not only seen it, but she's proud of it too." The amusement was back in his voice.

"Proud." I found that hard to believe.

"Yes, proud. She goes around telling people she taught you to stand up for yourself."

"Well, she got that right. By teaching me no one else would." The words came out of my mouth before I could stop them.

"Ginge." Joe's voice had gone soft and smoky. "You know that's not true."

"It's true enough." I snorted. "So, she's proud of the video but never let on that she knew about it?"

"I think she didn't want to embarrass you."

I almost said, "That's never stopped her before," but caught myself in time. I settled for a harumphing sound instead and changed the subject. "How long does it take a team to process a crime scene?"

There was a pause before Joe chuckled. "With as many bodies as you've found, you don't know the answer to that by now?"

"Now who's the comedian?" I glanced down the hallway, where the flash of photography blinked like Morse code from the inside of Amanda's unit. "I'm serious. I've never hung around for the whole process before."

Joe hummed a bit to himself as he pondered the answer. "It varies. Depends on the size of the community and its resources, as well as the complexity of the scene, exposure to the elements, that sort of thing. I'd say eight to ten hours on average for the initial examination and documentation, but it can take a couple of days to process the whole scene."

"Yikes. Surely not with the same team. I mean, they get to go home at the end of shift, right?"

"Again, it depends on the size of your department. There's usually more than one team involved in bigger communities, but here in Greenbrier, we've got a bunch of people wearing multiple hats. As to your question, they'll do as much as they can in one sitting before closing shop for the night. It will probably be a couple of days before you get access to the unit, though. And it sounds like you want a cleaning crew in there first anyway."

"Great. The crime scene techs are still banging around next door. At this rate, they'll be here most of the night." With every muffled thump and bump from Amanda's unit, Remy lifted his head and cocked it slightly. Once or twice, he puffed air through his lips in a stifled bark. "Liz and I should have taken a hotel room for the night somewhere else."

"You're just tired. It's been a long day with a series of shocks to boot. Make an early night of it. Things will look better in the morning."

Having just told myself the same only a little while earlier, it was good advice. If I could get any sleep that is. "Yeah. You're right." I stifled a curse when yet another text message from Liz chimed. "Look, that's Liz again. She's having a small cow—probably a Jersey—because I've been out with the dog so long. I'd better go."

"Maybe I should make sure Lucinda is still in the county." Joe waited until I'd snorted at his feeble joke before continuing. "No worries. I just wanted to check in with you."

"I appreciate that. It was a tough day, and it means a lot to me that you called to make sure we were okay." I hesitated. "I'm not good about acknowledging that sort of thing, but I'm serious. Thank you."

"Call if you need me."

"I will."

But we both knew I wouldn't.

Chapter Eight

WHEN I OPENED THE door to unit 1302 and released Remy, he shot to the kitchen and began dancing in circles, barking in excitement. I paused long enough to grab his bowls and a bag of kibble out of my duffle and followed.

Liz waited there, with a glass of red wine in her hand. Where had that come from?

"Where have you been?" She demanded with such ferocity, it felt like I was standing in my mother's kitchen again, having missed curfew. "You said you were only going to be gone a short while."

"I'm sorry." The simmering anger in her tone left me scrambling trying to figure out what I'd done wrong. "I got caught up talking to some people downstairs. Where'd you find the wine?"

"The Lewises left some stuff behind." Liz lifted her hand, the wine sloshing within the glass with the movement. "Didn't it occur to you I might have been worried? Here I am sitting alone in this apartment for over an hour, with a dead body next door and me thinking the worst has happened to you."

Whew boy. This was like the time I forgot to tell my mother I was going to a professional dinner meeting in Birchwood Springs—and when she couldn't get hold of me, she called the police to report me missing. After only two hours of me being out of contact.

I measured my words even as I asked Remy to stay while I poured out some kibble into his bowl. Between the run on the beach and the theft of the hot dogs, I decided to reduce the usual volume. I didn't want to risk having him bloat, especially with no easy access to emergency care. Anticipation made him quiver with the effort not to break his sit. I released him quickly and filled his water bowl as he dove on the dog food and chased the metal bowl into the corner to stabilize it.

I decided to ignore the fact Liz was having yet another glass of wine and focused instead on how much to tell her about my visit downstairs. "I met some of the residents. They have a bit of a happy hour on Friday evenings out back."

"And you didn't bother to let me know?" Liz squinted over the edge of her glass; her lips pulled down as hurt flashed across her face.

"I hadn't meant to stop at all, but they wanted all the grim details about finding the body." I opened and closed cabinets as I spoke. Liz was right. The Lewises had left quite a bit of food behind. "We'll eventually need to go to the store to pick up more kibble for Remy, but it looks like we're good for the time being. Anyway, the residents gather most evenings, so you'll get your chance to meet them. Bit of an odd bunch."

Liz's anger still hovered on the edge of boiling over. Obviously not done being mad with me. When she spoke, it was with tight dignity. "How so?"

I shot a glance at her. Her cheeks were still quite pink, and her lids were beginning to droop. According to my watch, it was only quarter to nine, but I had a feeling Liz would be out like a light soon. I could fill her in on the full details in the morning, so I gave her the Cliffs Notes version. "Oh, you know. A group of people with not much in common, I'd guess. Including Brinkman's ex-wife, who wasn't the slightest bit broken up over his death, either. And his current lover, who got upset with everyone and stormed off."

Liz tracked my movements with a slightly glassy-eyed stare. "I'd have liked to have seen that. Sounds like interesting dynamics."

I'd never understand people who enjoyed watching confrontations that made me uncomfortable. But then again, I couldn't stand reality TV.

Remy didn't normally bolt his food, but he inhaled his kibble as though someone might steal it, and then jerked his head up at the sound of a thump next door and galloped into the main living area.

"What's gotten into him?" Liz frowned somewhat owlishly at Remy's exit.

"They're still working the crime scene. Hopefully they won't make too much noise. Remy's not used to neighbors." I opened the fridge and discovered, among other things, bottled water. I offered one to Liz, but she retained her death grip on the neck of the wine bottle and clutched her stemless wine glass in the other hand as she followed me into the living room.

Remy sat at the balcony doors, a wolf-like sentinel peering out into the dark, his head cocked in the direction of the unit next door. I'd have to do a safety check of the railings in the morning before I let him out there. Probably a good idea to do a safety check in general—you never know when a property management company might have put out rat poison in a rental unit. I paused in the middle of the room and turned slowly. If I closed my eyes, I could picture Amanda's condo, and even though the image of Brinkman's corpse blocked out almost everything else, I got the sense that unit 1301 had been decorated with more color and flair than the condo we occupied, which had the feel of a generic hotel room.

"What are you doing?"

My eyelids flew open. I uncapped the water and took a sip before continuing my examination of the unit. "Just trying to get a feel of the layout here. From what little I saw, the units are identical, only this one is flipped from 1301. The kitchen and bedrooms are on opposite sides. Did you pick a room to sleep in?"

Liz had chosen the main bedroom for herself and had unpacked most of her belongings. No surprise, the units on this side of the building *did* have an ocean view. The room left for me was smaller, as it made space for a pleasant little bathroom beside it, complete with a walk-in shower. I brought my duffle in from the living room and placed it out of the way near the closet. I tended to live out of my bag the few times I went anywhere. Afraid of leaving something behind, I guess. Or maybe it was because I seldom stayed away long enough to get comfortable in a strange place.

Liz followed me on my tour, seething resentment still coming off her in waves. When I returned to the living room, she sat down on the couch so she could set the wine bottle and glass on the end table beside her. Oh well, she'd have to deal with the headache in morning, not me.

"So, you just hung out downstairs with a bunch of strangers, then?"

"Liz, I texted you back." I sat down in a wicker basket chair so deep, it would be a miracle if I could get out of it again without assistance.

"Only after I texted twice. I know you're used to living on your own, but a reasonable person with normal social skills would have invited me down. At the very least, explained what was keeping you."

That was a slap back so hard it smarted. And yet, there was probably more than a kernel of truth to it. Mother aside, I wasn't used to accounting for my every movement to anyone else. And as someone who enjoyed being alone, I'd needed the time on the beach with Remy after being with Liz all day long. Recharging was fundamentally necessary if I had to people on a regular basis. Today had been a day full of peopling. Guilt reared its ugly little head in a reminder that not everyone liked solitude the way I did.

But now was not the time to mention meeting Troy Doherty. As angry as Liz was, I knew she'd blow a gasket if she knew I'd met a celebrity and I hadn't invited her down to join us.

"I honestly didn't think I'd be gone that long. First, I ran into the Breakfast Club—"

"The what?" Liz blinked several times, slow to catch the reference.

"*The Breakfast Club*. You know, a bunch of relative strangers forced to interact with each other and then finding out they have more in common than they thought?"

"You had to have been what—three? Four?—when that movie came out."

"And yet, you've seen it too. Thanks to the miracle of Blockbuster video."

The John Hughes movies were classic for a reason.

"Anyway, I got snagged by that bunch, and then Mother called."

"No." Liz paused mid-sip, her eyes going wide over the brim of her glass. "You didn't tell her about the body, did you?"

"I didn't have to. She already knew. Seems Sheriff Mercer's boys called wanting to know what I'd been up to for the last few days."

"She already *knew*? Is she on her way?" Liz looked around in a blind panic, as though our mother were about to walk in at any moment, and she'd be caught having an illicit drink. Come to think of it, that might have a lot to do with why Liz was acting like a college student on spring break.

"I don't think so. I hope not, at any rate." I gave it some thought and shook my head. "She didn't seem primed to charge into battle. But she didn't know all the details, either. Mercer's people didn't share much, only that they were investigating a suspicious death. She warned us about an impending hurricane though."

Liz's shoulders slumped with her sigh of relief. "That sounds more like she's staying put. Thank God for hurricanes."

We both snickered at that. Given our mother's intense dislike for travel and her obsession with the weather, it was far more likely she'd nag us every day to come home rather than drive down to Hartberry herself.

"You realize you have a thing about calling her Mom, don't you?"

The non sequitur took me completely by surprise and I frowned. "What do you mean?"

"You call her "Mom" or "Mother" depending on how uptight you are about your relationship." Liz lifted her brows in a kind of superior manner and sipped her wine.

"That's ridiculous."

Remy left off staring out the balcony doors to come over and lay his big head in my lap. I took refuge in stroking his ears.

"It's true. Most people call their parents—or grandparents—by one name or another. Mom, Mommy, Mama, Mother. They're..." She struggled for the right word for a moment, then snapped her fingers. "Consistent. Take Dad, for instance. He was always "Dad" to you. But you go back and forth between 'Mom' and 'Mother', and you didn't used to. It's only since you moved back to Greenbrier that you call her Mother."

Well, that was a little piece of alcohol-driven insight I didn't need.

"Huh. I never noticed."

Liz tipped her glass at me as though I should have. "She's almost always 'Mother' these days."

"Our relationship is evolving."

"Devolving is more like it."

"Hey," I retorted, stung. "I'm working on setting boundaries with her. That's a lot harder when you actually live in the same town."

"Oh, my God. You're still pissed with me for not dropping everything and uprooting my family to go back to Greenbrier when Dad got ill."

"What me? Pissed? Why should I be pissed?" A little of that wine would be nice right now. Maybe even a whole bottle for myself. "I mean, as a single woman with no children, it was only logical that *I* give up everything and go home. Sure, there were no jobs available, but I managed to eke out a living anyway."

Remy pawed at my leg as though he'd like to climb into the basket with me, but I discouraged that by pushing him back when he attempted to clamber up. He huffed a long-suffering sigh and settled on my feet. There was no way I could move without him knowing it.

"A husband and two children. That's four people to relocate to your one. You were single. You were the one with the medical background as well, as if we could ever forget it. You *were* the logical choice."

"First of all," I held up a finger. "I have no idea what that crack about never letting you forget I'm a vet is about. Second, I don't resent coming back to Greenbrier. At least, not anymore. What frosts my cookies is not once have I ever heard a single word of thanks for doing so. Not from you. Not from Mother."

"Thanks." Liz blinked slowly, as if she had trouble processing the word. "You want to be thanked."

Put that way, with disbelief dripping in icicles off her every word, it felt churlish of me to want a little acknowledgement of the sacrifices I'd made. I don't regret my time spent with Dad, and my job *had* been killing me.

Liz stood up with great dignity. "If you hadn't moved back to Greenbrier, you'd never have met Amanda Kelly. I'd say you've been thanked enough by her."

I sat with my mouth open as she collected the wine bottle and her glass. Without looking back, she said, "I'm going to call my kids."

She marched down the hallway to the main bedroom with the slightest of wobbles.

Despite the air conditioning, it felt like I couldn't breathe, so I leashed Remy and slipped out the door. When we hit the ground floor, I took him out the back of the building. There was a faint glow from the fire pit, but the residents had packed it in for the night. I was glad. I didn't want to talk to anyone right now.

Remy and I walked for a long time on the beach, the wind ruffling my hair as the waves murmured soothingly. Always happy to go for a walk, Remy quickly settled from excited crow-hopping into a contented amble. He seemed to know I needed to calm down, and after we walked as far as I thought was wise, we sat in the dunes and watched the tide come in. I kicked off my slides and dug my toes into the cool sand. Remy flopped down beside me and when I rested my hand on his shoulders, he laid his head across my legs. I stroked his ears.

For a moment, I could picture myself living here on the island. An image of me and Scotty galloping along the shore sprang to mind, riding her bareback, my arms spread wide like I was flying as she thundered across the hard-packed sand, and Remy keeping pace alongside.

Yeah. Right. How would I actually get her—or the old, retired horses—to the island? And where would I keep them? Not to mention, I'd probably have to feed hay year-round. And then there was the feral cat colony... No. Moving to the island was out of the question. Whether or not I kept the condo was a different story altogether.

The thing is, Liz was right about the inheritance. Amanda had even said as much. In a letter delivered after her death, she said she was leaving me her fortune because she thought I deserved it for coming back to Greenbrier to take care of my dad.

What's the saying? *In vino veritas*?

I sat on the dunes with my dog until the sea worked its magic on me and I could return to the condo without wanting to punch the walls.

When I entered the unit, Liz's bedroom door was still shut and the light was off. Just as well. No point in trying to have a rational conversation with someone well on her way to being drunk. I picked up my e-reader and escaped to my own room with the dog.

Sometime during the night, I woke abruptly with a gasping start to feel Remy nosing me. The last time that happened, my house had been on fire. No smell of smoke now, but once it was clear I was awake, Remy danced backward toward the door. The hallway light I'd left on in case Liz needed the bathroom spilled into the room, silhouetting the brush of Remy's tail and the shuffle of his feet. He gave a muffled bark, the kind of noise that meant he needed to go out right away.

The stolen hotdogs. They must have upset his stomach. I shoved my feet into the slides I'd left by the bed and grabbed the keys from the nightstand to follow Remy into the living room.

Remy pawed at the outer door, and I snatched up his leash to prevent him from damaging the wood in addition to ruining the carpets.

I clipped it on his collar and opened the door. His sudden lunge nearly wrenched my shoulder from its socket, but before I could scold him for pulling, he let out a booming bark.

The hallway maintained low level overhead lighting at night. The crime scene techs had gone home at last. Someone dressed in all in black, with a hoodie pulled up over their head, was bent over the doorknob of 1301, head tucked under the yellow crime scene tape across the door. When Remy barked, they jerked upright, breaking the tape barrier. Whoever it was wheeled and ran, even as Remy tried to drag me down the hallway after them. The door to the stairwell clanged shut just as we reached it. I grabbed the handle and started to open the door, but then it was pushed shut from the other side. Remy barked again at the sound of someone dashing down the stairwell. When I gave the metal bar a good shove, I felt resistance. I tried it again, but it wouldn't budge.

Which was probably just as well. What would I have done if Remy had caught the person?

The door to unit 1304 opened with a bang. A hairy-chested man in boxer shorts stood in the doorway with arms akimbo, and a sleep mask pulled up over his forehead. "For heaven's sake, keep it down out here."

"I'm sorry—"

"The no pets rule is a good one," the man snarled.

Irritated, I snapped, "Someone was trying to break into the condo next door."

"Then call the police. Quietly." The man stepped back into his unit and closed the door with decided force.

I stood blinking at him for a moment. Remy pawed at the jammed door to the stairwell and looked up at me. Mr. Grumpy Hairy Man had a point. I glanced at my watch. Almost 2:00 a.m. A smile curved my lips. With luck, I was about to ruin Deputy Wilson's night.

Chapter Nine

A TEXT ALERT WENT off on my phone at 5:50 a.m. I groaned and reached for the phone. When I opened the text, a stark message in all caps greeted me.

GET OUT WHILE YOU STILL CAN

My heart froze for a second and rebounded back in double-time.

What on earth?

Was this related to Brinkman's death? Who would have my phone number anyway? I began running through a mental list of people who might have access to my contact information.

A second message explained the first, as it contained a screenshot of the latest weather forecast, and I realized that both were from my mother. Apparently, the tropical depression had strengthened into a named storm now. Edna was fairly weak and most of the projections showed it missing us entirely, but that wasn't good enough for my mother.

Thanks, Mother, for nearly giving me a heart attack.

Normally I ignore nonemergency texts that fall outside of time frames I consider socially acceptable, but my mother was likely to call out the National Guard if I failed to respond, so I sent her a brief text back citing the ongoing investigation as to why we couldn't leave. Reminding her I was here on business (even if it was really more of a vacation) wasn't good enough for my mother when weather was involved.

Fortunately, I wanted to be up early anyway to take Remy out for a run.

The door to Liz's room was still shut. When I peeked in to make sure she was okay, I was tempted to capture her snoring on camera for when she would vehemently deny doing any such thing. But I remembered the tension between us and opted not to take hostilities to DEFCON 3.

Remy and I crept out of the unit (as much as anyone can creep with ninety pounds of excited dog) and into the hallway. The door to the stairwell opened easily, unlike when I tried it the night before. Fragments of splintered wood lay near the sill. The metal bar that opened the door from inside the hallway told me nothing, but a patch of paint had been scraped off the inside of the jamb on the stairwell side. A piece of wood jammed into the door to prevent it from opening? If so, whoever had tried to break into the unit knew the building well. At least well enough to bring along something to jam the door.

That was a disquieting thought.

Walking outside into the cool, damp air managed to dispel some of the uneasiness. In the east, pink streaks lightened the gray predawn sky. Like the evening before, the surf tumbled in and subsided in a rhythm that was somehow both bracing and calming, unraveling tangled nerves I hadn't realized were knotted again. The stiff breeze made me glad I'd brought a windbreaker. We made the short walk to the beach front, with Remy charging forward only to leap back in place beside me when he got to the limits of the leash. His excitement levels were so high, I didn't mind. Technically, he wasn't pulling.

An hour later, after having watched my dog romp and play to his heart's content, the appeal of living at the beach finally got through to me. I didn't think it was for me—between the broiling sun and brutal heat, it felt like a steep price to pay for a scant amount of heaven—but I could see why others loved it. And it certainly was a nice place to visit. But enough to justify keeping the property? The sale of the condo could go a long way toward funding the new vet clinic I wanted to build without tapping into more of the principal from the estate.

Definitely things to think about as I walked my sandy, wet, tired, happy dog back to the main street. At the last second, I took a detour into town toward Bennie's. On the other side of the bar, there'd been a bakery. Fresh bagels and coffee would be a nice peace offering, as well as a wakeup call for Liz. Provided she was ready to get up, that is. A glance at my watch made me doubt it. Despite the rising heat, it was barely nine a.m. by the time we returned to the Sand Dollar.

Remy's damp coat still held several pounds of sand, so I looked for the expected outdoor spigot and was pleased to find one near the back of the first building. Most likely each building had its own rinsing station. I set the bag of bagels and cardboard tray of coffee down on a nearby table and took Remy over to the station.

Hosing off his legs and belly was a process, as he thought it more fun to bite at the water than get rinsed. I was nearly as wet as he was when we were done, and there was no warm water option at the station. Shivering a little as I coiled the hose, I noticed someone down by the little bridge I'd observed the night before. The graceful movements of the person on the bridge suggested they were doing yoga. The blonde ponytail suggested it was Emily.

I looked down at Remy. He stared back at me with a happy grin. Breakfast awaited both of us, but I thought it might be wise to let him dry off a bit before heading upstairs.

That's what I told Remy, anyway.

We ambled our way down the walking path toward the wooden bridge, a task much easier than it would have been before Remy had his run on the beach. We passed the long marshy area where the inlet moved in slow ripples out to sea. Tall reeds obscured most of the bank, and I made sure to keep Remy a safe distance back from the edge. No telling what was hiding in the rushes.

To my relief, morning yoga activities seemed to be winding down as we reached the base of the bridge. It was indeed Emily. She was dressed in a tank top and yoga pants. She glanced in our direction before kneeling to roll up her mat.

"Emily, isn't it? I'm sorry, I didn't catch your last name. We're not interrupting, are we?" I motioned over my shoulder. "We can go another way."

Emily fixed a hard look on me as she stood, and I fought the urge to shuffle and squirm. Clearly, if I was worried about being disruptive, I could have simply picked a different path in the first place. She tucked her yoga mat under one arm. "No problem. I'm done here."

That statement had an interesting edge of finality to it.

As she passed, I turned Remy and fell into step alongside her. She cast another sharp-eyed glance at me but didn't stop. "I thought you were going the other way."

"We were. That is, not particularly." I felt flustered for being called out and resisted the urge to smack my forehead for being so obvious. "I'm just walking the dog until he dries off some. I wanted to apologize for last night."

This time she pulled up abruptly. She turned her pretty face in my direction and said, with a brittle smile, "Apologize?"

This girl was probably half my age. Her older lover had died under suspicious circumstances, and she was as cool as a cucumber. I couldn't have managed the same when I was twenty. Or even now, for that matter. I cleared my throat. "Yes. For the way everyone spoke of Mr. Brinkman. It must have been terribly difficult. I understand why you walked away last night."

"Do you?" This time the smile was less hostile, but faintly superior.

You'd have thought she was the millennial and I was from Gen Z, supposedly naïve and inexperienced. I guess it shouldn't have surprised me. Most kids today seem a lot more grown up than I was at that age.

"It must have been hard listening to everyone speak so ill of your...um..."

She laughed and started walking again. I let Remy tug me along to catch up.

Her long legs let her close the distance between the bridge and the building in seconds, and I was running out of time to ask her anything. "Do you have any idea what he was doing in my unit? The condo was supposed to be empty."

She stopped again and this time I didn't imagine the cold stare. "What do you think a property manager does? He's supposed to check on the units, regardless of occupancy. Besides, didn't you ask him to look for some specific paintings? Mostly likely that's why he was there."

Interesting that he'd shared that information with her.

I tossed my head back slightly in wide-eyed understanding. "Oh, you're right. That must be it. I don't know why I didn't think of that. The whole thing was such a shock, you know? Finding him like that, I mean. Didn't anyone notice he was missing?"

Her eyes narrowed slightly but her nostrils flared. Emily No Last Name hid her anger well, but the signs were there if you looked closely enough. "Jeff often would leave on business for a couple of days here and there. We weren't joined at the hip."

"Oh, I wasn't suggesting—"

"Yes, you were." Her voice was slightly mocking now. "What are you trying to say? That I should have reported Jeff missing? I assumed he was out of town."

Remy whined, shifting uncomfortably at the growing antagonism between Emily and me. I soothed his damp head and said quietly, "I didn't mean to imply anything. I'm just trying to understand what happened. Was Mr. Brinkman in poor health?"

Emily made a choking sound, quickly suppressed. "Not that I was aware of. Look, this may be hard for someone like you to believe, but Jeff and I had a mutual understanding. It wasn't about love."

She spoke "love" with the kind of disdain some people might use when saying "politics." "Someone like me" obviously meant a candidate for AARP, since everyone thirty and older clearly had one foot in the grave.

Given that I'd been playing up the role of the dim-witted but well-meaning middle-aged woman, I could hardly be annoyed that's how she saw me, so I aimed for a sympathetic smile instead of baring my teeth. "You were still more upset over his death than Andrea."

"It was a useful arrangement." She shrugged in a manner that only the young and careless can pull off. "All things come to an end sooner or later."

She stepped off the path to cut across the wide space of grass, taking her in a different direction from the building. To follow at this point would have looked very odd indeed. Yet Remy and I hadn't taken two steps toward my abandoned breakfast before she called out, "If you really want to find someone who'll rejoice over Jeff's death, you should talk to Manny Hernandez. He's the manager at Bennie's. I'll bet he bought a round for the house when he found out."

Before I could ask why she thought I would want to speak with anyone who'd wish Brinkman harm, she strode off.

"A mutual arrangement." I watched her head toward the parking lot, her walk loose-limbed, athletic, and eye-catching. An unplanned change of course, given she probably intended to go back to her unit. "I wonder, what did a middle-aged property manager have on you, my sweet?"

Remy pawed at my foot, and I gasped when his claws found my skin. Normally I wore boots.

"Right, right." I lead the way toward the coffee and bagels. "Breakfast it is."

Chapter Ten

To my surprise, Liz was up when we entered the apartment. She'd showered, put on fresh makeup, and stood in the kitchen nursing a cup of coffee the way most people savored their hallowed beverage. Not like a woman who'd put away at least a bottle of wine the night before. Her eyes were a little puffy, but otherwise she looked as put together as always.

"What's that?" She gave a nod to the bag in my hand as I set the tray of coffee down.

"Breakfast. From that bakery we saw last night. I brought coffee as well, in case the stuff here wasn't very good." I placed the bag of bagels on the counter between us and went to the cabinet for plates. Remy headed straight to his bowl and began chasing it around the kitchen island, so I stopped to scoop some kibble into his dish.

She pulled the bag over to her and opened it. "Bagels. You monster."

"Monster?" I frowned as I put the plates on the counter. Was she ready to pick up the fight from last night already? My voice had a sharp edge to it when I asked, "How does bringing bagels make me a monster?"

She gave me an evil glare from over the brim of her mug. "Because they're carbs. Look at you. Eating bagels and cream cheese like it's no big deal. You haven't gained an ounce since we were teenagers. I so much as *smell* a croissant and it goes straight to my waist."

Whoa. Not what I expected at all.

"Okay, first of all, I've gained at least twenty pounds since high school. I should know because Mother reminds me on a daily basis how much I've let myself go." I put finger quotes around my mother's favorite phrase to describe me. "Second, you must be blind if you think I haven't changed. Not the least of which is I wacked all my hair off, remember? As far as most of the male population goes, that makes me an undesirable harpy. Third, I thought we were on vacation. Vacation carbs don't count."

I got out the cream cheese along with little plastic knives and placed the tub between us, cautiously, the way I might leave food for a feral cat I wasn't sure might attack me for the effort.

Lip still curled, Liz selected a bagel from the bag.

"Twenty pounds is nothing. Try having children back-to-back." She set her coffee down in order to slather a generous portion of cream cheese to her bagel slice, not even waiting to toast it. "I've put on at least fifty pounds and no matter what I do, I can't budge it. I've tried every diet on the planet. I lose five pounds or so and it comes right back."

Liz had been a junior when I entered my freshman year of high school. She'd spent hours practicing for the cheer squad and had a different crazy diet for each week of the month. Having a mother who didn't believe anyone should ever actually have to eat hadn't helped. Liz still looked fabulous though.

"You look amazing. You always do. Poised, polished, and professional."

"Thank you. Nothing says 'sexy' like looking professional."

Where was this coming from?

"You know what I mean. You don't look as though you've been mud-wrestling piglets at the State Fair." I slid into a perfect imitation of our mother, deepening my accent and sharpening its edge. "Ginny, dear. *Must* you smell like a dog?"

Liz snorted outright at that and then hesitated before saying, "I'm sorry about last night. The details are a little fuzzy, but I know I was rude."

I started to automatically wave her apology aside, but she continued before I had a chance to open my mouth. "It's just you were gone so long, and I didn't know where you were. And the crime scene people were banging around next door because someone *died* in there. I kept thinking about you finding a dead body and then imagining what that must have been like, and I gave myself the heebie-jeebies."

"Yikes." I winced. "I'm sorry, I really meant to come back sooner. Honest. I ran into the residents, like I said, and then Mother called, and Joe called—"

"*Joe* called?" She pounced on that statement like a cat spying a mouse, her eyes suddenly focused on my face. "Does he often call you?"

"He keeps a horse at my place, so yes, we talk on a regular basis." Annoyed that I was offering an explanation when I didn't have to, I hurried on. "He called last night because Mercer had contacted him about me."

I relayed Joe's concerns about Mercer's motivations and added my own. "I hope Brinkman's reason for being in the apartment doesn't come down to the paintings after all. And if it does, that the paintings are still there. I can see this turning into a national news story if the artwork is missing."

I made my fingers into brackets, as though outlining a headline. "Mysterious Death of Property Manager Connected to Stolen Paintings of Dead Artist."

"That would definitely get people's attention." Liz set down her unfinished bagel to absently twist her wedding ring set around her finger. "Look, about last night..."

For once, instead of automatically dismissing what was bound to be another attempt at an apology, I waited her out.

"You were right, and I was wrong." Her words rushed out, sluice gates opened, as though she might lose her nerve to say them. "Everyone assumed you were the best choice to go home and help out—I don't think we were wrong there—but it *was* taken for granted that you'd go, and no, I never really acknowledged what a big deal it was or how grateful we were that you did it."

I cleared my throat uncomfortably. "Yeah, well, you were right about the way things turned out with the inheritance. Are you... Are you okay? Because between the wine and the way you flirted with the sheriff—"

Liz went as red as a tomato and covered her heated cheeks with her hands. "Oh, no. I didn't. Please tell me I didn't."

I spread my palms up with a shrug. "And then you got angry and stormed off to your bedroom..."

Liz winced and rubbed her temples. "I just feel old, you know? I'm not Liz Grant anymore—I'm Liz, the mother of Livy and Lindsay. I'm Dave Grant's wife. I'm 'good old Liz', the person at work who gets the job done but none of the credit for doing it. I'm going gray. I have crow's feet and stretch marks, and I'm getting those stupid lip lines too. I'm thinking of having some work done."

"Work?" I repeated stupidly.

"You know. Like a tummy tuck or lip filler." She bit into her bagel like she was taking a chunk out of someone's arm. Her eyes went shiny—though with tears of rage, hunger, or sadness, I couldn't tell.

"At least you're curvy in all the right places, and you always look Instagram-ready instead of being a beanpole or, as Mother likes to say, looking like a teenaged boy." I waved my bagel slices at her before popping them into the toaster. This lapse into revealing her insecurities made *my* insecurities quiver in alarm.

Liz sniggered despite herself. "No one looking at you could ever mistake you for being male."

"Thanks. Tell that to Mother. She thinks I look like a troglodyte."

"She never said that." Liz lifted an eyebrow in patent disbelief and took another bite of bagel.

"She didn't have to." You'd have thought I'd have built up a thick-enough suit of armor by now, but words delivered with the best of intentions often contained sharp points that could slide right past links of chain mail. "It was implied. She's also of the firm belief that unless I make some kind of effort with my appearance, only dogs will love me."

Hah. She completely discounted cats. And horses. I was surrounded by love.

"It's not like you've never dated." Liz grew thoughtful in a manner that made me squirm. "You've had at least one long-term relationship that I'm aware of. What was his name? Cory?"

"Colin." I hoped my tone was repressing enough she'd let the subject drop.

She snapped her fingers in remembrance. "That's right. Colin. What happened between you two?"

"He didn't want to move to Greenbrier."

"Oh." She hesitated, then added more forcefully, "*Oh.*"

I shrugged. "It's not a big deal."

"Ginny, I had no idea. No wonder you were angry with me and Mom."

"It never would have worked between us. He told me he was allergic to dogs and wanted me to rehome Major so we could get a Doodle."

"Doodles being hypoallergenic, I take it?" She frowned as what I said fully registered. "It's not like your dog is a car you can just trade in for a different model."

"No." I bit off the word sharply. I was annoyed with myself for how long it had taken me to realize Colin simply didn't like my previous German Shepherd. The feeling between him and Major had been mutual. "Doodles aren't really hypoallergenic, though some people benefit from the decreased shedding. Colin wasn't allergic. He hated all the dog hair and he thought a little lapdog suited us better."

I put finger quotes around the word "us."

"Uh-huh." Liz arched an eyebrow at me. "And he's still alive?"

"Funny."

I was ashamed to admit I'd shunted Major to the side in the early days of our relationship in order to keep Colin happy. My workload those first couple of years out of school was so intense, I hadn't even thought about dating. Joe and I had gone our separate ways. Most of the guys I'd dated since had been defeated by the eighty-hour work-weeks and on-call schedules. By the time I'd met Colin, I thought love had passed me by, and I'd been determined to give it my all.

"At least a dog is loyal." Liz flicked a look of cool assessment at me. "Of course, Mom's right about the way you dress. I mean, with short hair, you really need to make an effort to accessorize."

"Not you too." That stung. Why is it family always knows how to push your buttons? "You know I have to wear practical clothing for work, and I'm almost always working."

"You're not working now. Really, Ginny, those shorts have seen better days."

Whatever mood had reduced her to tears had passed and the Liz I knew was firmly back in control. Maybe all it took was running myself down. I was well-versed in beating others to the punch. It hurt less that way.

Liz waved a hand about in my general direction. "Didn't you go shopping when you had to replace your entire wardrobe after the fire?"

"That was back in March." I sounded sulky, but I didn't care. "It was still cold then."

She rolled her eyes. "You're allowed to go shopping more than once, you know. That's what we'll do this afternoon. I can't believe you only brought that beat-up duffle bag with you, like you're an adventurer who must travel light. With just your fedora and a bull whip. We'll buy some luggage and get you some new outfits."

"Everything here will be so expensive." I would *not* kick the base of the counter, even though I felt like doing it.

My bagel popped up and I fished the hot slices out of the toaster.

"How fortunate you have plenty of money." Liz's drawl was so sarcastic, it reminded me of Joe. "Come on, this is what I do really well. I'll help you pick out some versatile pieces you can wear both here and back home."

She looked really excited by the idea, darn it. I realized that for Liz, shopping was fun. Going on a spree—on my dime to boot—would be a way of making up for fighting with her.

"No dresses. I look like I'm wearing a potato sack." I slapped cream cheese on my bagel slices with vigor.

"You just haven't found the right dress." She held up a placating hand when I started to speak. "Trust me. I won't let you buy anything that doesn't look good on you."

Which is how, later that day after having selected "the least disreputable" of my outfits to wear, I found myself being herded by my sister as effectively as a collie to go shopping.

I sincerely hoped I wouldn't regret it.

Chapter Eleven

"Is the dog going to be okay?" Liz asked as we locked the door and headed toward the elevator.

I suspected her question was less about Remy's mental wellbeing and more about how long we could reasonably expect to be gone from the unit. "He'll be fine for now. I took him out while you were getting ready and he had a good run this morning. We'll go out again for another walk on the beach when it cools off this evening."

We passed unit 1301. The door stood open and a couple of techs worked quietly within, looking up as we passed.

"I thought they were done." Liz shouldered her bag as though one of the techs might try to grab it.

"Joe says it can take days to process a scene." I pressed the button for the elevator.

"Joe says?" Liz was back to wearing shades and her shielded eyes made her seem perfectly secure behind barriers again. "So, we're quoting Joe now?"

I studiously adjusted my wristwatch and went back to staring at the elevator doors. "You specifically asked about working the crime scene. Last night I asked him how long it usually took. I'm relaying information, not hanging on his every word."

"You keep telling yourself that, sis."

Before I could muster a snappy retort, the elevator doors opened. Deputy Wilson started out of the lift, only to stop dead at the sight of us. He paused so long the doors almost closed on him, and he had to shove his arm out in front of him to stop the automatic closure. "You."

There was no question who he meant, but he followed up by pointing at me. "Sheriff Mercer wants a statement about last night."

"I gave my information to the dispatcher."

I could feel Liz burning holes in me with her eyes, even from behind her shades.

"That was before this officially became a homicide investigation." Still holding the door, he seemed to be reading my face for a reaction.

A sinking feeling in my gut caused a momentary sense of instability, as though I was already in the elevator and the floor had dropped beneath me. I spoke without thinking. "I was afraid of that."

That gave Wilson the opening he wanted. "Oh really? And why is that?"

Ugh. Hadn't Joe warned me to watch my step around the police here? "Just considering the odds, that's all. I hoped it would turn out to be natural causes."

"In the brief moment you glanced into the condo, that is." Sarcasm wasn't a good look on Deputy Wilson.

"How did he die?" Liz asked.

Wilson looked her up and down before saying, "We're not releasing those details to the public at this time."

He relayed the party line in a haughty tone. Aping Mercer, no doubt. Dismissing Liz, he turned back to me. "So, what about last night?"

"Someone wearing a hoodie tried to break into unit 1301. When my dog barked at them, they took off and ran into the stairwell. I tried to get a better look at them, but the door to the stairs wouldn't budge when I tried to open it."

Liz pulled her shades down with one finger to boggle at me, but thankfully said nothing.

"Yeah, well what were you doing in the hallway at 2:00 a.m. anyhow?" Wilson had an air of triumph, as though he'd caught me in the act of doing something illicit.

"The dog wanted to go out. He must have heard the intruder." I indicated the elevator, where Wilson stood still blocking the doors. "Are you leaving? We're going down."

Wilson stepped aside, holding the doors open with one arm. "By all means. Did you give Sheriff Mercer the details on the artwork that's supposed to be in the unit?"

"I emailed the list—including images of the paintings Amanda had added to the inventory herself—to him last night." Once I was inside the elevator, I turned to face Wilson. "Hold up. Supposed to be? Are you saying they aren't there? That someone has taken them?"

"I didn't say that." Trolls had a more pleasant expression than Wilson's scowl, which drew his heavy black brows together in a single ridge. "You were the one who sent Brinkman looking for the paintings. So that means you weren't sure they were there in the first place."

Liz hung back in the hallway, chewing at her bottom lip as if not certain she should interrupt by boarding the elevator.

"How many times do I have to say this? I've never been to Hartberry Isle or the condo. I have no idea if the paintings are there or not. That's why I asked Mr. Brinkman to confirm the presence of the artwork. Have the paintings disappeared?"

"You know I can't discuss the details of the investigation with anyone at this time." Wilson studied me for a long moment before giving me a smile that made me distinctly uncomfortable as he dropped his arm. "Oh, and Miz Reese? Don't plan on leaving the island any time soon."

Liz took that as her cue to get into the elevator. His position by the doors placed him in close proximity to her as she squeezed by him. With her sunglasses back in place, she led with a lifted chin as she joined me. He definitely ogled her rear when she brushed past. I pressed the "Close Doors" button as soon as she was inside.

He stood in the hallway facing us, giving Liz a slow once-over as he did so, one that was night and day different from the assessment he'd given me a moment earlier. The doors slid shut.

"Ugh." Liz wiped at her arm as though brushing off any lingering contact. "What a sleezy creep. Married, too."

"He is?" I guess it takes all kinds, though the notion astonished me.

"You didn't notice the wedding ring? Well, you wouldn't."

"What's *that* supposed to mean?"

Liz gave her hand a little spin in the air. "Only that it's not the sort of thing on your radar most of the time. You could tell me if Wilson had a calico cat because you'd notice the little tri-colored hairs on his clothes, but aside from that, you don't really engage with people like you do animals."

I had absolutely no idea how to respond to that.

She pressed the button for the ground floor. "Oh, don't look at me like that. I didn't mean it as an insult. Just an observation. Anyway, Deputy Wilson is an idiot."

While I couldn't agree more, Joe's warning regarding the local police came to mind. Why hadn't the police confirmed the presence or absence of the paintings? If they were there, why not say so? Unless Wilson just liked the power play of jerking my chain. "He might be an idiot, but I doubt his boss is. We need to watch what we say around the law enforcement here."

"By telling that deputy you suspected it was murder all along? Smooth move, there. By the way, when were you going to tell me about the attempted break-in? I'm not Mom, you know." The tightness in Liz's voice sounded a lot like hurt.

"I meant to. I just forgot. Lots of things on my mind. You know." I offered an olive branch. "Remember the young lover I told you about? The one Brinkman left his wife for? I ran into her as I was coming back from the beach this morning."

I shared the details of my conversation with Emily. This seemed to mollify Liz a bit and it gave me time to wonder if I was shutting her out intentionally or subconsciously. I suspect a little of both.

The elevator doors opened out onto the ground floor. We exited just as Andrea was coming in the front door.

"Andrea!" I waved as though she were a long-lost friend and tugged Liz over to her. "Liz, this is Andrea Brinkman. We met last night. Andrea, my sister Liz."

To her credit, Liz played her part as though she'd been coached. She clasped Andrea's hand in both of her own and said, "Oh, my *dear*. Ginny told me about meeting you. I am so terribly sorry for your loss."

Andrea initially seemed taken aback by this fulsome expression of condolences but pressed a hand over her ample bosom while extracting the other from Liz's grasp. "That's very kind of you, but your sister can tell you, there was no love lost between Jeff and me. We were getting a divorce."

"Someone can be the biggest jerk in the world, and it's still shocking if something happens to them." A touch of sympathetic sisterhood warmed Liz's voice. "You loved him once. You have history."

Andrea's expression softened and she suddenly seemed years younger. "Yeah, there's some truth to that."

"I was just telling Liz that I ran into Emily this morning—I'm afraid I don't remember her last name—and she said something about some guy named Manny who hated Mr. Brinkman's guts. It struck me as a kind of odd thing to say." I shook my head as if I couldn't understand it.

Liz's expression might have been hidden by her sunglasses, but she turned her head ever-so-slightly in my direction.

"Bledsoe. Emily Bledsoe," Andrea supplied automatically, before appearing to give my statement some frowning thought. "She's not far off, come to think of it. Manny Hernandez used to be good friends with Jeff until recently. They had a falling out not too long before I found out Jeff was cheating on me. They actually came to blows over whatever it was. Never spoke to each other again, as far as I knew."

Her brow cleared. "Huh. Never thought about it much before, but I bet Manny knew about the affair. The three of us were good friends at one point. That's probably what they fought about."

"That could explain a lot then." I smiled as though certain Andrea had hit upon the cause of the discord. "Emily said he worked at Bennie's, and Liz and I were planning to eat there tonight. I didn't want things to be awkward or anything."

Andrea rocked her head back slightly on her neck with a bit of a twisted smile. "I'm not sure why it would be awkward, but I wouldn't hesitate to go to Bennie's if you want. Great seafood."

Liz opened her mouth as if to say something—no doubt that we'd eaten there the night before—but clamped her lips shut when I kicked her in the ankle as subtly as possible.

"Terrific. Thanks for the recommendation." I smiled brightly, befitting the slightly dingy persona I'd used with Emily that morning.

Andrea tipped her head to one side thoughtfully. "I haven't seen Manny in a while. Maybe I should head to Bennie's this evening myself. It's karaoke night at the bar." She paused to smooth one hand down her waist and over her thigh with a grin. "He likes redheads."

"Oooh, karaoke." Liz practically trilled, taking me by the arm to tug me away. "Maybe we'll see you there? Now we definitely have to go shopping."

"What are you doing?" I muttered under my breath as she hauled me away. "I'm trying to figure out who might have been in on Brinkman's rental scam."

"You heard her. Manny likes redheads. We can see to it he talks to you tonight."

I rolled my eyes. "I'm guessing Manny prefers the tough bar chick look over the hulking Amazon."

"We'll see about that. You brought your credit cards, right? When I'm done with you, Manny won't notice anyone else in the bar."

The amusement in my sister's voice boded ill for both me and my wallet.

Chapter Twelve

TO MY SURPRISE, LIZ vetoed dinner at Bennie's in favor of grabbing a quick bite to eat at a café in town. "No point in showing up at the bar until later. Either Manny will be working tonight or he won't, and he's likely to be more talkative with the bar crowd than the dinner one. It will probably be less hectic then."

She had a point.

Our shopping expedition had also been far less painful than expected, largely because Liz had a good eye for color and putting outfits together, much like my friend Meg back in Greenbrier. If I could have a personal shopper all the time, pulling together a polished look wouldn't be nearly so difficult. The clothes were one thing. The makeup, skin and hair products, and jewelry were something else altogether. A simple jar of face cream cost at least half as much as my new car payment would run, and I vowed to return to the cheaper Oil of Delay when the jar of liquid gold ran out. But even there, Liz had chosen items with me in mind and not her own personal taste.

We talked as well. Miz Hattie wasn't the only one who thought I should open a clinic on the island. According to Liz, it would take me out of Mother's orbit, provide a much-needed service to the local community, and the sale of the property in Greenbrier would more than pay for building the clinic from the ground up. When I pointed out I would have to swim my horses across from Hilton Head like Chincoteague ponies, the sarcasm didn't register.

We didn't just shop for me, either. While Liz seemed reluctant to spend anything on herself, I persuaded her to accept some gifts for the girls, and we'd enjoyed picking out things they'd like. Truth be told, I wish it could always be like that between us. That was the whole point of inviting her on this trip, wasn't it? An attempt to reconnect and repair fences, if needed.

Which is why, after having taken Remy for a long walk and returning for a shower, I sat unresisting at the kitchen counter and allowed my sister to put makeup on my face.

The end result shocked me. Somehow, she'd made my eyes bigger and greener with what she called a "smoky" look. She'd teased my hair into standing up in short spikes that reminded me of Joe's metrosexual style and had paired a simple silver pendant with a lemon-yellow tank top and a short black leather skirt. I drew the line at stilettos, but the black ankle boots were sublime. How did she know I had a weakness for boots? Somehow, she also talked me into wearing an ear cuff with a small chain that connected to a set of dangling silver feathers in the primary piercing.

"Silver looks best on you, not gold. Short hair, long neck, great arms. A bit of an androgenous look, make the most of it. No, not that lipstick. It's too orange. Think 1940s *Victory Red*." She leaned back and studied her efforts like an artist considering a canvas. "You could be a contestant on one of those modeling shows."

"You watch too much reality TV. Besides, I enjoy eating," I groused, but I did like the effect. Maybe I could manage to recreate it myself, with a little tutoring and a lot of practice. On the rare occasions when I had a reason to dress up, that is. "You don't think the lipstick is a bit much?"

"Let your lips make a statement for you. Much like the short hair. Your makeup and hair need to be punchy if you don't want to look too masculine."

I'd never admit in a million years that for someone who chose her outfits based on what wouldn't show animal hair or mud, the idea of making a statement felt kind of good.

Remy, happily content to lie on the couch as we got ready to leave, gave two thumps of his tail when I petted his head to say goodbye. A tired dog is a good dog. A happy dog is the best dog.

Liz's own ensemble was hard to describe. Less soccer mom and more *Sex and the City*. She'd donned a burgundy wraparound top that showcased her cleavage in a spectacular way paired with a pencil skirt in the same shade that made her look like Marilyn Monroe. She'd even flipped the ends of her hair out in a style reminiscent of Marilyn's. No doubt about it. She'd stop traffic when we walked to the bar.

"What's the plan, Stan?" Liz asked as we stepped out of the building into the warm, humid night. "You're obviously looking into this murder on your own."

My protest was automatic. "No, I'm not. Well, okay, maybe a little. But just some mild poking around, that's all. It's really about the artwork. According to Laney there should be three of Amanda's cataloged paintings in the condo. That doesn't include any she may have painted on her last trip down. By all accounts, Amanda was good about indexing her works, but not always, particularly if she was in the mood to move artwork between her various residences. Since she'd been on Hartberry Isle a few weeks before her death, there's always a possibility there are some additional paintings we don't know about."

"What are we talking about here money-wise?" Liz flicked a sharp look at me. "And don't waffle around trying to avoid telling me how much you're worth now."

Ouch.

"It's not waffling. I really don't know for sure. Laney told me one of Amanda's paintings could run for anywhere between two to three grand a pop—but that was before her death. The last of Amanda Kelly's work?" I made finger quotes as I spoke. "We could be talking thirty to forty now. Possibly more. That is, according to the last gallery that contacted me begging for anything, even a charcoal drawing."

The little sketch of Remy Amanda had done last year was now worth an easy fifteen hundred dollars. To me it was priceless.

"And there may be more than the three in question?" She pursed her lips and whistled. "Ginny, that's some serious dough we're talking about here."

My wince was automatic. "I know. I should have come down here sooner. There was a lot going on in my life though."

"No use crying over spilt milk. They're either in the unit or they're not."

"That's just it. The police aren't saying. Until we can get into the unit, we won't know if they're missing or not. I get the impression Brinkman wouldn't be above walking off with some valuable paintings. His death could be related directly to his being in Amanda's condo or else it's where someone with a grudge caught up with him. Either way, I admit to some curiosity about the whole thing. Especially after meeting the residents last night and how they took the news."

"It's become an addiction with you now, hasn't it? This investigating murders thing. You always were a freak for puzzles."

As we walked toward the row of businesses, the street became more crowded. People were definitely looking for a night out on the town. If I'd worried about being overdressed, I needn't have done so. For every person wearing beach clothes, there was someone else dressed to the nines. "I think it's more than that. It's a bit like solving a diagnostic mystery. I see a sick cat; I want to figure out what's wrong with it and fix it."

"But unlike back home, you've got no personal stake in solving this one. So why get involved?"

She had me there. I had no good reason for sticking my nose in where it didn't belong and lots of good ones for butting out.

"Brinkman gave me the run around about getting into the condo," I said at last. "I'm sorry he's dead, but I'm more concerned about whether or not he's stolen the paintings. I hope not, but now that his death has been labeled a homicide, I don't have a good feeling about it. Anyway, as soon as we find out whether the paintings are there or not, my sleuthing days are over."

"Fair enough." Liz clicked along the sidewalk beside me in dainty gold lame sandals with needle-thin heels. "But what if the paintings aren't there?"

"They better be." I didn't like the thought of Amanda's artwork having walked out the door to wind up in some illicit collection. "If not, that's going to open another whole can of worms."

If the three original paintings were missing, there was a slim chance we might be able to track down the inventoried items. Any uncatalogued work would be in the wind, though.

The bars and cafes were doing a strong business, with music, laughter, and the scents of fried food wafting out onto the street. Lit business signs competed with halogen streetlamps and fairy lights over outdoor seating to create a festive air. The "we're on vacation" atmosphere was tempered by a sense of sophistication. No gaudy neon flashes. Even the music edged toward cool jazz and blues over country. A far cry from Main Street in Greenbrier, where a bar fight was likely to spill out of Lucky's into the road.

Was it weird that I would have been happier with the more rough and ready crowd back home? Maybe my fine feathers made me more uncomfortable than I thought.

We paused at the corner to cross the street. Tempting as it was to cross anyway, due to the lack of much traffic, we waited for the light.

"Anyway, I have no real excuse for meddling in the murder itself this time. No one I know is at risk of wrongful conviction. Brinkman was likely killed by someone he knew—and that's not us. We should leave it alone."

"Who are you trying to convince? Me or you?"

I sighed. "More me than you, I'd say."

"Especially since here we are on our way to Bennie's, where someone who hated the dead guy might be working."

The light changed, and we entered the crosswalk. A bit of a crowd gathered in front of Bennie's and we got in line. The bass of some song thumped its way through the open door of the bar.

"Emily knew about the paintings—she mentioned them this morning. Maybe Brinkman discussed them with his former friend, Manny, as well." Talking to him was worth a shot at any rate. If the paintings are gone, we might have a head start on tracking them down. "Kudos to you earlier for handling Andrea the way you did, by the way. But how did you know I wanted to pump her for information?"

Liz tossed her head back and laughed, the first genuine sign of amusement I'd seen since the beginning of our trip. "Oh, Ginny. You rushed us over to meet her like she was a long-lost friend. You actually *introduced* me to her. Social skills aren't exactly your forte. There was only one of two possible explanations. Either you wanted something from her or you were a pod person."

There was no point in taking offense at the truth. "Huh. Maybe the detective gene runs in the family."

"Maybe," Liz agreed. "You know Mom fancies she would make a good spy, don't you?"

"Do I?" I snorted and regaled her with how I'd taken advantage of our mother's yearnings to be Jane Bond. The truth was, however, that playing off my mother's deepest fantasies had been beneficial in many ways. Not only had I gotten her off my back when I needed space after Amanda's murder, but my mother actually came up with critical information—the nature of which I'd have never ferreted out on my own.

The group ahead of us was called to a table, and Liz and I were able to squeeze into the entrance, where a woman took our names for seating over the excruciating wail of someone murdering "Hotel California" on stage.

I'd been spelunking in caves with better lighting than the inside of the bar. The place was nearly pitch-black, with the exception of the large screen positioned facing the stage so singers could see the lyrics of the songs and a bright spot highlighting the stage itself.

"What are you going to say to Manny anyway?" Liz had to raise her voice to shout in my ear. "You can't exactly walk up to him and ask if he's glad good ol' Uncle Jeff is dead."

"I don't know." I indicated with my hand she should keep it down, but she only rolled her eyes at me. "I'm making this up as I go along."

Someone directed us to a small open table in the back. We edged our way through the crowd and took our seats even as an employee wiped the surface with a damp rag. We were lucky to get a seat at all; our table must have just become available. There was an empty table near the stage, but it had a small placard stating "reserved" on it, which surprised me. Bennie's didn't strike me as the kind of joint that lent itself to reservations.

I suppose it could have been worse. Our table was jammed up against the back wall, but at least there was reasonable access to both the restroom and the emergency exit. The crush within the bar had to be over capacity and the thought of trying to get out in the event of a fire made the pulse jump in my neck.

Liz leaned across the table to yell at me. "Speaking of Uncle Jeff—isn't that young Timmy over by the bar?"

I craned my head to look over the crowd and spotted him perched on a stool in front of the long counter, nursing a beer. I reflexively jerked and ducked my head when I saw who he was sitting beside. "Don't look now, but Deputy Wilson is with him."

Liz rose up in her seat to peer over the heads of the patrons. She sat down with a muffled curse and a thud. "Gah, I didn't notice him at first because he's out of uniform."

"I said don't look." The last thing we wanted was to get caught staring. "I'm guessing that's why he was annoyed with the crime scene tech—what was her name? The one who told us to come to Bennie's. This must be a hangout for him."

"Yay. The Creep Squad. Let's hope they stay clear of us tonight." She looked around for a server. "Do you think anyone is going to take our drink order?"

"Someone's coming." I nodded to a server winding his way through several dancing couples to make his way toward us.

"Good. Say, you know what this means, don't you?" Liz's eyes lit up as the thought occurred to her. "If this is Wilson's bar, then he's local to the immediate area. It means he lives around here."

I could see where she was going with this. "Which is probably why he was the first officer on the scene. Don't make more out of this than it is."

Even as I spoke, Wilson and Tim had their heads together, as though deep in conversation. Of course, they could have been talking about football, for all we knew, and shouting at each other to be heard.

Liz pouted ever so slightly before diving in again. "We picked the wrong time to come. I didn't realize it would be so busy. Manny won't have time for your questions about the murdered guy tonight."

Three things happened almost at once. The server arrived at our table, the music died, and Liz bellowed her last sentence into the lull in the sound.

Tim and Wilson both turned to glare at us, apparently trying to slay me with their eyes. Heat rushed into my cheeks. Fortunately, the lighting in the bar was too dark to reveal it. Liz crinkled her eyes and nose in order to mouth "sorry" at me.

"Karaoke night is always popular." The server flipped open a small notepad and stood poised with a pen. "You looking for Manny? That's him at the mic."

A big beefy man with a shaved head and a dark mustache and goatee asked the crowd to give a round of applause to the woman teetering down the steps off the stage platform to join her laughing friends. He glanced our way as though, he too, had heard Liz. I hoped not.

"Is it too late to sign up for karaoke?" Liz asked brightly, as though she hadn't shoved her size eight foot into her size big mouth. "We should do that."

"Absolutely not." The thought made my skin crawl. I turned to the server. "Can I have a glass of the house red?"

"Oh, come on, Ginny." The pout reappeared. "I've always wanted to try it, and it's never been the right time. We could do it together."

The next singer took the mic and we were back to yelling again.

"There are only two reasons to do karaoke," I shouted. "Either you're delusional about your skill set or you're looking to make your friends howl with laughter."

The server tipped his pen at me as if I'd made an excellent point before pivoting ask Liz, "Drink for you?"

"I want a shot of tequila." She glanced up at the server through her bangs with the kind of smile seldom seen outside the pages of one of the racier romance novels. "Keep 'em coming."

"Are you sure that's wise?" I asked when the server nodded and dove back into the crowd again. Anxiety caused the pulse in my throat to pick up double-time.

"Don't start with me." If I'd thought the glares I'd received earlier from Wilson and Tim were bad, they had nothing on Liz's death stare. "I'm here to have fun."

"I'm not against having fun." It was the "keep 'em coming" part of her request that bothered me. "I'm just thinking your liver isn't as young as it used to be."

"Are you saying I'm old? Because—"

"Oh look, Andrea's here." I grasped at whatever straw would get me out of the hole I'd dug with Liz. "I guess this place really is jumping on Saturday nights."

"Who's that silver fox with her?" Diverted, Liz squinted in the direction of the door.

It was obvious the moment she recognized him. I realized belatedly I'd never given her all the details about the night before.

"Is that..." Liz gasped. "It is. She's with Troy Doherty, the actor."

"Maybe they'll join us." I waved desperately at Andrea.

Troy saw my gesture, lifted a hand in return, and nudged Andrea toward our table.

"Hang on a second." Liz turned a glare on me that would have melted steel. "You met Troy Doherty last night and you *didn't tell me*?"

Enraged dragons sounded less furious. I half-expected sulfurous flames to shoot out Liz's nose at any moment. Mentally dope-slapping myself for not mentioning sooner, I said, "It slipped my mind."

Once again, the music ended abruptly, and Liz's shriek could be heard over the background noise.

"It slipped your mind?"

Heads turned our way at her outrage.

Thank God for Troy. He swooped over to the table, ushering Andrea in front of him.

"Ginny!" He seemed truly delighted to see us. "I'm so glad we ran into you. The food's great here, isn't it?"

He saw Andrea seated, and then turned a five hundred-thousand-watt smile on my sister. Lifting her hand to his lips, he murmured, "And you must be the lovely Liz. I've heard so much about you."

Liz simpered with her hand still in Troy's clasp. I might as well have not been there at all.

Chapter Thirteen

"I'M SURPRISED TO SEE you two here. I thought you'd be gathering back at the Sand Dollar." I raised my voice over the music, leaning forward across the table as I did so.

"What? And miss karaoke night?" Troy's smile was so blinding, he could have posed for toothpaste commercials. He probably had.

Andrea helped herself to a handful of pretzels from the little dish in the center of the table and looked around for the server. As soon as she flagged his attention, she swiveled back to face us again. "I told you this afternoon I wanted to talk to Manny."

The people at the next table were only too happy to give one of their chairs to Troy once he turned his powerful smile on them, and he placed the chair between me and Liz as he spoke. "What's this about Manny?"

From the frown on Andrea's face, she was a little put out by the seating arrangements, as she was wedged on my far side. "I think I figured out why he and Jeff had a falling out. It's sweet, really."

When the server came with our drinks, Andrea ordered a screwdriver. Troy ordered an IPA, and my sister, heaven help her, knocked back her shot of tequila and asked for another one. I took a sip of my wine and made a note to ask the server about the label because it was considerably smoother than the average house brand.

"Mr. Doherty, it's such—"

"Please, call me Troy." He neatly cut Liz off mid-gush and patted her on the hand. "We're all friends here."

He leaned forward, raising his voice so Andrea could hear him. "What do you mean about Manny? What's sweet?"

"Manny and Jeff. Huge fight about six months ago—right before we split up." Andrea tapped a finger on the table. "Manny must have known about Jeff's affair with little Miss Yoga Queen. He was standing up for me."

Troy's jaw dropped slightly, but he had the smarts to shut his mouth quickly. "My dear, that's brilliant. Of course, you must be right."

"Miss Yoga Queen being..." Liz asked with her head cocked to one side like a robin spying a worm.

"Emily Bledsoe," I volunteered. "She was the one I ran into this morning, remember?"

Turning to Andrea, I said, "Does she take yoga or teach it? Or both?"

I had to repeat myself to be heard, as another singer took the stage.

"Oh, who knows," Andrea said in disgust when she finally understood me. "She doesn't teach at a studio nearby, for what that's worth. She claims to be an influencer, whatever the heck that means."

"It means she has a social media presence." Liz took out her phone from her bag. She and Troy bent their heads over it as she began checking various platforms. "I'm not finding anything right off the bat. Maybe she goes by a handle instead of her actual name."

Andrea suggested a name that combined both Emily's flexibility and presumed promiscuity and Troy said, "Andrea" in a tone that said he should disapprove but he found her amusing.

The server came back with the drinks. Andrea took hers like someone desperately needing oxygen who'd discovered an O2 line. Troy took a sip from his beer and set it in front of him. Liz downed her shot glass in one gulp and slapped the glass upside down on the table beside the first one. Bouncing up out of her seat, she gave us all a beaming smile. "I'm going to sign up for karaoke!"

"Oh dear." I watched her thread her way through the crowd toward Manny.

"Your sister seems like a lot of fun." Troy gave me one of those little boy grins that sent a frisson of alarm up my spine.

"My sister is married with two children," I said loudly. In order to be heard, of course.

Troy merely lifted an eyebrow and smiled even wider.

Holding a conversation in the noisy bar was challenging, but we tried our best. On her return, Liz took to placing a hand up to Troy's ear to speak to him, the result of which had both of them laughing. At one point, Troy caught my eye and had the effrontery to wink. That left me to speak with Andrea, even though she seemed perfectly content to watch the singers.

Between the heat in the room, the laughter of well-lubricated people, and the booming bass of the karaoke machine, it didn't take long for a jackhammer of a headache to take residence at the base of my skull. I hadn't brought any ibuprofen with me—my little clutch purse barely held my phone and credit card. After the events of the past year, I never left the house without pepper spray, and I'd had to clip it to the chain link strap for lack of space in the purse.

"Do any of you have something for a headache?" Yelling was becoming old and it only made the jackhammer worse.

Troy shook his head. Both Andrea and Liz began rooting around in oversized bags. Liz found a travel packet of ibuprofen. I took it with gratitude and excused myself to get something to wash it down. At the bar, the bartender filled a plastic cup with cold water and pushed it across the counter at me.

"You."

The word came from behind and was said with enough force that I turned to see who was speaking.

Tim, cheeks flushed from a combination of alcohol and anger, stood with clenched fists, clearly looking for a fight.

I didn't give him the chance. I took my water with me instead of drinking it at the bar. That proved to be a mistake, as dancers threatened to knock it out of my hands when I tried to cut in between them to return to our table. How did the servers manage to navigate the floor with entire trays full of drinks? Giving it up as a bad cause, I ducked into the long narrow corridor that led to the bathroom so I could tear open the packet and wash down the pain meds.

No sooner did I crumple up the cup and toss it into a trashcan did I hear someone call my name. I whipped around with my hand coming to rest on the clutch at my hip, and my fingers closing around the tiny container of pepper spray.

"Well, don't you clean up nice."

Deputy Wilson's bulk filled the hallway, almost blocking my exit. He gave me a leisurely once over that made the hair on my arms rise. If I'd been a dog, my hackles would be up.

"The difference between driving all day and going out with friends." My smile felt stiff and unnatural, but I hoped it would pass for pleasant.

"Friends." The word rolled off his tongue as though he savored it, and he placed one hand on the wall, effectively eliminating my ability to pass. "You seem to make friends easy."

"Thanks."

I held both my ground and my eye contact. This close, I could see the redness in his cheeks and nose, which spoke of more than one drink this evening.

"Well, here's a bit of friendly advice, Miz Reese." His eyes narrowed as he cocked his head slightly to one side. "I hear you've been nosing around, asking questions. I've also heard this isn't the first time you've been involved in a homicide. You need to butt out. Before you find yourself in a heap of trouble."

"I don't know what you're talking about." Best to let him think he was barking up the wrong tree. "If you'll excuse me—"

He dropped his hand to step in front of me, preventing me from leaving the corridor. "I'm talking about you chatting up the locals. Coming here to talk to Manny about Jeff."

I couldn't help it. The words came out of my mouth before I could stop them. "Oh, it's Jeff, now? Did you know him well?"

Wilson pointed a finger as thick as a sausage in my face. "This here's exactly what I'm talking about. You shut your mouth and mind your business, or we'll throw you in a cell for obstruction of a police investigation."

A pair of giggling women stumbled their way into the hallway, only to pull up short behind Wilson.

"We need the restroom," one of them said, placing her hands on her hips and looking distinctly put out by the delay.

Wilson stepped aside to let them pass, and I cut behind them to leave the corridor. When I glanced back, Wilson was watching me. I shivered despite the heat in the bar.

Andrea stood up when I reached the table.

"Where are you going?" No matter where it was, it had to be better than watching Liz flirt with Troy.

Andrea jerked a thumb at the back exit. "I need a smoke."

"I'll come with you. I need some air."

Troy and Liz were still deep in their amused conversation and barely looked up when I told them we'd be right back. I followed Andrea down another corridor to the back door and watched as she pinned a matchbook over the catch so we could get back inside.

"Aren't you going to need that?"

"Got another." She grinned, stepped a few feet away from the door, took out another matchbook, and lit up her cigarette. She puffed a few times and then took a hard drag, causing the end of the cigarette to glow red.

The alley was typical of its kind. A bulb over the back door of the bar cast a pool of light near the door that faded away into a narrow passageway between the buildings out to the street. Outside of the light, the shadows were as fathomless as the bottom of the sea. From a row of trash cans, the odor of old fish wafted, but mostly the air was fresh, damp, and laden with salt.

I took a deep breath and felt the tension in my chest ease. My phone made the communicator noise from the original *Star Trek* series, and I dug it out of the tight confines of my purse.

"Cute," Andrea said, watching as I checked the text message.

"I'm lucky we came outside. I'd have never heard it in the bar," I responded, frowning as I read the text.

"Problem?"

I looked up from the phone. "No. Not really. An old friend checking on me."

The text was from Joe, asking where I was. Not sure why he cared, my fingers flew over the keypad.

Drinks with Liz at the local bar.

I put the phone back in my purse, half-listening for another text but not hearing anything. Weird.

Andrea held out her pack. "You want a smoke?"

I shook my head. "No thanks. I just needed to get out of the bar for a bit. The noise in there was getting to be too much."

Andrea gave half a laugh and leaned back against the wall to continue smoking, bringing one foot up behind her to rest on the brickwork. "Yeah, but if you stick around, it'll be worth it. You'll see."

"I will?"

She nodded as she savored the cigarette. "I'm not spoiling it for you though. Wait and see."

I started to run my fingers through my hair, encountered the stiff spikes Liz had created with gel, and dropped my hand back to my side. The temptation to ask Andrea for a cigarette after all was strong; it would have given me something to do besides watching her pull smoke in through her lips and breathe it out in whisps from her nose. Suddenly it dawned on me how I might be able to question Manny without actually doing so.

"Have you thought about what you're going to say to Manny?"

"What do you mean?" Andrea half-closed her eyes, making her expression harder to read.

"Well, obviously he didn't say anything to you about the affair. What makes you think he wants to talk about it now?"

She took a long drag on the cigarette, the end of which burned brightly like a red warning signal. "Why not? Jeff's dead. Manny has no loyalty to him now."

I shrugged. "Seems to me, his loyalty to Jeff would have ended as soon as they had the big fight."

"Yeah?" Her nostrils flared and this time I didn't think it had anything to do with smoking. "Maybe he didn't see the point in bringing it up once I found out about Emily."

I made a kind of noncommittal noise. "That makes sense, I guess. Though, do you think the fight could have been about something else?"

"Like what?" She lowered her hand slightly to stare at me through a wreath of smoke.

I leaned in slightly. "You know it was murder, right?"

She ground out the cigarette against the wall and flung the butt away. "I spoke to Deputy Wilson after I ran into you and your sister."

"Well, stop me if I'm wrong here, but I got the impression your husband's business practices might have been a little shady."

"So?" She stuffed the pack of cigarettes back into her purse and then flicked a sharp glance at me. "And he was about to be my *ex*-husband, if you please."

"Right. Ex." I laid extra emphasis on the qualifier. "Anyway, if they were good friends and Jeff was into something crooked, Manny might have found out and *that* could be what the falling out was about."

I spread my hands palms up as though this was a brilliant conclusion.

"I doubt it." She hefted her bag's strap across her shoulder in the manner of all women who were preparing to leave a situation. "They were as thick as thieves. It makes more sense that Manny was defending my honor."

"Thick as thieves? You think Manny was in on whatever Jeff might have been up to?"

"It's a figure of speech." Annoyed now, Andrea turned for the door.

"You should ask him then." I adopted my best girlfriend voice. "Maybe you're right. Maybe Manny's been biding his time before asking you out."

She glanced back as she opened the door to the bar. Sound washed out in a tide over us, but her expression seemed somewhat mollified. "Maybe I will."

Chapter Fourteen

"WHERE HAVE YOU BEEN?" Liz shouted over the karaoke machine when I returned to the table.

I didn't answer at first, instead watching Andrea cut through the crowd in a beeline toward Manny. Between the music and the lighting, it was difficult to read their body language, but the stiffness of their posture didn't come across like potential lovers rekindling a romance to me.

Though what would I know about that?

"I told you, I stepped out for some air."

"Headache better?" Troy asked with patent solicitude.

I used my hand as an indicator, wobbling it from side to side. "A little bit. We may need to leave soon, though."

"No, we can't." Liz's voice bordered on shrill. "Troy says we have to stay. We can't miss it."

I might have glared slightly at Troy. "Not you too. What is this special surprise we can't miss?"

"Soon," he promised, and somehow the word was infused with a languid sensuality that made the promise seem worth it. He added with a boyish smile, "Besides, you don't want to miss our performance."

"Your what?" I said, realizing belatedly he held Liz's hand clasped in his own.

Liz lifted their joined hands like a prize fighter declaring victory but spoke only to Troy. "Should we tell her? I don't think so. I don't think she'll approve."

"Tell me what?" I didn't like the sound of this. I started to reach for my wine but stopped at a flutter of movement near the stage.

Troy let go of Liz's hand and leaned forward with both hands outstretched, as though breaking up a fight between us. "Hush now. This is it."

Manny stood at the mic. Andrea was nowhere to be seen.

"Ladies and gentlemen," Manny announced, much like the ringmaster of a circus. "We have a special treat for you tonight. Please put your hands together for the one, the only, Hattie King!"

He stepped back with a sweep of his arm, the spot highlighting the mic. After a smattering of applause, the crowd quieted. In the shadows just outside the spotlight, a broad-shouldered man helped a white-haired older woman up the stairs onto the stage. Before I could ask Troy if it was who I thought it was, Hattie Olsen entered the brilliant light of the spot. Her face wore a serene smile as she approached the mic, clasping it with familiar confidence.

"Thank you all," she said. "You're so kind. Manny, if you would?"

She glanced offstage at Manny, who nodded and pressed buttons on his karaoke machine. A jazzy kind of syncopated rhythm played over the speakers, and then Hattie opened her mouth. A golden voice streamed out, as though someone had opened curtains and let the sun in. Rich like coffee, warm like melted honey, her voice washed through the room like the sea, ebbing and flowing with the music. She sang of strange cargo, the face her heart could not erase, and empty dreams. Her voice wove magic with music, holding the entire room in thrall.

I sat with my mouth half open, mesmerized by the sound, holding my breath as the final strands of "Key Largo" hung in the air. The spell was broken only when the crowd erupted in wild applause.

"That was amazing." I breathed at last. I turned to gape at Troy. "You knew."

"Oh yes." His smile was that of the Cheshire Cat, sly and enigmatic. "Hattie King never got as big as say, Aretha Franklin or Roberta Flack, but she was a highly sought-after backup singer for years. Even had an album of her own out in the late seventies. She'd married Gordon by then, but she kept her stage name for singing."

"I can't believe she didn't make it as a solo artist. She's incredible."

Troy gave a philosophical shrug. "That's show business. You can be talented, beautiful, charismatic"—he turned his palms up and gave his shoulders a little wiggle to indicate his own strengths here—"but sometimes it just boils down to luck."

"I'm sure it had far more to do with talent in your case." Liz placed a hand on Troy's arm and gave a little squeeze, before looking around with a pout. "What happens now? Is karaoke over for the evening? They didn't call our names."

"I can't imagine anyone will want to follow that act," I said with a laugh.

"Too right," Troy agreed. He patted Liz's hand. "Never fear, they're only taking a break so that no one has to come right after Hattie. The first night she showed up and walked out on stage, the audience laughed at her. You could tell what they were thinking. Little old granny making a fool of herself. Then she sang the first note and brought the house down. Now, Gordon brings her on karaoke night and Manny has a table waiting for them."

"That's really nice of him."

"Don't grant Manny sainthood just yet. Hattie brings in a crowd. After a bit, she'll do another number. She'd sing all night, but Gordon won't let her overdo." He turned to Liz. "I'm sure we'll be up soon."

"Wait, what?" I eyed the upside-down shot glasses in front of Liz, which now numbered four. What on earth was she planning?

"I knew she'd be a party pooper," Liz announced loudly, rolling her eyes so hard I was sure she'd dislocate something.

Several people looked over at our table, so I said, "I'm pretty sure you don't need to shout anymore. The music's not playing."

"I'll have you know I'm doing this for you." She pointed at me dramatically. "You wouldn't sign up to sing, so I asked Troy to be my partner. All so we'd have an excuse to talk to Manny and you could ask your questions."

"Hold up now, what's this about Manny?" The smallest of frowns marred Troy's brow.

The cynical imp inside me wondered if Botox prevented his expression from being more pronounced even as the rest of me cringed at Liz's attempt at being helpful.

"She has questions." Liz went to rest her chin in her hand and missed. The resulting wobble forced her to sit up straighter. "You know, about Jeff. He was *murdered.*"

She pronounced the last word with wide-eyed emphasis, loud enough to cause the couple at the next table to turn around.

"Jeff was murdered?" Troy's mouth dropped open and his eyebrows shot up. He turned to me in disbelief. "Are you sure?"

I nodded. "Deputy Wilson told us this afternoon."

Speaking of Wilson, I glanced around but didn't see either him or Tim. As impossible as it seemed, the crowd was even denser than before. I didn't see Andrea either. To my surprise, however, I spied Emily across the room. She saw me as well, holding eye contact until the bartender brought her a drink and then she melted into the shadows.

Troy took a slug of his beer and sat staring at the table. Clearly, the news that Brinkman had been murdered had shaken him. After a moment, he seemed to pull himself together. When he met my gaze, there was a flash of something calculating and unfriendly in his eyes and then it was gone, replaced with his smiling urbanity once more. "So, you're playing Nancy Drew then? Questioning the suspects. Rather brash of you, isn't it? I can't think Sheriff Hollywood will care for that very much. But why Manny?"

I blanked out a second at Troy's nickname for Mercer and then floundered at how to answer his question. Annoyance at his condescending tone flooded me, causing my cheeks to heat. I didn't even have the excuse of knocking back tequila to blame for my flushed face. The thought of possibly having lost thousands of dollars if the paintings were gone stiffened my resolve to get some answers, however.

"I'm concerned about the inventory of Amanda's artwork that's supposed to be in the condo. It should have been secured properly after her death, and I'm afraid at the time, I didn't consider how valuable it would be now. Brinkman was murdered in my unit and Andrea said he and Manny used to be as thick as thieves. What if the two are connected? You knew Brinkman better than I did. Did he strike you as an honest man?"

"He struck me as a man who was always eager to make a quick buck." Bitterness tinged Troy's voice, whether he knew it or not.

"We're talking at least ninety to a hundred thousand in paintings here. Maybe more." Liz placed her hand on Troy's arm again, drawing his attention back to her.

Troy whistled with lifted brows and cocked his head to look over at me. "I can understand your interest then. What do the police have to say about the art?"

Ugh. I would have preferred to keep the actual value of the paintings out of the picture, but Liz had let the cat out of that particular bag. I shook my head. "Nothing so far. We only just heard this afternoon it's murder."

Troy shrugged and rolled both hands out palms up. "You'll find out one way or another soon. Until then, you might want to leave things to the police. Mercer may look like Hollywood's idea of a cop, but I get the impression he'd be a nasty customer if you get on his bad side."

"Of course, you're absolutely right." He was. Either the paintings were there, or they'd gone missing. It was pointless to speculate until I knew. But Emily's hint about Manny had been so provocative, and as attractive as Andrea was, I still had a hard time believing the two men had fallen out over Jeff's infidelity. Especially since Manny hadn't made a move on Andrea once it was clear they were getting a divorce. Which reminded me that I'd hoped Andrea would find out what the big fight had been about. "Where's Andrea, by the way? She'd hinted to me earlier that Hattie's performance wasn't to be missed, and yet she hasn't returned to the table."

Troy's lips flattened briefly before he shrugged. "Andrea's not the most reliable of people."

No surprises there.

"Well, I'm glad I didn't miss hearing Hattie sing. It was amazing." I pushed my chair back from the table to stand. "I'm going to go tell her how wonderful a singer she is."

Liz had propped her head up on her hand and was blinking slowly at the crowd. Leaving her seemed like a bad idea all the sudden.

"Don't worry, I'll keep an eye on her." As though reading my thoughts, Troy laid a casual hand on Liz's shoulder, and she beamed at him.

That's what worries me.

At least I didn't say that part out loud. With a stiff nod, I pushed my way through the crowd over to Hattie's table. There was quite the crush surrounding her, with patrons gushing enthusiastically and asking for autographs. She seemed to be in her element: a queen holding court with Gordon as her consort. He even held her purse for her.

Hattie was deep in conversation with an adoring fan, so I came around to Gordon's side of the table.

"She's fantastic. But then I guess you know that."

Gordon's face lit up at the praise. "She's still got it, that's for sure. A lot of singers lose their voice with age, but not my Hattie. Of course, she'd be here all night if I let her. Two, maybe three songs I tell her. Leave 'em wanting more."

"They certainly do." I nodded toward the crowd. "I'm surprised no one has contacted you about doing a reunion thing. It would be wonderful."

The light in Gordon's eyes shuttered slightly at my words. "They have, actually. Not sure she'd be up to that, truth be told. I wasn't sure about her singing down here at first, but she found this place and marched up onstage as bold as brass—after that, what choice did I have?"

His smile appeared like a photographer's flash, there and gone in an eyeblink, leaving only the impression of it on my retinas.

Hattie glanced in our direction and stared at me for a long, frowning moment before a smile broke free on her face. "You're Amanda's friend. The one with the dog. Oh goodness, help me out, Gordon. I'm terrible with names."

"I'm Ginny, Miz Hattie. I had to come over and tell you how much I loved your singing. Are you going to do another number later on?"

She bounced a little in her seat like a young girl. "Oh yes, though something more my time. Perhaps 'Respect.' That really gets the toes tapping."

"I'm looking forward to it." I started to say I was here with Liz but thought better of introducing her to my sister just now. "I'm with Troy and Andrea. I'd better get back to them. I just wanted to say hello."

I gave them both a little wave and spun to head back to our table, only to plow nose-first into an immovable wall. Said wall turned out to be a hard-muscled chest. I clutched my nose and, with watering eyes, looked up at the owner of the chest who frowned with intimidating intensity.

The bluish light in the bar gleamed off his bald pate. "I'm Manny. I hear you've been looking for me."

Face to face with this hostile man, I decided I didn't really need to talk to him after all. "Um, no. Not particularly."

He put a hand under my elbow and tried tugging me along until I whipped my arm out of his grasp.

"Let go of me," I snapped.

He wheeled to face me. I'd seen friendlier Rottweilers. "Were you the one who told Andrea I knew about her husband's affair?"

"No!" Honesty made me waffle. "Well, not really. She was convinced that must have been why you and Jeff stopped being friends. I merely told her if she wanted to know the truth, she should ask you."

"My beef with Jeff had nothing to do with Andrea." He jabbed a finger at my chest. "I'll thank you to stay out of my business."

"Is there a problem?"

Gordon materialized beside me, as steady as an old oak tree.

Manny tempered his snarl into a semblance of politeness. "Ask her. She's been nosing around, asking questions about Jeff."

"I don't th—"

"The whole club is buzzing about how you wanted to grill me tonight."

If looks could kill, they'd be shipping me home in a box right about now.

"There's been some kind of misunderstanding—"

"I don't want to hear it." Manny got up in my face so close I could count his nose hairs. "You want to interrogate someone about Jeff, I suggest you ask that pretty boy sitting at your table."

I blinked at that and reared back from the beer-breath blasting my face.

"Ginny, why don't I walk you back to your seat." Gordon cupped my elbow, but unlike the manhandling I'd suffered before, his touch felt like a cloak of protection.

Manny huffed a few times like a dragon working up a head of steam to flame the village but spun on his heel and stomped back to the karaoke machine.

"Thanks," I said somewhat shakily, as Gordon guided me through the crowd.

"What was Manny going on about?" Gordon spoke in my ear, close enough that I could hear him over the background noise. "You're not really asking questions about Jeff, are you? Why on earth would you do that?"

"I'm not. I mean, not really. It's complicated. Sheriff Mercer was already on my case before Brinkman's death was declared a homicide. I have reason to believe Brinkman may not have been on the up and up, and I'm worried about some property that's supposed to be in the condo. Then Andrea said Manny and Jeff had a big falling out. I wanted to know if the two were related."

"Jeff was murdered?" Gordon stopped in the middle of the dance floor to stare at me. "Forgive me for saying so but poking around doesn't seem to be a smart thing to do."

"Smart or not, I have a lot at stake. Amanda left some valuable paintings behind. Hopefully, they're still there in her unit. If not..." Given the fact Liz had spilled the beans to Troy about the paintings' worth, sharing this much with Gordon didn't seem unreasonable. What Troy knew tonight, the rest of the residents would know tomorrow, if my suspicions about the local gossip mill were right. I rubbed my forehead. Nope, headache still there. "What do you think Manny meant by that crack aimed at Troy, though?"

"My dear, you know what they say." Gordon had begun moving again, using Hattie's purse to clear a path through the patrons for me to follow. "Curiosity. Cats. It's a bad combination. Though if anything's missing from your unit, I'd definitely put my money on Jeff knowing something about it."

I pulled up just as we reached the table. Andrea still hadn't returned. Liz leaned on Troy's shoulder, and Troy lifted a hand in greeting at the sight of us. I couldn't face introducing my snockered sister to Gordon, so I pleaded the need to use the restroom and bolted.

By the time I returned, the table was empty. Across the room, Gordon sat beside Hattie, smiling as he leaned in to speak with her. The music had started up again, each familiar thud of the bass reverberating in my aching head. I had just enough time to think *I know this song* before Troy's voice rang out with "I got chills, they're multiplying." I watched in fascinated horror as he and my sister belted out "You're The One That I Want", playing the roles of John Travolta and Olivia Newton-John respectively.

Downing my glass of wine would have helped to ease the embar-rassment, only someone else had already beat me to it. My glass sat empty among the other dead soldiers on the table.

On stage, Troy gave John Travolta's open-mouthed hound dog ex-pression a run for its money as he pretended to hang on every note my sister sang. Of the two of them, Troy was the only one who'd probably watched Grease in the movie theaters when it was first released. Her over-the-top flirtatiousness lit the crowd on fire, and they stamped and clapped to the beat, egging both performers on even further.

It wasn't half bad, to be honest. Liz nailed the coy, sly, and yet some-how awkward delivery of Newton-John, and there was something about watching a soccer mom cut loose that appealed to the crowd. The song came to its conclusion with a rousing round of applause. Liz collapsed into Troy's arms, laughing as he helped her down the stairs offstage.

They weaved their way through the crowd. Troy guided Liz back to her seat. She sat down heavily, still holding onto his arm and giggling. "That was so much fun!"

"It was." Troy seemed genuinely pleased, not just giving lip service. He remained standing, however. The wattage dimmed on his smile slightly as he continued speaking. "I'm afraid I must call it a night."

"Oh no." Liz pouted but her eyelids were drooping, and she listed to one side, despite being pushed gently back in her seat. "Not so soon. The night's still young."

Troy laughed and shot me a rueful glance. "The night may be young, but sadly, I'm not."

"I'm with Troy." Aside from Hattie's performance and some il-luminating insight into my sister's desire to break bad a little, this evening had been a bust. "My head's still killing me. The ibuprofen didn't touch it. Why don't you wait here, Liz, while I go close out our tab."

Troy stopped me when I would have risen.

"I'll get it. No, I insist." He waved me back into my seat. "My treat. I had a lovely evening and the two of you to thank for it."

He bent over Liz's hand, brushing it with a kiss. He took mine next, but when his eyes met mine over my knuckles, a kind of weariness flickered there for just an instant. It caught me by surprise, and for once I didn't make the usual protests over who was paying the bill.

"Thank you, I appreciate the generous offer." I glanced over at Liz, who weaved a little in place. "How about I spring for an Uber? Troy, you'll share it with us, yes?"

"No, love." He squeezed my hand before releasing it. "The walk will do me good. I believe a ride is a good choice for you two, however."

He gave a nod at Liz, who listed to one side before I pushed her upright again.

"Right. Thanks. Well, as fun as this has been, we should be heading out ourselves."

Troy raised his hand in a wave and melted into the dance crowd. Another hopeful karaoke singer took the stage, this time too drunk to do Taylor Swift justice.

Liz slumped into my shoulder again.

"Come on, sis. We need to call it a night." I gave her a little shake. As loud as it was in the bar, we'd be better off if I waited until we were outside to order an Uber.

"Stop." Liz protested weakly. A convulsive movement rippled through her. Swaying, she said, "I don't feel so hot."

She slapped a hand over her mouth as she clutched her stomach.

"Oh, no, no, no." I hauled her up by the elbow, making sure I had both of our purses. A quick glance at the line waiting for the restroom told me we'd never make it to the toilet, but there was a clear shot to the back door that Andrea and I had used before. "Come with me."

I hustled Liz down the narrow corridor, with her stumbling along behind me, making ominous retching noises. We burst out into the street, and Liz managed to take three or four steps past the exit before she spewed the contents of her stomach all over the alley. I held her partially upright and kept her hair back out of her face.

"Come on, sweetie," I said when she seemed to be done. "You'll feel better once we get back to the Sand Dollar."

I tried walking with her to the end of the alley, but she sank into me, barely able to stand. Oh heck, this wasn't good.

"Liz. Come on. You have to keep walking."

An explosive shot of sound made me look over my shoulder to see the back door of the bar bang open against the side of the building. The light from within illuminated the two figures who had exited the building, only for them to disappear into shadow again. The door opened a second time, and a third man slipped out to join the first two.

I had one arm around Liz's waist, but she slithered out of my grasp. My other hand was on the pepper spray attached to my purse, but I couldn't hang on to that and Liz too.

The three figures stood just outside of the light, a predatory phalanx that rang all my alarm bells as it slowly moved forward.

"Liz." I hissed in her ear. "Get up. We need to get out of here."

In response, she groaned and sank to the ground. It was all I could do to keep her from banging her head on the pavement. The bass beat of the karaoke machine bled through the walls of the bar as the singing started up once more and my pulse jumped in rhythm to the sound.

Three against one. Moving Liz was out of the question unless I wanted to drag her behind me like a corpse. My tiny vial of pepper spray would only go so far. Same with the limited moves I'd learned in the self-defense class back home. Bruce Lee, I was not. The odds of anyone hearing me yell over the noise of the music was low. I braced myself in front of Liz in a defensive stance and closed my fingers around the small container of pepper spray once more.

"Looks like you could use a little help." The voice that came out of the darkness was mocking and someone snickered.

"No thanks. We're fine." Thankfully, my voice didn't crack at the outright lie.

The two men in the lead stepped into the small pool of light cast by the lamp at the back door. The third had disappeared entirely, so deep in shadow he could have been part of the building.

The first man laughed without humor. "Doesn't look like things are fine to me. Looks like your friend has had a little too much to drink."

"Yeah." The second guy piped up, a thread of excitement strumming through his voice. "You're never going to move her without help. Why don't we give you a lift?"

"No thanks." I had to get Liz off the pavement and out of the alley. Our chances were better on the street than out of sight of any passersby. I tried tugging her to her feet, but she was dead weight.

Things One and Two took the opportunity to move in.

I wheeled on them with a snarl, holding out the pepper spray in front of me. "Back off. I said I don't need your help."

"Now that's no way to be. All unfriendly like." Thing One nudged his pal.

"The lady said back off."

The drawl came out of the shadows from behind them, so familiar, so infuriating, so wonderful to hear. A form split from the darkness, and Joe Donegan stepped into the light. "I suggest you do as she says."

Chapter Fifteen

DRESSED IN A BLACK T-shirt and dark jeans, it was a small wonder Joe had been practically invisible. Coming as he did from out of the darkness, his sudden appearance gave my would-be attackers pause. The pinkish light above the door cast a spot around him, illuminating a smile that should have made their skin crawl. With two-day stubble and his trademark tumbled hair, this was Lucifer looking for a fight that he knew he would win. When the two men merely gaped at him, Joe thumped his fist on the edge of the nearest trash can, and the lid flipped up into his hand, where he caught it like a shield.

It was such a boss move.

The two men stammered and blustered.

"We were only trying to help, man," the first guy said.

"Yeah," the second one whined. "We saw they were having trouble and came out here to help."

"Leave. Now." The words came out with clipped precision. The two losers didn't even stick around to see if Joe was a threat to me or not. They bolted like scalded cats, bumping into each other in their haste to get past me and out of the alley.

Joe chucked the metal lid aside with a clatter and joined me. He rested one hand on his knee and knelt alongside while I checked Liz. "Is that your sister? What happened?"

"I don't know. She's passed out. She had a lot to drink this evening, but she usually holds it better than this. I think she's been drugged." I had my phone out and used the flashlight to examine Liz's pupils. "What are you doing here, anyway?"

Joe ignored my question and leaned in for a closer look. The clean, citrusy scent of him took me straight back to high school with a jolt as if I'd been slammed into a time machine. I bet it was the same stupid cologne I'd bought him back then. It went a long way toward offsetting the stench of the alley.

"I think you're right. She's doped up with something."

Liz's pupils were like black holes, dilated despite the bright light of my phone shining in her eyes. I took hold of her wrist. "Her pulse is slower than I'd like. We need to get her to a hospital."

Joe called for an ambulance, requesting assistance in the brisk, authoritative manner of a first responder, down to giving the street address of the bar, and telling the dispatcher we were in the alley behind it. When he ended the call, he touched me on the shoulder. "I need to go back inside. It's possible they haven't cleared your table yet. We might be able to get some information from the glasses."

"You let the guys responsible for this go!"

He blew out his breath with a small sound of frustration. "You don't know that. They came out behind you, yes, but for all you know they were the Good Samaritans they pretended to be."

"Obviously, you don't believe them." For once I wished he thought less about the law and more about justice. He was right, though. We had no proof. "Then why bother with the glasses?"

"You never know. It could help with treatment if they do a rush on the screen. Will you be okay here for a minute by yourself?"

"I'll be fine."

A surge of anger flared like a faulty wire that would electrocute anyone who touched it by mistake. My blood was up now. Someone had drugged my sister and the two of us had almost ended up as a nightclub statistic. My pulse thundered in my ears, looking for a release valve.

He held up a finger. "I'll be right back."

"The door won't open from the outside," I warned as he headed for the exit. "Not unless you jammed the lock on your way out."

Cursing, he took off toward the front of the alley at a jog and disappeared around the corner. I held Liz's head in my lap and fumed. The rough concrete dug into my knees, and I vowed never again would I be so stupid as to go out wearing anything but durable, practical jeans.

As the minutes ticked away, I felt so completely useless. I didn't even have a jacket I could use to cover Liz and keep her warm. When had Liz's drink been spiked? I never should have left the table this evening. First I'd gone to the bar for water, then outside with Andrea. I'd also gone to speak with Hattie and Gordon and to the restroom as well. The tampering could have occurred at several points during the evening. Liz hadn't been in a position to pay attention to her glass. I should have been watching out for the both of us.

The back door of the bar flew open with a bang again, and Joe came out, followed by Manny. In the distance, I could hear the sound of sirens.

"Is she going to be okay?" Manny hovered alongside Joe as they reached us.

"Paramedics are on the way." Joe's voice was taut as a wire, but it wasn't clear what the source of the tension was. "You saved those glasses for me, right?"

"I told the server to set them aside until you could pick them up. Look, I run a nice place. This kind of thing doesn't happen here."

Manny's conciliatory tone was night and day different from the aggression he'd shown me earlier, and I looked up with a snarl. "That's the stupidest thing I've ever heard. Lots of money here. Lots of entitlement. What makes your place any different from the rest?"

"Because I pay attention. I watch my crowd, okay?" Manny's irritation boiled over on me. "I know what's going on most of the time. Your sister was knocking them back ever since you arrived. Maybe she's just drunk."

"Or maybe the police need to take a closer look into how you run things."

Manny took a deep breath and stepped forward with balled fists, but somehow Joe was between him and me.

"Won't hurt to check the glasses for drugs. What's important now is getting her treated." Joe indicated Liz and then maneuvered Manny toward the street. "Why don't you show the rescue squad where we are?"

"Yeah, right. Of course. Anything." Manny wiped his mouth as though the whole idea made him queasy. He trotted down the alley to the street as though he wanted nothing more to do with the scene. For all his tough guy looks, he seemed to be taking this hard. Maybe he had a boss who would come down on him like a ton of bricks for an incident like this.

I eased Liz out of my lap in preparation for the paramedics to take her. Her head lolled to one side; she was out cold.

"She'll be okay."

Joe's quiet voice came like a beacon on a foggy night. Solid, dependable. Evidence of dry land and a safe harbor somewhere ahead.

It brought tears to my eyes. I hadn't realized how much I needed to hear some sort of reassurance until then.

"How do you know?"

He knelt beside me and took my hand. "Because she was still mobile and functioning a few minutes ago. Because she got sick to her stomach in the alley, bringing up anything left that she drank. Because you got help right away."

"People die of drug overdoses—" I held on to his hand as though dangling from the edge of a building with only his grip to pull me back up.

"Heroin. Fentanyl. Stuff injected. Things taken in combination with no one else around to intervene." He spoke into the stiff spikes of my hair.

"Be careful." My warning came out half-laugh, half tears. "That gel I put in my hair might put an eye out."

"I'll have to introduce you to less lethal styling products." His words landed on my ear like a soft cashmere sweater—light, warm, and comforting.

"I *knew* you didn't come by that casual, careless look naturally." I appreciated his comment for what it was: a distraction. I pushed back to look up at him. The teasing note in my voice faded away when I spoke. "You were already on the island when you texted me."

It was a statement of fact, not a question.

He let go of me and nodded. "Luckily, I figured out where you were."

Flashlights bobbed at the end of the alley, forcing both Joe and me to shield our eyes from the paramedics hurrying to our location.

Thankfully, Manny chose to manage the street traffic, rather than head back into the club. His glower and imposing presence made the rubberneckers move on, and probably saved me from going to jail for assault when I came up growling like a bear at someone trying to record Liz being loaded into the back of the ambulance. The paramedics almost refused to let me onboard with them, citing regulations, but I quickly pointed out my car was back at the condo and I was without transportation to the hospital. Rather than argue, they gave in.

I shot a worried glance at Joe as I settled in beside Liz in the back of the ambulance.

He seemed to read my mind.

"Give me your keys. I want to talk to the local authorities. Then I'll go by your unit, let Remy out, and bring your car down to the hospital."

With a nod, I fished out my keys from my purse and tossed them at him. He caught them one handed and shut the door behind me, giving the side of the vehicle a couple of thumps to let the driver know we were all in.

As someone who has spent a lot of time at the bedside of ill relatives, I hate hospitals. I hate the soothing fish-green or pond-blue walls and the smell of burnt vending machine coffee. I hate the blaring, nearly unintelligible sounds of announcements over a PA system, and the moans of people in discomfort. The steady beeping of monitors that failed to soothe and the hard, plastic chairs that inhabited most of the waiting areas.

But it was an environment I knew how to navigate. I provided the triage nurse with Liz's information, including the insurance card from her purse, and confirmed my status as her sister. I remained calm when questioned about how much Liz had drunk, and whether or not she was on any prescription medication. I waited patiently while they wheeled her away, presumably to start IV fluids and run tests.

No, she hadn't hit her head. Yes, she'd vomited. No, she didn't take any pills. Yes, she'd had a fair amount to drink.

The triage nurse pushed on the question of medication. As a medical professional myself, I knew why she did, and also why she had a hard time believing my answers, but after the third time the question had been asked and answered, the anger that had been simmering on the back burner threatened to boil over.

"I'm telling you. I was with her most of the evening. She doesn't take any medication. She had to dig around in her purse to find me a dose of ibuprofen."

The doctor, a young dark-skinned man who wore his weariness like his lab coat said with a sigh, "Look. She's not going to get in trouble. But I can't treat her properly if I don't know what she's taken. She has all the signs of a barbiturate overdose. Blue angels. Yellow jackets. Or she may have been prescribed something to help her sleep. Just tell me so we can focus our treatment."

I gaped at him. "Barbiturates? No. Nothing like that—at least—"

He pounced on my hesitation. "At least what?"

"I don't think she's taking anything like that. I know she hasn't taken anything like that tonight." Did I though? I wasn't with her the entire evening. What if Liz *had* popped some pills? No, that wasn't like her at all. But then again, she'd been acting out of character the last few days. "I'll call her husband though, to make sure she's not on any prescription medication I don't know about."

"You do that." The doctor returned to the treatment area and left me trying to remember Dave's contact information. In the end, I had to use Liz's phone to call him. His phone rolled over to voice mail, and I left him a message asking him to call back right away, as it was urgent.

Ten minutes later, I called again. And then texted after another five. A half hour passed after my first call, and it was clear wherever Dave was, he wasn't checking his phone. My finger hesitated over the contact information for Liz's in-laws. Surely if Dave was off somewhere, the girls would be with their grandparents. I *couldn't* call the children. I found myself oddly reluctant to call Liz's mother-in-law. What would I tell her? "Hey, your daughter-in-law got roofied at a bar, and the doctor wants to know if she's on any prescription medication."

That would go over well.

Would her in-laws even know if she were on any medication? It's not something I would share with my own mother, let alone someone else's. This was Liz's life we were talking about, though.

In the end, the risk of opening a can of worms better left closed made me fire off another text to Dave in all caps with my phone number that it was an emergency and he needed to call me.

I was still seething when Joe walked into the waiting area.

Chapter Sixteen

"WHAT DOES THE DOCTOR say?" Joe handed me a cup of real coffee, one procured from a shop rather than the vending machine.

I took it gratefully. Until then, I hadn't realized how cold my hands were. Not just my hands, actually. A tank top and short skirt meant for a hot night out on the town didn't cut it in the frigid air of the hospital. It was like being inside a freezer.

"He thinks she took something herself. Some kind of barbiturate, most likely."

Joe's expressive eyebrows climbed into his messy hairline. "Is that likely?"

"No." I hesitated, then tried to run my hand through my hair, only to be defeated by the styling gel. "I don't think so. I can't really say for sure. I would have said definitely not if you'd asked me last week, but she's been acting odd on this trip. I didn't get an answer when I called her husband. I left several text messages."

"Ouch." Joe winced appropriately and took the empty chair beside me. "So, not GHB or ketamine, then."

I shook my head. "They don't think so. The doctor said something about sleeping pills."

The more I thought about Dave's lack of response, the angrier I got. "I've got her bag right here."

I picked it up from the floor and upended it over the empty seat beside me. The purse contained the usual things for a night out: her wallet and ID, her cell phone, a single credit card, another travel packet of ibuprofen, a hairbrush, lipstick, a compact with mirror and face powder, and a travel-sized bottle of hand lotion. No prescription bottles of any kind.

"Of course, we both emptied our purses of anything we didn't want to carry when we left the unit," I said, continuing to poke around in Liz's bag. "Hardly anything would fit in mine."

"Yeah, I noticed."

Something in Joe's voice made me glance up at that. He stared at me with what I could only describe as an appreciative eye. For a long shivery moment, his gaze ran the length of my body, as though trailing a finger across it. "I see you only brought the bare minimum with you tonight."

"That's the last time *that* happens. Next time I won't leave home without a full medical kit."

The corner of his mouth twitched and he started to say something, only Liz's doctor appeared in the doorway. "She's awake and asking to speak to you."

I leapt to my feet to follow the doctor down the hallway. When I glanced back at Joe, he half-lifted a hand. "I'll wait here. No need to overwhelm her."

I left him guarding our respective purses and hurried after the doctor to Liz's room.

"How is she?" I asked as we walked.

"Reasonably well, all things considered," he said. "It's just as well she threw up when she did. It limited how much of the drug got into her system and we didn't have to pump her stomach. The combination with alcohol is the biggest issue, but she's responding to the fluid therapy nicely, though still a little sleepy. She'll be able to go home in the morning, as long as we're confident this wasn't self-inflicted."

He pushed open the door to her room and stepped back so I could enter first. The room was divided by a curtain into two patient areas. The person on the far side of the door was asleep. Liz's eyes were closed as well, but she opened them, blinking several times when I spoke her name.

"Ginny." She ran her tongue over dry lips before speaking again. "What happened?"

"I could ask you the same." I kept my voice light, resting my hand beside hers without touching it. "What do you remember?"

"Shopping. Going out to Bennie's." She sighed and reached for her hair, only to stop short when she realized she had an IV line attached to her arm. "Um, having a few drinks. Singing karaoke with Troy. After that, it's a bit blurry."

I sensed the presence of the doctor hovering just beyond my shoulder, but I didn't acknowledge him. "That's good. You got the highlights. Do you remember getting sick in the alley?"

This time she brought her hand up to cover her eyes. "Oh Lord, yes. How embarrassing. But then what? How did I end up here?"

"You passed out." I tucked a lock of hair around her ear and met her gaze when she lowered her hand. "That was kind of scary, so we called an ambulance."

"Oh, for heaven's sake." Her eyes filled with tears. "I'm sorry."

"Nothing to be sorry about." I kept my tone light. "I guess four shooters is your limit."

"Ugh. I'm never drinking tequila again." She gave me a shaky smile. "Chasing it with your wine was probably a bad idea. I'm not surprised you didn't finish it though. It was so bitter."

"Excuse me, what?" I leaned in to take her by the shoulder. "Liz, are you sure? That wine was fantastic. I intended to ask the server what brand it was."

She wrinkled her nose. "You can't be serious. Honey, if you want the names of some great wines, just ask me. Though I'm not sure I'll ever drink again after tonight. You... you didn't call Dave, did you? This is going to upset him."

Her brow furrowed with worry, and I had to tamp down my resurfacing anger with her loser husband.

"Sweetie, I had to. The doctor wanted to know if you were on any medication, and I couldn't be sure." At the look on her face, I hurried on, conscious the doctor was listening. "He didn't answer. I left him a message saying you had a bad reaction to something, which is the truth. I didn't want to overly alarm him until I could speak with him directly."

Tears pooled and spilled over, dragging a line of mascara down her cheek. A tiny frown made a pucker between her eyes, which had the effect of damming the flow. "You couldn't reach Dave? That doesn't make any sense. Why wouldn't he answer his phone?"

I squeezed her hand. "I don't know. But since you're better, it doesn't matter right now. You should get some rest. I need to speak with your doctor. You're sure about the wine, though?"

A touch of her former imperiousness entered her voice. "Of course, I'm sure. The wine was dreadful."

"And you didn't take anything else during the evening? No medication of any kind?"

She pulled her hand away from mine. "Medication? What are you talking about? I'm not on any medication."

Her indignation was good enough for me. "Just had to be sure."

I turned to the doctor, pulling him aside to whisper, "See? No medication. Furthermore, that wine she's talking about? It was mine and it was delicious. I think someone put something in it. Something bitter."

I thought back to when I'd returned from the restroom and found the entire table empty. I'm not sure Liz would have noticed if someone had spiked the wine, but Troy would have—if he wasn't the person doing the spiking, that is. I started to ask Liz if she'd left Troy alone at the table at any point before she drank my wine, but she'd already dozed off again.

The doctor escorted me from the room saying, "I'm satisfied she didn't take anything on purpose. It sounds like a matter for the police, however."

More than he knew. Because no one could have predicted Liz would drink my wine. That glass had been meant for me.

Chapter Seventeen

I UNLOCKED THE DOOR to the condo, bracing myself for Remy's enthusiastic greeting.

He did not disappoint, leaping and corkscrewing in the air, all while giving little squeaks of excitement as Joe and I entered the unit.

"Knock it off, Remy." Irritability sharpened my voice. "It's too late for this, and you'll wake the neighbors."

Remy managed to keep all four feet on the floor, but still whined and bumped into us, delighted with our arrival. As far as he was concerned, Joe's unexpected arrival was grounds for throwing a party.

I tossed my keys on the kitchen counter. The clock on the stove read 2:48 a.m. My head still pounded and the late-night coffee had my pulse singing. I went to the fridge and pulled out a bottle of cold water. I drank half of it down in a few gulps before setting it on the counter.

Joe dropped his travel case by the door and greeted Remy quietly, apparently waiting for me to speak. He'd waited a long time. I'd said almost nothing to him at the hospital after I told him about the wine. He'd disappeared for a while, only to come back to tell me that the police had the glasses he'd preserved from the bar and that Mercer would want to talk to me in the morning—not being very happy with me at the moment. Mercer, that is. Or perhaps Joe. Maybe both. It was hard to tell.

I wasn't happy myself, for that matter. If there was enough merlot left to sample, they would probably discover barbiturates in the remnants of the wine. If drugging my wine wasn't a deliberate attempt on my life, it had certainly been done with the intent to cause harm. What had started out as a desire to protect my financial interests had become personal now. And Liz had gotten caught in the crossfire.

"There's no point in you taking a hotel for the remainder of the night," I said at last. "You can sleep in Liz's room for now."

"Are you mad at me?"

I whipped around to face him. He leaned against the kitchen island the way he always does, legs crossed at the ankles, arms folded over his chest. It was a deliberately disarming pose, and I was having none of it.

"You in particular? Don't flatter yourself. I have plenty of reasons to be angry and they don't all center around you."

Remy's ears drooped to half-mast, and I could see the hesitation in the way he froze. It wasn't his fault it had been a terrible evening. I hated that my long-simmering rage had this effect on my dog, and I made an effort to control it.

"Don't take this wrong, because having you show up when you did was a lifesaver, and we both know it. But why are you here, Joe?"

The pallid glow of the light over the kitchen sink cast Joe's face into strange relief, picking out the angles of his cheekbones and deepening the shadows under his eyes. It had been a long day for him too.

"Mercer called me this morning asking questions about you."

"That's it? The local sheriff here has some routine follow-up questions about me, and you decide to leap in your car and drive down here? Where's Toad?"

Joe's heeler pup was only about seven months old. If I thought traveling with Remy was challenging, it was nothing on a long car trip with a teething, hyperactive puppy.

Joe pushed off the counter to wipe his face with his hands, a gesture that felt chock full of exasperation. "I left her with Deb, and before you ask, she's also taking care of the horses and Ming. And no, I didn't just leap in my car and drive down. I flew."

"You flew." I gaped at him.

"I haven't taken any leave since I'd started as sheriff and this seemed as good a time as any. It was just a short hop from Birchwood Springs to Charlotte, and then another puddle jumper to the island." He gave a little deprecatory shrug. "No big deal."

"It probably cost you and arm and a leg." It was on the tip of my tongue to offer to reimburse him for the plane ticket, but something in the lowering of his brows suggested I shouldn't.

"My choice," he said crisply, before that little half-smile made an appearance on his face. "Of course, I'm hoping for a place to stay while I'm here. And a lift back when you leave."

"You still haven't explained *why* you're here."

He turned his hands palms up. "Mercer's questions weren't routine. He wanted to know about your reliability as a witness and whether you'd falsely report a crime to jerk his chain. Or even go so far as to fake a crime."

"What?" Okay, that line of questioning was definitely disturbing. "Is this about me calling last night about the attempted break-in?"

"Probably. At least, that's bound to be part of it. He also had a bunch of questions about the murders in Greenbriar. Guess he's been looking into them as part of investigating you."

"Which just so happens to call into your integrity as an investigator as well. Why am I a person of interest to him?" I exploded. "I wasn't even here when Brinkman was murdered. I never even met the man."

"My guess is it's about the paintings. Mercer probably figured you came down here—or sent a representative—to confront Brinkman and things got out of hand." He yawned suddenly. "If it's any consolation, between driving to Birchwood and the layovers, flying here took almost as long as driving. And unless you have fake ID lying around somewhere, there's no way you could have made the flight down and back without someone noticing."

"Which should completely let me off the hook!"

Remy pressed into my leg and whined. I took one of his silky ears and pulled it through my fingers several times, soothing myself as well as him.

"You personally, yes. But my guess is he's leaning toward an accomplice now. Look, from Mercer's perspective, it's the strongest lead he's got. There's reason to believe Brinkman was scamming you—not just over continuing to rent out the unit after you told him to stop but possibly over valuable artwork as well—and here you are with a history of being involved in a couple of homicides."

"This is just insane." I rubbed my own face and then glared at Joe. "So, you took it upon yourself to hop on a plane and come down here. How did you find us at the bar?"

"Oh, that." The corner of his mouth quirked upward. "Longshot. If you remember, I texted as soon as I got off the plane. You said you were at a local bar, so I got an Uber to the Sand Dollar. I started to text you again but played a hunch instead."

The grin had decidedly smirky overtones now.

"A hunch?"

"I asked the first person I met where I could find the best calamari closest to the condo. Figured they might be one and the same."

I pinched the bridge of my nose. How was it he still knew me that well? Either I was that predictable or incredibly boring to have changed so little since we dated. The fact he remembered my thing for fried squid was a little unsettling. "You shouldn't have come."

He nodded several times as though he'd expected my answer, working the muscles of his jaw as though biting back a retort. The drawl had been wiped from the face of the earth when he responded. "Right then. I guess I'll be off in the morning. You can follow up on the glasses I submitted to the sheriff's department for testing, though since Liz is doing better, I doubt they'll put a rush on it."

Now I felt like a heel. I might have thought about having the glasses tested, but would Mercer have listened to me as well as a fellow member of law enforcement? Not likely. Joe still had gravitas with the police, even if his involvement with me made him a little suspect.

"Joe—"

Instead of replying, he headed to the front door. For a split second when he took the handle of his bag, I thought he was going to walk out, but instead he tugged the suitcase behind him as he headed down the corridor to the bedrooms. Remy followed him, wagging his tail the entire time.

He paused in front of the main bedroom. It didn't take a detective to be able to tell which room Liz had been staying in. The mountains of pink luggage had been a dead giveaway.

I tried again. "Joe—"

He stopped me with a lifted hand. When the silence fell between us, he ran his hand through his hair. His jaw clenched and tension coiled his muscles, almost as taut as when he'd been about to take on the two men in the alley. When he finally looked at me, I felt pinned by his intense stare. "I get that you're not used to asking for help. That you wade into everything with the knowledge that if you don't get it done, it's not happening. That it's better to try on your own and fail than to ask for help and be disappointed. But let me ask you something."

I held my breath for a second, not sure where this was going.

"Those times when you were in trouble. When someone was trying to kill you. Did you for one moment tell Remy to back off, to stay out of it, that you had everything under control?"

He made air quotes with his fingers around the words "under control."

"No, but—"

"No buts about it, Ginny. The people in your life deserve as much chance as a dog. It's okay to ask for help sometimes. Anyone who really cares about you wants to help. I hope you learn that someday."

He went into Liz's bedroom and shut the door. Remy wilted, his ears and tail drooping at being shut out from Joe.

I stood in the hallway, not sure of what just happened, as tears burned my eyes.

Chapter Eighteen

MORNING CAME FAR TOO soon, but I was in the habit of rising early. I showered to remove the last of the spiky hair gel and took Remy out for a run as soon as the first pink streaks of dawn painted the sky. As usual it served to clear my head and put me in a much better frame of mind by the time we returned to the condo. Joe entered the kitchen as I was unloading the coffee and bagels as a peace offering, just as I'd done with Liz the day before.

I really needed to get better at not needing peace offerings in the first place.

The sight of Joe pre-coffee, pre-shower and shave took me aback for a second. He cruised into the kitchen with a yawn, wearing his clothing from the night before, scratching at his belly from underneath the black T-shirt. His hair was beyond its usual messy disarray, straying into bedhead territory, and his stubble had that "I'm on vacation" effect that made him impossibly sexy. His eyes lit up at the sight of the coffee and he made "gimme" motions with his hands.

I pushed a cup of strong coffee across the island toward him, remembering he liked it as black as the devil's soul and as potent as jet fuel. To my surprise, he dumped a container of creamer into it, and then smiled with his eyes closed over the brim as though saying a benediction.

He opened his eyes as he took a sip. "What?"

"Creamer?" I said, indicating the little empty cup. "That's new."

"People can change, you know. Are those fresh bagels too? Yum."

I shoved the bag toward him and watched as he fished out a sprouted grain bagel and popped it in the toaster. He got out some plates and some silverware and brought them back to the island while his bagel toasted. He perched on one of the tall chairs along the island, hooking his bare feet over the rung. "Have you heard anything from the hospital?"

I nodded as I blew on my own coffee before taking a sip. "Yes. They're releasing Liz this morning. I'm about to head over to pick her up. Listen, about last night..."

He waved me off, still savoring his coffee. "Forget about it. Not to worry, I'll be out of your hair before you get back from picking up Liz."

"That's just it." I held the sturdy paper cup with both hands, staring into my coffee as though it held the power to change my life—which given that it was coffee, it did. "I overreacted last night. I was pissed on many levels, and you happened to catch the brunt of it. I'm sorry."

He merely stared at me until his bagel popped up in the toaster. Turning away to fetch it, he stood with his back to me as he slathered cream cheese on the slices. The stiff line of his shoulders seemed to relax after a moment. Almost as though coming to a decision, he returned to the counter with his plate. "I might have overreacted a bit myself, coming down here like I did without even running it past you."

"Maybe a bit." I held up my thumb and forefinger in close proximity to each other. "But you're here now. Seems a shame not to take advantage of your time off. Catch a few waves. Work on your tan."

He snorted softly and bit into his bagel. He chewed in companionable silence for a moment, swallowed, and said, "I'll find another place to stay."

It was my turn to snort. "You don't even want to know how much it costs to stay on the island or how far in advance things book up. Trust me. Most likely that's why Brickman ignored my request to cancel the bookings. He'd probably have had to refund deposits he might have already spent. There's plenty of room here. It's not a problem for you to stay."

Remy had inhaled his own breakfast and was now sitting hopefully at Joe's feet. Every now and then he rested his chin on Joe's knee, as if to remind him of how patient he was being. Fortunately, Joe was made of stern stuff and resisted the urge to slip my dog some of his bagel.

I crossed behind Joe to put my own slices in the toaster. "It won't hurt having you run interference with the sheriff's office, either. I'm not sure they would have taken seriously any request from me to run tests on the glasses from Bennie's."

"Once they accept that I arrested the right people back in Greenbriar, you mean." A man could die of thirst listening to Joe's dry drawl. "Don't hold your breath on the drug testing panning out to any great degree. There wasn't much left in the wine glass. And even if they determine the drugs were in the wine, it's not likely to nail down where they came from."

"Wouldn't knowing the type of barbiturate be useful?" I stood frowning beside the toaster. My appetite had returned with a vengeance now that the atmosphere in the condo had lightened, and I was ready to fall like a hungry wolf on my toasted slices as soon they popped up.

"Only if they have another sample to compare them to. Despite Manny's protests to the contrary, we're talking about a bar here. One situated in the playground of the rich and famous. Half the clientele probably brought their own recreational drugs, and odds are the other half could have held out their hands and gotten anything they wanted." He took another bite of his bagel and chewed thoughtfully.

"How long were you at the bar last night? I didn't see you come in."

He licked cream cheese off a fingertip and wiped his hand on a paper napkin. "Not long. I got there just about the time you hustled Liz out the back door. What you haven't told me is why you think someone spiked your drink."

My bagel popped up with the warm smell of toasted bread. Gingerly, I fished the hot slices from the toaster and spread them with cream cheese as I gave Joe the recap on the residents of the condo and everyone I'd seen at Bennie's last night. "After Emily and Andrea both mentioned Manny as someone who used to be tight with Brinkman but then had a beef with him, it struck me that he might know more about Brinkman's business dealings than the others. Like you said, I think the paintings are probably missing, though I don't know why the police haven't said anything yet."

It was odd that the sheriff's office hadn't been in touch with an update on my accessing the condo, or the status of its contents, or even to ask further questions.

"When I called the department this morning, there'd been a big fire down at the harbor. Mercer was probably tied up there most of the night. As for not informing you about the status of the paintings...I get the impression he believes you capable of insurance fraud."

Joe's words rolled like tumbleweeds across a bone-dry landscape as he continued eating.

"Great." I balled up my napkin and tossed it onto the counter between us. "Well, regardless of what Mercer thinks about me, I thought it wise to start tracking down anyone Brinkman may have had dealings with."

"I think the real issue is who might have wanted you out of the picture last night—even if it was just a temporary measure to stop you from asking any more questions." He ticked off people on his fingers as he listed them. "You mentioned seeing the assistant manager and he was openly hostile. The ex and the actor, of course, were at your table at least part of the night and had the greatest opportunity to spike your drink. And the older couple from the Sand Dollar were there, too."

"Yes. I'm sorry you missed Hattie's turn at the mic. It was amazing." I frowned as I tried to recall when, where, and who I saw the night before. "I could swear I also saw Emily—the yoga teacher—for a brief moment. I don't think I'm mistaken about that. And, of course, Manny. Not to mention Deputy Wilson, who was less than pleasant."

It was Joe's turn to frown. "The deputy? Not there in an official capacity, I take it. And certainly gone by the time Liz collapsed—or at least chose not to do anything about it when it happened."

"I can't say whether Wilson was still in the bar by then or not. I don't remember seeing him after he spoke to me. For all we know, he got called in on his night off to help with the situation at the harbor. In all fairness, if you hadn't walked in when you did, would you have noticed us leaving out the back door? Or followed if you weren't trying to catch up with us?" I shook my head. "Nope, I'd already gone out into the alley once with Andrea and no one blinked twice. I'm glad Wilson *didn't* follow us out though."

I barely refrained from shuddering.

"And that would be because?" Joe's voice had gone silky smooth. I'd heard that tone before and it never boded well for the person responsible for triggering it.

Great. It would probably be best if there wasn't an additional source of friction between Joe and the local police, so I weighed my words carefully. "Earlier in the day, he seemed to enjoy telling us that Brinkman's death was a homicide and not to leave town. Then, at the bar, he...uh... cautioned me about asking too many questions."

"For heaven's sake, Ginge." Joe looked disgusted. "Did everyone at the bar know why you were there?"

I lifted my shoulders with a grimace. "During a gap in the music, Liz sort of blurted out we were there to see Manny. Oh, and that Brinkman was murdered, too. Loud enough that people around us reacted. Andrea and Troy were both right there. I'm sure it didn't take long for word to get around to Manny himself. Wilson seemed to know as well, and I saw him talking to Tim at one point, too."

A little twinge of pleasure at being called "Ginge" shot through me, however. It was the first time since Joe's arrival. Don't bother reminding me that I'm always telling him not to call me that. It's like having a normally evil patient feel well enough to try biting you again. It's a good sign.

"That doesn't help narrow down the list of people who had a reason—and the ability—to spike your drink, does it?"

With a sinking feeling, I had to agree. We were no closer to finding the answers than when we started.

Chapter Nineteen

I'D BROUGHT LIZ A change of clothing, along with her purse and makeup bag when I went to pick her up at the hospital. To my relief, the person who stepped out of the bathroom looked like the sister I knew, armor once again in place. Aside from the hospital bracelet, she looked nearly as polished and precise as ever.

"Let's get out of here." She studied her face in the mirror and fluffed her bangs before turning to face me. "I suppose they're going to insist on my going out in a wheelchair."

"It's probably a liability thing."

"Honestly, as long as I get out of here, I don't care."

She sat like a princess on her throne, belongings grasped primly in her lap, and allowed me to wheel her to the front entrance.

"Let me bring the car around." I locked the wheels on her chair and dug my keys out of my pocket.

"Oh, don't be silly. I can walk to the car. I'm perfectly fine." She got up out of the chair and waited as I took it back inside.

On returning, I found myself hesitating to tell her about Joe and she picked up on my reluctance immediately, narrowing her eyes in suspicion. "What aren't you telling me?"

"You're feeling fine? No dizziness? No residual nausea?" I couldn't help fussing a little.

"I'm fine. The doctor said not to get overheated and no alcohol for a few days, but otherwise I can do what I want."

"Have you heard from Dave? I sent him my phone number last night and he never contacted me."

Liz sniffed but I couldn't tell if was because she was upset or annoyed. "Oh yes. He finally called. First thing this morning. Apologized again and again for missing your messages. Asked me to apologize to you, rather than risk waking you up this morning. Seems he decided to leave the girls with his parents and have a golfing weekend with his buddies. Told me they had a no phone, no work email policy. I get it. I do. Now that work from home is a thing, it seems like you're expected to be available twenty-four/seven. I had to put an "out of office" message on my own work email to come here. Even so, I brought my laptop with me just in case I got an urgent ticket to solve."

She seemed to be protesting a bit too much, though it was hard to say if it was for her benefit or mine.

"I thought maybe...I guess it's not reasonable to expect him to drive down here, particularly when I made it clear I was fine when I spoke to him this morning." Her lips pursed for a second before she continued briskly. "Right. Let's go back to the condo."

"Yeah, uh, about that..." I didn't know how to tell her that Joe was waiting for us at the car. There was no telling how she'd take the news or what kinds of erroneous conclusions she might leapt to about his presence here.

"About what? What aren't you telling me?" That had more of her usual snap to it. She put one hand on her hip and lowered her brows in annoyance.

Honestly, it was scary how much she could look and sound like Mother at times.

"Joe came down last night. As a matter of fact, he arrived just as you...as you got sick."

Her face shuttered as effectively as a portcullis shutting down on the palace gates. You could almost hear the barriers lock into place. "Joe came down. Here. To Hartberry."

"Um, yes. But here's the thing," I rushed on when I could see storm clouds building beneath her brows. "We don't think this was a random attack. We think it was targeted. On me. You drank my wine, remember?"

Her forehead furrowed in memory. "Yes. It was terrible."

"Not when I drank it. I think something was added to it later. When I wasn't at the table." At her blank look, I added, "Do you remember anyone messing around with the glasses?"

She rolled her eyes with a dramatic sigh. "I can barely remember singing karaoke. Maybe Troy will know."

Or maybe Troy was behind it. He certainly had the greatest opportunity of all. But how was I supposed to prove any of this? I'd have to gather all the principal players somehow and pick their brains.

In the strong sunlight, Liz looked rather wan under her makeup. I took hold of her arm as we began walking across the parking lot. "Maybe you should think about going home."

"Are you kidding?" She bridled at the suggestion of quitting. "Obviously we were getting close enough to worry someone. If this was an orchestrated attack, then what happened last night just means we're on the right track. You can't just send me home while you remain here on your own—oh wait. You *aren't* here alone. You have Joe now, is that it? You want me out of the picture?"

She drew herself up with a stiffness that screamed injured dignity.

"No. That's not it at all. You're not the third wheel here, you're the buffer." I smiled to indicate there was a little bit of a joke to the truth—or the other way around. "I just don't want you to get hurt again."

"I don't know which is worse. Thinking I was the victim of a random act of violence against women or finding out that someone is deliberately out to get you and I was just collateral damage. Let me tell you, I never—" She broke off suddenly, her mouth dropping open as she stared.

I glanced over at the Subaru. Joe leaned up against the dusty side of my car, talking on the phone. He wore a form-fitting royal blue T-shirt and lightweight khaki pants, complete with belt. Even his shoes were business-like, being loafers instead of his usual trainers. Earlier, I'd ribbed him about dressing like he was about to take a photo shoot for GQ, but he'd merely given me a tigerish smile and said that he wanted to look semi-professional when dealing with the local authorities.

Mirrored aviator lenses hid his eyes. There was no mistaking the distinct three-day stubble, or the artfully tousled hair, even at this distance. When he saw us, he ended his call. Pocketing his phone, he lifted a hand in silent greeting.

"Mindy wasn't kidding when she said he was as hot as ever."

Mindy being one of Liz's cheerleading buddies from high school. I was surprised they were still in touch.

"Yowza." Liz boggled at him a second longer, then said, "He came all the way down here from Greenbriar."

"I told you this already." Frowning, I failed to see her point. "The police—"

"The heck with the police," Liz snapped, pointing briefly in Joe's direction. "He didn't come down here because of the cops. He came down here because of *you*."

"Yes, but—"

"No buts." Liz turned to face me, shading her eyes with her hand. Despite her expert makeup job, I could see the dark circles under her eyes. "Dave didn't drive three hours to be here despite the fact I'd been hospitalized. This man drove six hours to be here because he thought you might need him."

I wished one of those rare sinkholes might open up and swallow me whole. "Er, flew."

"I'm sorry, what?" Liz looked at me as though I were speaking a foreign language.

"He flew down." The look on Liz's face made me rush on. "Which means he's kind of expecting to drive back with us. And sort of staying with us as well."

Liz punched me in the shoulder hard enough to leave a bruise.

"Ow, what's that for?" I rubbed my arm and glared at her.

"If you let him get away from you a second time, you're dumber than I thought." She straightened her cotton top and walked toward the car, leaving me to catch up.

"Like I had any choice the first time," I hissed as I closed in on her, aware that Joe was watching us both. "Besides, I don't need—"

"Oh, shut up. Need and want are two different things. I don't *need* chocolate cake. But you can bet your bottom dollar I won't turn it down if it's offered to me on a plate." She pulled up abruptly to poke me in the arm. "The right person is worth making room in your life for them."

"Stop poking me. I swear, it's like we're kids again." I thrust my chin at her. "What if they're not the right person?"

She opened her mouth, closed it again, and shook her head. Lifting her head with a look of determination, she finally answered. "Then you cut them out of your life and move on. Even if moving on hurts like the very devil or forces you to make choices you don't want to make."

"Oh, Liz," I said softly.

Darn it, I was terrible in these kinds of situations. Give me a frenzied wild cat ricocheting off the walls, trying to attack everyone in the room, and I knew exactly what to do. But relationship stuff was out of my comfort zone, mostly because I understood animals a lot better than people. Still, I had to say something. "Do you want to talk about it later?"

She lifted her chin with rigid pride. "There's nothing to talk about."

Joe greeted Liz as though we were picking her up from the airport for a fun-filled weekend, and not as though he'd appeared out of nowhere from a nearly twenty-year hiatus just when someone had given her enough pills to knock out Secretariat. He took her things and opened the passenger door for her. She shot me a glance and mouthed "wow" at me as he made his way to the back seat.

By way of showing Liz support, I put my "angry women singing" playlist on low for background noise as we drove. Ignoring me for the most part, Liz engaged Joe in conversation, asking about his return to Greenbriar and how his family was doing, but at least twice, she flicked a glance in my direction, her slight smile seemingly acknowledging my choice in music.

Once back at the development, Joe hung back as Liz went up the stairs in front of us. He lifted an eyebrow. "Interesting song choices. Trying to tell me something?"

"Not you," I spoke out of the corner of my mouth. "Liz."

He lifted his head in a nod of understanding and mouthed "ah" silently. "I was worried there for a second. That line about "sleeping with one eye open" seemed a bit pointed."

"The Reese women aren't particularly known for their forgiving natures."

"No," he agreed solemnly. "And yet they're worth the effort all the same."

I avoided making eye contact with him. We caught up with Liz at the elevators.

"You'd better let me go in the unit first. Remy is going to be so excited to see you both, he may jump up on you."

"I don't care if he puts his sandy feet all over me and deposits a pound of dog hair." Liz pushed the "Up" button again. "I'm starving. Please tell me we still have some bagels left."

"I got some fresh ones this morning. We should probably go grocery shopping today, though. Especially if they're calling for any kind of major storm. I think a cookout for the residents tonight is in order. Get everyone together with a little liquid lubrication and see if anything slips."

"I like the way you think." Joe's lips curved upward as he nodded a few times.

We got into the elevator and exited on the third floor. As we passed until 1301, I glared at the yellow tape still up over the door.

"I have half a mind to hire movers to box up the whole place sight unseen and put the condo on the market as soon as they give me access again."

"Aw, c'mon Ginge. It's not that bad. I'm sure the sheriff's office will clear the crime scene soon."

Liz stopped in front of 1302 and waited for me to tug the key out of my pocket. "What happened to your thoughts about moving here full time and opening a practice?"

"Excuse me, what?"

The shock on Joe's face might have been comical under other circumstances. It made me realize that short of when he set out to be charming, or when he was in serious law enforcement mode, there seemed to be a dampener on most outward displays of emotion. Liz's question had definitely caught him off-guard. "You're not serious about moving to the island, are you?"

"No." I narrowed my eyes at Liz. What was she playing at? "I might have toyed with the idea for a minute or two when walking on the beach the other night, but only in a fantasy kind of way. Horses, Joe. What would I do with the horses?"

Liz knew that, too.

Joe let out his breath softly, which was an interesting reaction.

"You say that," Liz continued, as though my moving somewhere had already been decided and the decision set in stone, "but you know Mom is right."

Scrabbling sounds came from inside the unit. I unlocked the door with haste and caught Remy's collar as he would have bowled either Joe or Liz over, or both, like pins in a lane. I'd hoped Remy's excitement would have been enough to change the subject, but once we were all inside the unit, Joe said, "Right about what?"

"Inheriting all that money." Liz went straight into the kitchen and tossed her purse down on the counter so she could pour herself a cup of coffee from the carafe still sitting in the coffeemaker. "If she sinks her fortune into building a state-of-the-art veterinary practice in Greenbrier, no one will ever forgive her for trying to make it pay its way."

I winced briefly at her words, recalling a previous argument with Joe over the fact I undercharged and devalued my services. Clients might expect even more underselling since I was no longer struggling to make ends meet.

The glance he shot my way suggested he remembered the discussion too. "That's going to be an issue no matter where she sets up. Her money will go a lot further in Greenbrier."

"It will be less of an issue if no one knows who she is and that she inherited money. She'd be better off starting a practice in Charlotte than back in Greenbrier." Liz lobbed her statement at him with the efficiency of a strong backhand on the tennis court.

"Where she would be competing with twenty or so other animal hospitals. She has an established base in Greenbrier."

Liz bridled slightly and opened her mouth to say more, only I forestalled her by changing the subject. "Right now, I'd just as soon be done with Hartberry Isle and everything on it. I'm not even sure keeping the condo as a rental unit is a viable idea. I wish we knew whether the paintings were in there or not, though."

Liz's phone pinged. She dove on her purse with unusual haste, but when she pulled out her cell and looked at the screen, her face fell. She opened the text message and rolled her eyes.

"Not from Dave, I take it?"

She held her phone out to me. "Did Mom text you with one of these?"

It was an image of the weather forecast, indicating that tropical depression Edna had strengthened into a hurricane, and showed its predicted path up the Atlantic Coast. Most of the previous weather models showed it making landfall near Wilmington, North Carolina, but this new one indicated a possibility of it hitting the Outer Banks instead.

The second text read in all caps: **COME HOME NOW**.

"I got one yesterday morning promising dire consequences if I didn't return home immediately. It read like a warning in a fantasy novel. 'Abandon hope all ye who enter here.'" I showed Joe the current message and handed the phone back to Liz. "Biggest mistake I ever made was teaching her how to screenshot things."

"That was you? Thanks a lot, sis."

"We can't exactly tell her what's going on. If she thinks we're persons of interest and not allowed to leave, she'll bombard the sheriff's office with complaints. I'll text her that I'm having car trouble and we have to wait for parts."

"That she'll believe."

I ignored the dig at my loyal Subaru. To my surprise, Liz placed her phone in her purse and shouldered the strap as she stood up.

"I want something more substantial than bagels. Let's grab an early lunch. You said something about a cookout tonight. If we're doing that, we need food. We can run by the store on the way back."

Remy shoved his muzzle up under my arm, forcing his head into the crook of my elbow. Exhaustion swamped me in an unexpected tide. All of it was just too much: the long trip down, finding the body, the hostility of the sheriff's department, the possible hurricane, Joe's sudden appearance, being up half the night worrying about Liz. She seemed to have gotten a second wind from somewhere. Maybe the hospital had included caffeine in her IV drip.

Joe said in a quiet voice, "Why don't you and I go, Liz? Ginny looks beat. She can take a nap and you can drop me by the sheriff's department. I want to check in with them this morning. On the way, you can tell me what you remember about last night. It will help me get a clearer picture of what we need to ask the residents when we get them together tonight."

"Kind of like gathering the suspects in a Poirot story." Liz nodded and linked her arm through Joe's. "You going to be okay here, sis?"

"I should be asking you that. You're the one that just got discharged from the hospital."

"Best night's sleep I've had since the girls were born. Apparently, all I needed was an overdose of sleeping pills and a ton of IV fluids," Liz quipped. Clearly, she was in better shape than I thought. "You stay here. Get some rest. You'll need to be on your toes later."

"They confirmed it was sleeping pills?" I didn't expect sleep aids to be used recreationally. Though I guess if you used drugs to jazz you up, you might need something to bring you back down.

Joe came to subtle attention. I doubt Liz even noticed and she was holding his arm.

"Yep. That's what my tox screen said, according to my doc. I assured him I hadn't taken them myself. Not the sort of thing I want around the house with small children. Otherwise…" Liz gave an elegant shrug, as though she could see the appeal.

Joe met my stare with a lifted brow, and I knew he would follow up on this when he went to the sheriff's department. He guided Liz to the door with a glance back over his shoulder, but I put Remy in a sit/stay to prevent him from following.

As Liz went out into the hall, Joe paused at the door, one hand on the jamb. "Ginny. Don't leave Greenbrier without at least talking to me about it."

"Huh?"

His statement came like a wild pitch out of left field and I nearly missed catching it. As if he had any right to tell me what to do. I opened his mouth to say as much, when he added, "I did that to you twenty years ago, and I know now how it felt. Just…talk to me, okay?"

He shut the door behind him and I released Remy.

It was a relief to be alone in the sudden quiet of the condo.

Chapter Twenty

TRY AS I MIGHT, I couldn't settle after they left. My phone also buzzed with an updated weather report from Mother, and I had to tell her we wouldn't be leaving the island right away in a manner that wouldn't make her send the family lawyer—and a wills and estates man who shuddered at the idea of criminal cases—down by the nearest plane to defend me against possible incarceration. After that, my brain ran in circles like a squirrel on crack trying to figure out what Joe had meant by more or less asking me not to leave Greenbrier.

My body desperately cried out for a nap, but I'm not a napper by nature, preferring to stick it out until bedtime as opposed to facing a night of insomnia. Those years in vet school when I could fall asleep on a pile of laundry were long behind me. I picked up the book I'd been reading instead, trying first the basket chair, then the couch, and then my bed in effort to get into the story—which wasn't nearly as compelling as the events of the last few days. Why was Brinkman killed in the condo? If he'd been there for legitimate purposes, it could have been for one last look around after the previous renters had left, to make sure there was no evidence of continued use after I'd forbidden it. If his reasons for being there were less than honest, then surely the presence or absence of the paintings would be vitally important to the case.

Annoyed that I couldn't get a straight answer on the artwork, I called the sheriff's department, only to be informed that Mercer was busy dealing with the aftermath of the harbor fire and the county-wide prep for the possible hurricane.

"The chief's got more important things on his plate right now than the death of some property manager." The person on the phone could have been the president of Mercer's fan club. "Someone will be in touch once the crime scene has been cleared."

Maybe Joe would have better luck getting information out of the department than I had.

Remy went over to the door and laid down with his head on his paws. That was his sign he needed to go out, so I gave up on the idea of trying to relax and grabbed his leash. He jumped up, dancing with excitement when I clipped the lead onto his collar.

"I hate to tell you, bud, but it's too hot to stay outside long."

I took him out back to an area designated for dogs to relieve themselves and then hustled him inside the building. Just the short time we were outdoors had him panting.

We met Deputy Wilson as we were coming back toward the elevators.

"Miz Reese. Just the person I wanted to see."

He cast a wary glance at Remy, who wagged his tail but made no effort to go over to greet Wilson.

He held out the key to 1301 at arm's length. "I stopped by the office, but Timmy wasn't in. I was going to leave the key with him, but seeing as I ran into you, I can hand it over directly."

As it wasn't possible to take the key without bringing Remy into range, and as Wilson was clearly uncomfortable with the notion, I put Remy on a sit/stay and dropped the leash to step forward.

Wilson eyed Remy to make sure he wasn't about to move as he handed me the key, and then fished a card out of his pocket to offer as well. "Sheriff Mercer told me to give you the name of some crime scene cleaners. They do a good job, though you'll need to replace the carpet in the main living room."

"Thanks. That was kind of him." I pocketed both the keys and the business card. "I take it with the fire and everything, he's a busy man."

"He's responsible for the entire county, and we're coming under a hurricane watch, so yes. Also, you may have heard this by now, but the fire was probably arson, so there's a big investigation going on." Wilson's chest expanded as he squared his shoulders. "I'm in charge of the Brinkman case now."

"I see." The killer was probably doing a happy dance somewhere. Wilson didn't impress me as an investigator any more than he did as a human being. I had to ask, though. "Were the paintings accounted for?"

"The ones you emailed Brinkman about? Yes, all three of them are in the unit, hanging on the walls."

"Oh, thank goodness." My breath whooshed out of me in relief. "I was really worried about that."

Wilson seemed to be gauging my reaction, and it dawned on me that had the paintings been removed, he'd have already hauled me in for questioning.

"Seems foolish of the former owner to leave such valuable art lying about." He shook his head. "Dumb thing to do with rental property."

Bristling at his opinion of Amanda's intelligence would do no good. "That's my fault, I'm afraid. When Ms. Kelly was murdered, the last thing on my mind was the rental unit or any artwork that might be there. And of course, the paintings didn't become truly irreplaceable until her death."

He shrugged, though whether it was at the idea of art being valuable or the fact it was all a moot point, I couldn't tell. It dawned on me the presence of the paintings meant there was no art theft, no insurance fraud, no big case. Small wonder Sheriff Mercer suddenly found it possible to delegate the investigation. Especially with more newsworthy events taking place on the island.

But then why spike my drink? It didn't make sense.

My phone chirped. I made my apologies to Wilson and gave the phone a brief glance. Hurricane Edna had been upgraded to a Category 2.

"My mother," I explained. "She's worried about the weather. Do they think the hurricane is going to track this way? Is there likely to be a mandatory evacuation?"

His tiny eyeroll could have been aimed at my own parent or all mothers in general, it was hard to tell. "We have to be open to all possibilities."

"Well, I hope that's not the case." I deliberately sighed. If I wanted answers, I had to make sure I wasn't part of the problem. "Now that I have access to the condo, I hope to be able to tie up my business here before I leave. The last thing I want to do is come back because of loose ends. I'll give those cleaners a call as soon as I get back upstairs. This hasn't exactly been a great trip for either my sister or me. I don't suppose there's been any word on the testing of our glasses from Bennie's?"

"Like I said, we've been busy." Wilson's lips flattened as he hitched his belt. "You tell your Sheriff Donegan we'll take it from here, but frankly, a spiked drink is low on the list of priorities right now. My understanding is that your sister was treated and released."

My Sheriff Donegan? What exactly has Joe been saying to the local police?

I nodded in what I hoped was convincing sympathy. "I understand. For what it's worth, the hospital said it was sleeping pills and not GHB or anything like that. Liz drank from my glass as well, you see. So, it's by no means certain she was the target."

Wilson frowned at that. "Sleeping pills? Not your typical choice for spiking a drink."

"I thought the same thing." And wasn't it interesting that Wilson seemed surprised by the information? Maybe my dislike of the man made me read more into his actions than what was really there. We both eyed each other as if rethinking our initial impressions.

"Of course, everyone and his brother knew you were at Bennie's to poke your nose where it didn't belong."

Any softening of my opinion toward him hardened into concrete again.

"That doesn't mean the business with the drinks had anything to do with Jeff Brinkman's death, though." Wilson seemed to be speaking more to himself than to me. "Manny Hernandez is no Boy Scout."

I tucked that piece of information away for future reference. "You're right. And we can't rule out the possibility my sister was the target without testing the glasses. But you can't say for sure it's *not* related to Brinkman's murder, either."

"Yeah. I'll keep that in mind."

The acknowledgement was definitely grudging.

Remy shifted his front feet in boredom but didn't break his stay. The movement caught Wilson's attention, however.

"Well-trained dog."

The compliment seemed almost grudging as well.

"We're working on it. I confess, I've been a bit lax with him. Cobbler's children and all that, you know." I cast a fond glance at Remy and reinforced the "stay" with a slight hand gesture.

"The shoemaker's children go barefoot?" Puzzlement furrowed Wilson's brow until he got it. "Oh, right. You work with animals all day. Must be hard to go home and do it some more."

"Sometimes." It was more complicated than that, but Wilson didn't need to know about my struggle with burnout, or how being my dad's caretaker for so many years had eaten into all my free time. I changed the subject. "So, if there won't be any problems if we decide to leave early? Because of the hurricane?"

"You're as bad as my wife. The storm won't hit here." He spoke with pompous authority, signaling that whatever slight understanding we had between us was gone. "But the ferry can't dock for the next few days anyway."

"But what about the hurricane?"

All of the sudden, my mother's warnings seemed critical.

"They're working as fast as they can to clear the investigation and begin repairs, but unless you can line up a private plane, I guess you're stuck here with the rest of us."

He obviously enjoyed jerking my chain. I had to believe his previous statement that the storm wasn't tracking in our direction. But it made sense that Mercer had his hands full elsewhere now.

Wilson left with a smirk, and I collected Remy to head back upstairs. Feeling guilty about using the elevator so much since our arrival, I opted to take the stairs. By the time we reached the third floor, I was huffing a bit. Heat and humidity were not my friends. Curiosity made me inspect the door to the third floor from the stairwell side. At least, that's how I justified pausing to catch my breath. A few splinters still lay scattered on the landing.

Untreated lumber, not gray driftwood. Probably swiped from the construction going on in Building Four. Relatively easy to jam the handle, at least long enough to mount an escape.

But what did it matter? The paintings were safe. Hurricane notwithstanding, I could get my business done here, enjoy the rest of our time at the beach, and we could return home. I'd better call the cleaning crew as soon as possible, just in case the storm did head this way, though.

As Remy and I walked down the corridor, I came to a stop in front of Amanda's condo. Remy took a few steps toward 1302, then turned his head to look back at me.

"We might as well take a quick peek," I told him as I unlocked the door to 1301. "So we can tell the cleaners what to expect."

Remy accepted the change in plans with his usual good nature at the notion of being able to explore some place new.

The smell was bearable. Not great, but not nearly as bad as it had been before. The carpet had been cut away from where the body had laid. Not a problem, as it would have had to be replaced anyway. The staining went down to the subflooring, however, and that was going to take some powerful cleaning or replacement. I didn't have enough knowledge to say which, and I hoped the professional cleaners would be able to tell me.

I shut the outer door, and after a moment's hesitation, decided to unhook Remy's leash. He focused immediately on the patch of bare subflooring, but eventually came away when I called him off it. I left him to explore the unit while I did the same.

I'd been right about the reversal of the layout of the unit. I'd also been right about the differences in personal style. Unlike the condo we were currently staying in, Amanda's unit was decorated with an eye to color. Mostly white furniture stood out against walls the color of pale grass, and blue accents in the form of glass bottles, lamps, and throw pillows made the entire room seem like a seascape.

The painting hanging over the sofa was in perfect harmony with the décor. It was a view from a balcony, glass doors partially open, and curtains billowing in. Beyond, a gray wave crested as a beam of golden sunlight turned the water translucent green. It was a gorgeous piece of art, and I knew at once I had to display it at the house back in Greenbrier, no matter how much it was worth.

As I stepped in closer to examine the painting, I found myself frowning. No oil painting I'd ever seen had quite the flat sheen to the surface this one had. I carefully touched the canvas. All the Amanda Kelly elements were there. The composition, her magnificent ability to convey light, her recognizable signature. It *was* an Amanda Kelly painting.

But there was not a single brush mark on the canvas. I'd bet my bottom dollar it was one of Amanda's limited-edition pieces that had been printed on canvas. I knew her online store sometimes sold products that way for buyers who wanted the look of a real painting without paying the full price. I had my phone out to call Laney about whether this painting was in the online inventory or not when a noise made me look around for Remy.

To my surprise, he was pawing at the side of the island in the kitchen. Thinking he'd found a bit of food left behind, and not wanting him to eat whatever it might be, I tried calling him, but he continued to nose and paw with determination at the side of the counter. When I realized he was actually pawing at an electrical outlet, I hurried over.

"Stop that. You're going to hurt yourself." I took him by the collar. What had gotten into him? The only time I'd ever seen this kind of behavior from him before was when he was trying to eviscerate one of his toys to remove the squeaker, or that time when he discovered

Ming's treat ball and he tried to destroy it rather than roll it to release the goodies.

Remy whined and stretched his nose toward the outlet while I frowned. So far this place was an exact replica of unit 1302, just reversed. But there wasn't an outlet on the kitchen island in the unit we were staying in. I was sure there wasn't.

I had one of those multi-purpose tools on my keychain that included a piece of metal that doubled as a screwdriver. I pushed Remy aside to access the outlet cover, but the screws turned easily with my tool. As soon as I got the plate off, I realized it was a fake. No electrical works inside, just a dark gaping hole.

Why would someone put in a fake outlet, and why was Remy interested in it? He kept trying to shove his nose into the hollowed out square, making loud sniffing noises as he did so. The idea of sticking my hand in the black hole gave me the willies. You never really outgrow the idea there might be a monster hiding in the closet to grab your hand. A pair of latex exam gloves would be nice right about now, but I'd emptied my car of all my supplies in preparation for this trip.

Using the light from my cell phone, I gingerly reached into the opening, trying to angle the beam to show as much of the interior as possible. I had to press my cheek against the wood in order to peer down to the bottom, which Remy took as permission to lick my nose. His actions made me laugh, if a bit nervously.

Ah. Lying in the bottom of the kitchen island was a mouse curled up on its side. Had it not been for the general odor of the unit itself, the smell of this small death would probably have been more apparent. I sat back on my heels and withdrew my hand. At least the little corpse was accessible. I could come back with a plastic bag and dispose of it.

One mystery solved. Hopefully, the presence of the deceased didn't mean there was rat poison present in the development. I'd have to ask

Tim about that the next time I saw him, and I hoped it wasn't the reason Hattie's little dog had died. People don't seem to realize mice will often move bait from the location you placed it and most pets will eat it.

"Sorry, old man," I told Remy as I started to replace the cover. "Not for you. I'll get you something nice to chow on later."

I paused, tiny screws still in my hand. Clearly, Remy had been attracted to the island because of the dead mouse, but I still didn't know why anyone would put fake outlet there in the first place. The interior had appeared empty when I swept it with the light. But I had only checked the bottom and far side of the hiding place.

Grimacing in anticipation of touching something icky, I reached back in the hole and felt around toward the top of the counter. Almost right away, my fingers brushed something, and I squeaked and jerked my hand back. Laughing at my foolishness, I reached back in to see what I'd touched. A small object was taped to the wood inside. The tape gave with a tearing sound as I tore it off the pressed wood panel and pulled the item out.

A flash drive fit in the palm of my hand.

Chapter
Twenty-One

I TOOK MY DISCOVERY with me back to unit 1302. Remy flopped down on the cool tiled floor in the kitchen, and his eyes drifted shut as he panted.

The flash drive was the standard device you'd plug into a computer. I hadn't thought to bring my laptop with me, and Liz's tablet was unlikely to have the right port. Hold up, though. Liz had mentioned bringing her laptop with her.

Indecision made me tap my finger on the counter a few times. A tiny image of Joe poofed into existence over my right shoulder, dressed in his dark brown sheriff's uniform, sporting a halo with his unruly hair impossibly slicked back. This vision informed me the right thing to do would be to call Wilson and tell him of the find. It was evidence in an ongoing murder investigation and I was obligated to turn it in.

The little Joe angel was right. I had every intention of calling the sheriff's department, no question there. I'd report the substitution of the paintings at the same time.

A little Joe devil appeared over the other shoulder. Three-day stubble, messy hair, black leather jacket, and a knowing smirk. Of *course*, I was going to turn the evidence over to the authorities. But what was the harm in checking out the contents of the drive before reporting it? What if the drive contained information about the missing paintings? There was no law about checking the contents of the drive, was there?

The devil Joe won out, and not because he was so darned irresistible.

I stood up so fast, Remy rolled to his feet with a look of confusion on his face, but settled when I assured him there was nothing to worry about. I hurried into Liz's bedroom. She'd unpacked the bulk of her luggage, but inside the biggest case I found a black laptop bag. Finding that it was password-locked almost put an end to my scheme, but after I entered a combination of Livy and Lindsay's birthdays, I was in.

Suspecting that the real Joe might not be as forgiving as the imaginary devil Joe, and the knowledge Liz could return at any moment, made me fumble as I tried to plug in the device. Why is it that you never put it in the right way the first time? I had to flip the drive to get it to pair with the laptop. Fortunately, the drive itself wasn't password-protected and the laptop recognized it, granting me a menu option. The total amount of data wasn't that large. I didn't want to copy any of it to Liz's laptop, as I wasn't sure if it belonged to her company. I used a cloud service for my photographs, so I logged in to my server and opened the drive.

There were fifteen subfolders on the drive. A couple of the folders were much larger than the rest, which meant they probably contained images or video. None of them took long to copy, however.

I breathed a little sigh of relief once that was done and logged out of my cloud service. This way, if I got interrupted, I could still review the files later.

The use of a flash drive was a bit old school these days. Either the material on it was a backup for something important, or it was so hot the owner didn't want it out there anywhere.

The first folder labeled "accounts" appeared to be a spreadsheet of some sort. Column one recorded the date. The second listed account names, but unfortunately only described them with nicknames, such as "Big Shot" and "Cutie Pie." The third column tallied sums of money in varying amounts. As I scrolled through the spreadsheet, most of the listings were repeated on a regular basis. Several of the entries went back years. The whole thing reeked of regular payoffs, but for what, I couldn't say. For all I knew I might have been looking at bookmaking on racehorses at Hialeah Park, except that money only seemed to come in, and not go out.

We were talking about a lot of money, too. Thousands of dollars coming in each month in dribbles and drabs from each of the listings, averaging about three thousand per name.

Some of the remaining folders contained what seemed to be a series of random photos and articles collected from the internet. When I came across a grainy image of a couple clutched in an intimate embrace as taken through a bedroom window, I turned my head sideways in order to get a better view. I couldn't make out the man's face, but the silver mane of hair looked terribly familiar. Kept himself in good shape too, judging from the breadth of his shoulders. The secret photographer, however, had captured a perfect, if embarrassing, shot of the woman. And given that it was Andrea Brinkman, I suspected she was the focus of the spying all along.

One folder only contained images of credit card applications under a wide variety of names. Some sort of scam? All the names were female, but the addresses were from all up and down the east coast. Many were from South Carolina. Five listed different units within Sand Dollar Cove, most of them from building four, which I believed was mostly closed for construction. Someone had made use of the empty condos to "borrow" their addresses.

I hit pay dirt with the fourth folder, which contained the images I'd emailed Brinkman of the three paintings in question, along with three separate receipts to Amanda's online store—each made out for the purchase of a print to be placed on canvas. The same folder held receipts for a frame shop on the mainland. Interestingly enough, the names on the purchase orders matched some of the names I'd seen on the credit card applications. All three paintings were shipped to Hilton Head, but not to the same address.

For an initial outlay of about two grand for a printed version on canvas, the thief could make upwards of thirty to forty thousand on each substituted painting. It only took three names from the "regular payment file" to generate that kind of investment money.

A fifth folder contained an old article about a young woman who committed suicide. Her name and face didn't ring any bells with me, but I made a mental note to look her up later. Another folder included a scanned copy of a newspaper article about a hit and run about twenty-five years ago. There were few details, only that the victim, an older woman, had died at the scene.

One of the remaining folders contained various property leases in the name of Hartberry Island Realty, Inc. The addresses matched the ones where the prints had been sent. Manny was listed as one of the company directors. What were the odds Brinkman was a silent partner? Three condos withing Sand Dollar were listed along with the other properties on Hilton Head—but not the ones used on the credit card applications. Trying to figure out the complicated web of schemes made my head spin.

One folder was just a list of names and addresses, but the addresses themselves were in some pretty swanky locations. Park Avenue, New York. Beverly Hills, California. That sort of thing. I recognized one name as being that of a collector who'd tried unsuccessfully to buy an

Amanda Kelly painting soon after her death. I remember Laney telling me he hadn't been happy that we couldn't sell any of her works until the probate went through, by which time the value of the artwork had shot up dramatically.

The last folder I opened tracked the income from unit 1301 that had continued after I told Brinkman to cancel the rentals. The fees charged were 20% higher than Amanda's list price too. Even with a good lawyer, the odds of me recovering any of that money were slim to none, especially if Brinkman and Manny had been playing a shell game with fake corporations. I'd need a good forensic accountant to find the funds if Brinkman had been smart enough to hide them, rather than spend them outright. Either way, the thousands in illegal rent payments combined with the stolen paintings would put me back on Wilson's radar, even if he didn't have any direct links to me.

There were more folders, but it was going to take time to go through them all.

The scrabble of toenails on the kitchen floor and Remy's excited whining alerted me to Liz's return. A quick glance at my watch told me I'd been absorbed with the files a lot longer than I'd realized. I shut off the laptop and pulled the drive, shoving the computer back into its bag so I could hurry into the living room. Liz staggered in with a load of grocery bags on each arm and I went to help her. Remy followed as we took the bags into the kitchen, leaping around us as if on pogo sticks.

"I've got more bags in the car." She tipped her head to the side to look give me the kind of look of calculated suspicion only a mother could produce. "What have you been up to?"

"I'll tell you in a minute. Let's get the rest of the groceries in first. Where's Joe?"

"I dropped him off at the sheriff's department. He said he'd make his own way back."

I left her to start putting food away while I went down to get the rest of the bags. She'd bought enough food for a small army. I grabbed anything that was perishable, leaving the paper plates and such for later. I smiled at the large jugs of bottled water. She was our mother's daughter, after all. Thankfully, she'd also bought more dog food, and I hefted the bag over one shoulder while carrying the rest of the purchases upstairs.

"It's a good thing I went to the store when I did. Things were already getting picked over. Guess some people in the area are taking this hurricane threat seriously."

"Good thing you bought more alcohol, then." I nodded toward the stack of wine bottles lined up on the counter. No wonder she had a hard time bringing her bags in.

"It's not as bad as it looks, and yes, I remember I'm not supposed to have any." Liz eyed the hoard of alcohol with a somewhat disparaging glance. "Because it's Sunday, I was limited to beer and wine and we're planning for a party, remember? We want everyone to be happy and relaxed when we start picking their brains. Besides, you know how it is during storms. Bread, eggs, milk, and alcohol sell out fast."

"Deputy Wilson doesn't seem to think the hurricane will be a problem."

Her head snapped up at that. "Wilson was here?"

She got the *Reader's Digest* version of events, culminating with finding the flash drive. By the time I finished, her eyes were alight with interest. "We should see what's on the drive."

Clearly, she was willing to bend the rules a little.

"Material evidence in a murder investigation," I said, as I popped a grape in my mouth. "Be sure to keep the grapes out of reach. They can be deadly to dogs."

"Grapes?" Her head rocked back on her neck. "Seriously?"

I nodded. "Yep. Grapes, raisins, cream of tartar, tamarind paste...they all contain tartaric acid, which causes kidney failure in pets."

"I had no idea. I bake sour cream cookies every Christmas and they call for cream of tartar. If I'd known about the toxicity thing, I wouldn't have bought any grapes. Remy is a bit of a sneak thief, isn't he?" She shoved the bag of grapes in the refrigerator. "Hold on. Did you just change the subject on me?"

She spun round from the fridge. "You've already looked at the drive, haven't you?"

Heat rushed into my face. "Maybe."

"How? You need a laptop for that and you didn't—" She shot me a fierce glance. "How did you get past my password?"

"The girls' birthdays? Little obvious, don't you think? At least no one but me knows when my dogs were born." Her exaggerated eyeroll made me continue without further teasing. "The less said about me opening the drive, the better."

"You're worried about what Joe will think."

Her smug expression caused me to grit my teeth before I responded. "As a duly elected sheriff, it puts him in a bad position if I run around obstructing justice. It's not fair of me to make him an accessory to my crimes."

"Oh pooh," Liz said, sounding exactly like our mother. "It's only obstruction if you don't turn your findings over to the law, which I'm assuming you're going to do. It can't possibly hurt to take a peek at the files first."

Since I felt pretty much the same, I said, "Not just peek, I made copies. There's a bunch of shady stuff there."

I told her about some of the things I'd discovered, including documentation of purchasing prints to swap out with the real paintings. "I was just about to call Wilson to tell him about finding the drive. What I can't understand is why anyone would possibly think they could pass the prints off as the real thing. I saw the difference almost right away."

"I bet you'd have been fooled if Brinkman had sent you *photos* of the paintings in their proper place on the wall, though."

I smacked my forehead. "You're a genius. Of course! That's why he went through the trouble and expense of hanging the fakes in the condo. I bet he planned to send me photos of the fakes to fob me off and delay my coming down until he'd milked the rental train as long as possible. Then he could have shrugged and said who knows when the paintings were swapped out. Anyone could have done it."

"What I don't understand is why Amanda would have left any of her original paintings behind in a place she rented out in the first place." Liz continued to shelve the groceries with frowning efficiency.

I lifted both shoulders in a helpless shrug. "She liked looking at them?"

Liz's sniff spoke volumes for Amanda's lack of security measures. "The smart thing to do would have been to hang copies. It's not like she lacked the technology."

Changing the subject, I told her about the dozens of credit card applications, and how the prints had been paid for by some of the applicants. I also told her about the extra fees Brinkman had skimmed from the rental. "If he did it to Amanda, he could have done the same to any absentee owner whose unit he managed."

"The rest of what you're telling me sounds like straight up blackmail, though." Liz placed several two-liter bottles of soda in the fridge to chill. "Greedy little sleazebag, wasn't he? This doesn't narrow it down much. Sounds like a lot of people could have wanted him dead. Look at all the income he was raking in!"

"Yes, but someone on the spreadsheet had more to lose than the others. We just need to figure out who. Speaking of blackmail, there was a racy photo of Amanda Brinkman in flagrante delicto."

"Wait, you mean with someone else? As in naked?" Her eyebrows lifted as she pulled the corners of her mouth down and shook her head slightly from slight to side. "Do tell."

"I'm not 100 percent sure about the man in the photo because you can only see him from the back, but I think it's Troy Doherty."

"Troy." Liz's voice went flat with disappointment before she gave a decidedly disinterested shrug. "Oh, well. It's not like I'd turn him down if he made an offer."

"Liz!"

"If I wasn't married. For heaven's sake, Ginny. They're both consenting adults and single—" Her eyes went wide, and she snapped her fingers. "Andrea was going through a divorce, right?"

"So?"

"So, you've obviously never thought about this kind of thing." She rolled her eyes, as though the answer was so obvious. "Brinkman may have wanted to torpedo Andrea's divorce settlement, particularly if he had assets to hide. It depends on if South Carolina is a no-fault divorce state."

She had her phone out in an instant and looked the information up. "Huh, this is interesting, South Carolina is not just a community property state like North Carolina, which means it allows for a fault-based divorce. That incriminating image could have blown Andrea's chances for getting a quickie divorce and possibly more than 50 percent of the settlement."

"You think it was about her and not Troy?" I had to play the devil's advocate.

Liz rolled her eyes even harder. If she wasn't careful, she'd lose a contact lens. "Okay, as disappointing as it may be to find out your heroes have feet of clay, does the fact that Troy Doherty is a hound dog affect his status in any way? The tabloids might have made a short run of it if they'd gotten hold of this photo, but honestly, it would probably be a booster for Troy at this stage of his career."

An unpleasant thought occurred to me. "The timing is awfully convenient. You don't think there's any way he engineered it, do you?"

"Troy?" The question clearly took her aback. "You mean, he planned to seduce Andrea, knowing that someone was hiding in the bushes taking pictures? Just to jumpstart a flagging career? That's pretty low, don't you think?"

She looked sick at the thought.

"You're probably right." The bitter look on Troy's face when the subject of Brinkman came up at the bar had seemed real. "I got the impression Troy didn't like Brinkman very much."

On the other hand, if Brinkman had a hold over Troy, he might have coerced Troy into doing his bidding.

Liz seemed to read my mind. "Yeah. Well, you can't trust actors. We'll have to figure out a way to bring the subject up at the cookout without letting on how we know about it."

The furrow between my eyes had grown deeper at the thought of teasing information out of these people during a social gathering when I didn't have a clue how to go about doing it. I rubbed my forehead. Maybe it was like taking a patient history from a client. People with sick pets usually wanted to help you get to the bottom of things, but frequently they weren't aware of what was important or not. I'd just have to figure out how to ask the right questions.

"Given that it looks like Brinkman may have hidden some assets under Manny's name, Manny may have even more motive than Andrea for wanting him dead."

Liz frowned at that. "If they were really on the outs, Brinkman would have moved those accounts ASAP. Maybe the falling out was all an act."

"For Andrea's benefit. Or maybe she and Manny are in on it together." Somehow, that didn't feel right to me. "No, if Andrea and Manny were working behind the scenes against Brinkman, she'd have never called attention to any potential relationship between them."

"But she didn't." Liz pointed at me excitedly. "That was the what-shername, the Yoga Queen, who brought Manny into this in the first place."

"Emily only said Manny hated Brinkman. It was Andrea who decided it had to be over her."

"Ugh. You're right. And it's nothing but speculation anyway. Then again," she added, "what's the statute of limitations on a hit and run?"

She didn't wait for me to shrug. She tapped the mic on her phone and asked the question, pausing to read the answer. "Huh. Two years. That doesn't seem like very long, given the offense. Doesn't matter if there's a wrongful death involved or not."

"It could still destroy a reputation. But how would anyone prove that after all this time? With so little to go on? How would you even know who to accuse?"

"The articles must be a threat. Not proof per se, but something you can use to intimidate. If you do something horrible and someone says they know you did it, the threat of going public alone could be enough to make you cave in."

"Make someone think you know more than you do, and then trick whoever it is into giving themselves away." I looked at my sister with new appreciation. "You have a decidedly devious mind. You know, that's exactly the kind of fishing expedition we're going to make at the cookout this evening."

"I'm all for it, but what are you going to tell Joe?"

I blew my breath out slowly. "He was the one who requested a tox screen on the glasses from the bar, and earlier, he thought the cookout was a good idea. The only thing that's changed is we have a little more information now. I think he's still on our side as far as doing our own investigation—up to a point."

"That point being staying within the letter of the law."

"Exactly. I hate the idea of turning over the blackmail information to the sheriff's department, though. These people have suffered enough already."

"If the articles are truly significant, not all of them are innocent victims." Liz lifted her hands, palms up toward the ceiling. "And at least one of them may be a killer."

"You're right. I know. I still don't like it." I straightened my shoulders to shrug off the imaginary weight of tough decisions. "I'll get the rest of the groceries out of the car, and then run the flash drive over to the sheriff's office."

Liz shook her head firmly. "Just call them. They can send someone here. You need to talk to Laney, let her know about the paintings. When Joe gets back, we'll have a council of war. In the meantime, if you give me access to the file on your cloud, I'd like to look through it myself. Maybe I'll see something you missed. If I can stay awake, that is."

She yawned as if to punctuate her point. The dark circles under her eyes appeared like bruises.

"Yeah, go for it. You have a better head for numbers than I do." I used my phone to send her a link to the file and headed out to get the rest of the groceries. Remy wanted to come, but I told him I'd be right back, and he took his toy up on the couch to continue chewing it.

The door to Liz's room was shut by the time I finished unloading the car. I put away the rest of the party items, and then went out on the balcony to call the sheriff's department. The dispatcher said in a snippy tone they would send someone when they could, they were still swamped with all ongoing situations and don't hold my breath unless it was an emergency. In my opinion, this attitude completely justified making my own copies of the files.

I called Laney next, and not surprisingly, got her voicemail. It was Sunday afternoon, after all. She was probably out enjoying her time off. Using a combination of voice-to-text and typing on the tiny keyboard on my phone, I drafted an email explaining the situation, and asked if she could contact the people who ran the online store for sales receipts and shipping information on the prints, as the police would probably want that anyway. I hoped she checked her phone as religiously as I did. She had a lovely, no-nonsense way about her. She'd probably have some pretty good ideas about how to track down the stolen paintings and who the most likely buyers would be.

After I sent the email, I sat on the balcony facing the sea. The sun hadn't hit this side of the building yet, and it was pleasant sitting in the shade with the wind ruffling my hair. Remy lay at my feet with his big head on his paws, one ear occasionally flicking as he watched seagulls wheel and dive with their keening cries. My lack of sleep the night before must have caught up with me because it wasn't until a loud bark and squawk jolted me upright that I even realized I'd dozed off.

A large seagull had landed on the balcony railing on the off chance I might have some food, which caused Remy to leap up after it with a sharp "woof." The bird flew off screaming raucous obscenities. I reflexively grabbed Remy's collar but needn't have worried. The balcony railing was too high for him to go over.

With a jaw-cracking yawn, I rubbed my face and checked my watch. I'd been asleep nearly a half hour. Highly unusual for me. Hopefully, the impromptu nap wouldn't keep me up all night.

Surprised that Joe hadn't returned, I sent him a text. While I waited for a response, I checked my email. Nothing from Laney yet. An alert came through as Remy and I went inside. A man of few words when it came to texting, Joe's reply merely said he was on his way back.

I'd just opened a cold bottle of water when Liz came out of the bathroom. Her damp hair and change of clothing spoke of a recent shower. She looked better, not as tired as she had before. Spying my water, she went to the fridge and got a bottle for herself.

"Joe's on his way back. I'm going to take Remy for a short walk since we'll be doing the cookout thing when I would normally take him on the beach."

She nodded as she drank half her water down, then capped the bottle and said, "I'll come with you. I want to stretch my legs a bit. Has someone from the sheriff's office come for the evidence?"

"Not yet."

As we came out of the elevator into the lobby, however, a deputy entered through the front door. Not the dark haired one that had reminded me of Joe, but the other one from the first night of the investigation. He raised his hand to catch our attention and crossed the lobby toward us.

"Dr. Reese? I believe you called about something you found at the crime scene?"

"Darn it." His timing was less than perfect. "It's a flash drive. I left it upstairs."

"Go back for it." Liz held her hand out for Remy's leash. Remy whined and danced in place like a Grand Prix dressage horse, already primed with the excitement of going outside. "I'll take the dog out and you can join us when you're done."

When I hesitated, she immediately took offense. "I've raised two children, Ginny. For pity's sake, I'm perfectly capable of walking a dog."

"It's not that," I was quick to say, though it really was. "It's just that he can be quite strong and—" At the look on her face, I stopped myself. "Okay. But slip the loop over your hand. Oh, and you'll need poop bags."

I transferred Remy's leash to Liz and fished around for the poop bags out of my back pocket. The deputy looked irritated about being made to wait, but it was either that or hang around until we came back from our walk.

Shoving a fistful of plastic baggies at Liz, I added, "They open at this end, where the little arrow is located—"

"I think I can figure out how to manage a poop bag." She added the worst possible insult. "You're as bad as Mom."

Before I could protest, she went on. "The sooner you go, the sooner you can come back."

"Keep an eye out for Joe, will you? I'll be down in a minute." I called out over my shoulder with another reminder. "Be sure to stay away from the waterways!"

"Jeez Louise, you'd think I'd never walked a dog before. C'mon, Remy."

Remy was reluctant to go without me, but I shooed him on with her and turned toward the deputy, who insisted on going with me to the unit to retrieve the drive. He tutted a bit over the fact I'd handled it without gloves, so I didn't mention I'd actually looked at it as well.

I merely pointed out that I hadn't known what it was until I pulled it out of the wall. That led to his wanting to see the fake electrical socket, which I showed him with mounting impatience.

The deputy didn't seem pleased with my desire to cut this visit short. He listened as I explained about the fake paintings, leaning in to take a closer look as I described how it was possible to order copy from the online store and have it printed on a real canvas. He documented the swapped-out paintings with his phone, and then knelt to inspect the fake socket. Noticing my obvious fidgeting, he asked, "Need to be somewhere else, Dr. Reese?"

"My dog is young and strong. My sister isn't an experienced dog handler. I should really get downstairs. Take as long as you need here in the unit. You can return the key later."

Perversely, the fact I was willing to leave him behind made him decide he didn't need to inspect the unit further. He did give the standard warning about making the condo and myself available should Deputy Wilson decide further inspection was warranted.

I didn't care. I just wanted to get him out the door and go back to Liz before Remy got into trouble somehow.

Just when we reached the lobby, the deputy pulled a Colombo on me by suddenly asking about the replacement of the paintings. "Why do you think someone would go to the effort of creating fakes when you spotted the difference in seconds?"

I shared Liz's theory about the fakes having been meant to pass a photo ID only, in order to make me believe the real ones were still in the unit.

"That seems plausible. But leave the investigation up to us, ma'am." He agreed to pass the information—and speculation—on to Deputy Wilson.

He touched the brim of his hat as he took his leave. "You'll be hearing from us again."

Well, *that* didn't sound ominous at all. I watched him exit the building before hurrying out the back door.

As usual, the heat smacked me in the face like a wet blanket when I stepped outside. The oppressive humidity was tempered slightly by the breeze coming off the nearby ocean, but if I'd needed any reminders why living at the shore year-round was a bad idea, this would have done it. It probably didn't help that summer dresses or shorts and sandals weren't my idea of comfortable clothing. I glanced down at my boots and jeans and knew I should change clothes before the cookout tonight.

Shading my eyes with one hand, I scanned the area for signs of Liz and Remy. When I didn't spot them, I crossed through the patio space and over the short, browning grass that had been burnt to a crisp by the summer sun. Ahead, I spied an egret walking slowly among the reeds at the edge of the marshy body of water that ran toward the sea. Too large to be called a creek. Too small to be a river. The sluggish water smelled of mud and rotting organic matter in the heat of the sun.

The egret took off as I approached, lifting white wings in a noisy ascent as it cleared the water, headed for the other bank. An alfresco meal was set up at some tables among the loblolly pines, and small groups of people were scattered about the little park. The path led to the small wooden bridge that arched over the murky waterway, the same bridge where Emily had been practicing yoga just yesterday morning. Liz stood with Remy—a little too close to the water for my comfort level—facing the bridge.

I headed in their direction, about to shout at her to get back from the creek, when I realized she was pointing her cell phone at the bridge, where a couple stood in what was clearly a proposal in the making.

Several people gathered off to the side, apparently videoing the scene as well. I didn't want to spoil their moment, so I hurried down the slope to catch up with Liz and take over dog patrol.

Several events converged all at once.

The man on the bridge dropped to one knee, offering an open ring box to the woman covering her mouth with her hands. Remy alerted on something in the reeds, and pulled hard on his leash, causing Liz to jerk sideways. And I spied the ripple of movement in the creek that was faster than the surrounding water.

I took off in a hard sprint toward Liz, who was scolding Remy and trying to refocus her phone on the couple. The water moved faster, creating a wake on the surface.

"Run!" I bellowed, arms and legs pumping as I ran toward them.

Liz pivoted to face me, annoyance clearly written on her features, while Remy continued to tug her toward the reeds. The couple on bridge froze with their mouths hanging open.

"Run!" I shouted again, my voice breaking in desperation. Waving my arms, I tried to force Liz off, but Remy turned, delighted to see me, and began dragging her in my direction with the enthusiasm of a sled dog running the Iditarod.

The alligator exploded out of the water and onto the bank, headed straight for my family.

When you see gators sunning themselves, you wouldn't think they could move so fast. They look like prehistoric creatures, leftover dinosaurs basking in the warm glow of the sun. But think velociraptor, not brontosaurus. Gators come out of the water like a bullet and can run up to twenty miles per hour.

Liz shrieked like the last banshee on earth and dropped Remy's leash. He danced to one side while she went in the other direction with the alligator snapping between them, thrashing his body from side to side as he hesitated between his choice of prey. Liz was slower, but Remy was closer to the water. The gator leapt forward again with a great clash of teeth. Remy wheeled away, barking furiously.

I had no choice. I threw myself on the gator's back and clamped both hands around his snout.

Lord have mercy, this wasn't even that big a gator, but he was monstrously strong. I dug my toes into the soft ground to prevent him from rolling and held on for dear life. I used my knees to mash the front of the alligator to the ground, but the rest of his body writhed behind me like a bucking bronco. Something in my lower back twanged like a sour note from a guitar string, and I gasped with pain as the gator lurched again.

What now?

I didn't have an answer. I couldn't even look up. Every fiber of my being was concentrated on holding the alligator's muzzle shut, and I was only dimly aware of Remy barking and people shouting. Liz continued to wail like a siren somewhere off to my left. The gator was about six or seven feet long. Only the fact that we probably were close to the same weight allowed me to keep it pinned to the ground, but I couldn't hold onto it much longer. One more good thrash from the alligator and I would lose my grip. I had a close-up view of the gator's eye as it rolled back at me, simmering with untold generations of hate and fury.

"Cover its eyes!" I panted commands in staccato bursts. "Tie its mouth. Somebody catch my dog!"

Someone landed on their knees beside me. There was the sound of popping threads, and then strong forearms came into my line of sight as a blue T-shirt was stuffed between my arms and around the gator's eyes. Familiar hands knotted the shirttails to hold the blindfold in place. I recognized the hint of that citrusy, woodsy stuff Joe wore.

"Belt?" I ground out, glancing up to see that Joe had sacrificed his shirt to blind the alligator.

"Better." Without further explanation, he wound Remy's leash around the snout of the gator with the speed and expertise of a former rodeo champion—which he was. Within seconds, the alligator's mouth was completely immobilized, and with the leash tied in a knot, I could relax my grip on its face. Joe sat back on his heels; his tanned, bare chest glistening as he brushed a forearm across his forehead to block the dripping sweat. He shook his head slightly, a wicked grin creasing his face. "What am I going to do with you, Ginge?"

I pushed myself up by my elbows and then into a sitting position on the gator's back, still using my hands to hold the gator's head down. "See, I *do* know how to ask for help."

Joe tossed his head back and gave a short bark of laughter. A feral light gleamed in his eyes as he leaned forward.

"Yeah, I don't see any other way around it." He cupped the back of my head, pressing his forehead to mine. "I think I should kiss you right now."

"Well, don't take all day about it. In case you haven't noticed, I'm sitting on an alligator."

He was still laughing when his lips brushed mine. No, I wasn't going to settle for a quick peck out of old affection. I opened my mouth to let him in, inhaling sharply as I did so. It was just me, him, and the sun beating down from a blazing hot sky. Something inside caught like dry brush when lightning sparked, and I would have gone up in flames right there, only the eruption of cheers made me realize we weren't alone. I jerked back as though singed by fire.

A small crowd surrounded us, which included the would-be proposal couple along with the videographer and every single one of them were holding cell phones pointed at us. Even Liz, who struggled to hold Remy back with her hand through his collar, was still recording.

"Don't look now," Joe murmured close to my ear. "But I think you're about to become TikTok famous again."

I couldn't be bothered about the crowd just then. I'd ducked my head when I realized we were being taped, but now I spied what had attracted Remy to the reeds in the first place, the reason the alligator had been defending this spot of the riverbank.

Poking out of the tall marshy grass was a foot wearing a red canvas sneaker.

I recognized that shoe.

Chapter Twenty-Two

NEEDLESS TO SAY, THE cookout was cancelled.

"It seems like really poor taste to think about having a barbeque now," Liz commented while we watched in horrified fascination as animal control dealt with the gator and the sheriff's office dealt with the remains of poor Tim. "At least, not tonight, anyway. Maybe tomorrow evening."

"Liz!"

"What?" She eyed me with an astonishing lack of concern. "Do you really think Tim just happened to have a fatal encounter with an alligator? After all the cautions he gave us about staying away from the inlet?"

She had a point. At the same time, I wasn't sure if I was envious or appalled by her cool assessment of the situation.

"No, you're right. I have a feeling Tim was bashed over the head and helped into the water." I watched as Joe, still shirtless, spoke with the deputies down near the brackish inlet. "It's too much of a coincidence to think otherwise."

By the time animal control had arrived to deal with the gator, my back had seized up. I'd had to be lifted off the alligator, still in a sitting position, like one of those pitiful ash-covered corpses from Pompeii after the eruption of Mount Vesuvius. The first couple of steps hurt like the blazes before I was able to move again. Once the paramedics had checked me out (making sure to tell me several times how stupid I'd been to jump on the back of a gator), Liz and I were escorted to the cookout area (along with another lecture about the stupidity of gator-riding from the deputy who took us there) to take our statements.

Remy lay at my feet, panting in the shade. The proposal party had been seated at the wooden tables near the bridge. If the gods ever had a reason to smile favorably on me, hopefully all the cell phones with video of the scene had been confiscated for evidence, as Liz's had been.

A young deputy came rushing up as I eased into a chair.

He held out the Magic Elixir of Life, otherwise known as a cold cola to you and me.

"Compliments of Sheriff Donegan, ma'am. He said you'd need it after the whole, you know..." The deputy waved in the general direction of the chaos down by the water.

I forgave the 'ma'am' as I snatched the soda from him with hands that shook like a desperate junkie craving a fix. Nothing ever felt as blissful as that first, frosty, foamy sip going down my parched throat. Nirvana.

Joe knew me so well.

"Hey, where's mine? I was almost *eaten* by the gator." Liz sank into a plastic chair and lifted her hand, still bearing the bandage from her IV catheter, to her brow. "And I only just got released from the hospital this morning, too."

The young deputy stammered apologies and dashed back inside to the vending machine in the lobby. On his return, Liz accepted his offering as her due, and after another apology, the young man hurried back to his superiors. We watched the action from a distance, almost as though it were a scene from one of those crime scene shows. That reminded me of Troy. I cast a glance around at the crowd that had gathered. No sign of him, but I did spot Andrea smoking a cigarette on the other side of the police barricade.

The rest of the area was cordoned off with crime scene tape. Most likely the only reason Liz and I had been allowed back to the barbeque pit was because the deputies wanted to keep the various witnesses separated by groups, and because I'd begged to get both myself and the dog out of the broiling sun. I'd have preferred to have taken Remy back upstairs, but the law seemed to want everyone where they could keep an eye on them for now.

"Uh-oh." Liz took a long sip of her soda. "Don't look now, but Wilson is headed our way."

Deputy Wilson, red-faced and blowing like a steam engine, huffed his way up the slope to the barbeque pit. He came to a halt in front of me, arms akimbo as he leaned down to my level. Little flecks of foam flew from his mouth as he spoke, and I drew back to avoid it.

"Miz Reese, jumping on that alligator is the dumbest thing I've ever heard of anyone doing. People get killed by gators all the time around here. What were you thinking?"

Remy lifted his head and let out a low "woof." Muted for him, but it still pulled Wilson up short. He took off his Stetson and practically wrung it in his hands.

"That'll do, Remy." It was important to let Remy know I had the situation in hand, and he didn't need to come to my defense. "Believe me, Deputy. Everyone else has told me what a bad idea it was. It won't happen again."

Unless something threatened my family or my dog, that is.

"You're lucky it didn't tear you apart. Of all the addle-brained things to do—"

"It was trying to eat me." Liz snapped. "Or the dog. Of both of us. Something had to be done. Did the alligator kill Tim?"

A pained expression crossed Wilson's face as he straightened. "You know I can't... What makes you think the victim is Timmy anyway?"

Spots swam before my eyes, and I closed them quickly in an effort to blot out the image of that sneakered foot lying in the reeds. It only brought it into sharper focus. "The shoes. Red Converse. They were his, right? Was it an accident?"

Indecision puckered his face, but only for a moment. He glanced over at the parking lot, where several news trucks lined up, reporters in front of cameras, holding out microphones to anyone who might speak. "Oh heck, it'll be all over the news soon enough. The medical examiner won't confirm until an autopsy—and a necropsy of the gator, which will be euthanized." Wilson blotted his brow with the back of his hand. "A little more time with the alligator and we might have never known the cause of death. But the ME seems to think the head wounds are consistent with a deliberate blow."

With the release of the information, some of his swaggering self-confidence seemed to return. "I need an accounting of your whereabouts since this morning."

Liz caught my gaze for the barest of seconds, and then calmly recited her movements since waking up in hospital, being discharged, and then how she'd dropped Joe off at the sheriff's office while she grabbed lunch and went grocery shopping. "I'm sure the time-stamped receipts are upstairs in the condo."

I explained that after I took the dog out for an early run, Joe and I had been together until we picked up Liz from the hospital, but that I'd stayed behind to get some rest while they went out and had been alone until Wilson himself had given me the key to unit 1301.

His nostrils flared slightly at the reminder that if called upon, he might actually provide me with an alibi. My heart rate picked up as I wondered exactly when Tim had gone into the water. Could it have been this morning when I was out with Remy? Or when I was alone upstairs looking through the files? I'd spent a long time poking around in the drive.

I picked up my narrative where I'd left off. "After I made the discovery about the fake paintings, as well as finding the flash drive, I called the sheriff's department."

Wilson jumped on that.

"That's a pretty long gap between your sister leaving and when you reported finding the flash drive. Can you explain that? Did anyone see you during that time period?"

Ugh. This was going to suck, but I didn't see any way out of it. "I emailed the agent in charge of Amanda's art to tell her about the theft, and to see if she could find a paper trial."

I explained about the prints and how the swap was most likely made.

"That's still a lot of time between you finding the drive and calling it in." His lips thinned into a tight line. "You looked at it, didn't you?"

I shrugged, spreading my palms up to the sky. "I'd found a hidden drive in my condo, one left to me by a friend. How did I know it wasn't something personal and private of hers? It was only natural to look."

Wilson appeared to be grinding his teeth, an effect I seemed to have on law enforcement personnel on a regular basis. "You ladies stay here until I say otherwise. I'm going to want to talk to you again later."

Joe climbed the same slope that had made Wilson pant, with nary a change in breath. Somehow, he managed to exude more authority striding up the hill half-naked than Wilson did in full uniform.

The sight clearly irritated Wilson. "Where's that man's shirt, anyway? He looks ridiculous."

"The gator has it." I indicated the alligator, still blindfolded with Joe's shirt, but now wearing duct tape around its snout instead of Remy's leash. Four men were attempting to load it into the back of the animal control truck. Its powerful tail lashed furiously, almost knocking over one of the handlers.

Wilson blew out a disgusted sigh before shooting me a glance full of pointy daggers. "You people are the biggest goldarned idiots I've ever met."

He stormed off down the slope to intercept Joe before he reached us.

Behind them, animal control drove off with the gator, which signaled a good portion of the rubberneckers to disperse, no doubt thinking about how they could dine out this evening on their eyewitness accounts of the tragedy.

"Tim seemed harmless enough." Liz sipped her soda as the coroner's team loaded up a black body bag onto a stretcher and struggled to push it up the grass to the waiting van.

"Think about it. Either Tim had access to the information on the drive and tried to make use of it—or someone thought he did and killed him to stop any more blackmail attempts." I shifted in my seat as a thought occurred to me, catching myself just in time to prevent another back spasm. "Oooh. How much you want to bet Tim was the one who photographed Andrea and her lover together? Won't that be interesting if those photos turn up on Tim's phone?"

"I doubt those were taken with a phone. He needed a telephoto lens. You're right though. If Tim knew about the blackmailing pictures, he could have known about all the schemes." Liz sat up sharply. "That fits with why he was killed."

"Would you have trusted Tim with that kind of confidential information? He could barely manage the phones here at the Sand Dollar."

But why else kill Tim unless he knew something about Brinkman's activities?

"If Brinkman got him to take the blackmailing photos, that would be enough for Tim to realize his uncle wasn't on the up and up. Maybe he wanted to pick up where Brinkman left off but needed what was on the flash drive to do it. He could have been the person who tried to break into 1301 that first night," Liz suggested.

"Possibly." It seemed a stretch. "But as property manager, wouldn't he have had another set of keys? He wouldn't have needed to break in."

"He had to turn your key over to the police. In order to get into the unit, Brinkman used his own set and they went into evidence. Tim might not have had any other way to get into 1301."

"Makes sense." Also, the attempted burglary had been carried out by someone who knew the building well enough to bring something to jam the door. "Photos aside, if Tim found something that indicated what Brinkman had been up to, he might have decided to take over the family business."

"And the killer, having already dispatched Uncle Jeff, probably didn't hesitate to get rid of Tim too." Liz's expression softened into sympathy as she looked out in the direction of the medical examiner's truck. "Poor little idiot. He didn't stand a chance."

"Poor little idiot blackmailer, you mean." It bothered me, though, that Brinkman's killer had struck so openly and viciously, too.

We must have been on similar brainwaves because Liz suddenly said, "Promise me you won't say anything to anyone about the flash drive. Anyone outside of law enforcement, that is. We don't want anyone thinking we've gone into the blackmailing business."

"I hear what you're saying, but leaking information about finding the drive might making flushing out the killer a bit easier."

"True, but I'd prefer it if we were still alive at the end of the day. Besides, I thought this was about finding the paintings, not nabbing a murderer." When silence stretched between us, she added, "Ginny..."

"I promise."

We didn't want to tip our hand too soon anyway. At least, not until we'd had a chance to go through the files.

I shifted in the uncomfortable plastic chair. My back was screaming at me, along with everyone else, that riding alligators had been a really stupid idea. I desperately wanted a fistful of ibuprofen and an ice pack. If we had to wait here much longer, there was a strong possibility that I'd need help getting out of the seat.

"That was some kiss back there."

Liz waggled her eyebrows at me in sisterly glee.

"I'm not talking about that right now."

"Ginny and Joe, sittin' on a gator, K-I-S-S—" Her grin became a mock-pout. "Shoot. What rhymes with gator?"

"Hater, mater, later... As in we are never having this conversation later."

Joe appeared to have ended his conversation with Wilson and headed in our direction again.

"Oooh, here comes the conquering hero now." Liz straightened in her seat at Joe's approach.

Unconsciously, I attempted the same, only to squeak in pain as my back protested. When Liz shot me a look with raised eyebrows, I said through gritted teeth, "I'm fine."

Remy lifted his head and thumped his tail as Joe closed in with Remy's leash in hand, but thankfully, temperatures the equivalent of the devil's armpit had a dampening effect on my dog's overly enthu-siastic greetings.

"Animal control returns your leash with their thanks."

I started forward to take the leash, only to hesitate when my back objected to the movement.

"You okay?"

Those discerning hazel eyes missed nothing. Right now, they held me in a gaze both warm with affection and tight with concern. There were a lot of people who thought Joe only had one or two facial expressions. Charming Heartbreaker and Stern Sheriff. They'd be wrong. You had to pay attention, because his expressions were as subtle and fleeting as the shadows cast by clouds passing by overhead.

"I'm fine." I took the leash and carefully folded myself over to clip it on Remy's collar.

Joe made a little noise of exasperation, and when I looked up, he was miming shaking and strangling something.

"Clearly, you're not. They practically had to use the jaws of life to pry you off the gator, and I saw how you moved coming up this hill."

His eyes went sharp now, and while I was still protesting that it was nothing, he spun on his heel and went back to the deputies. A few moments of tense conference, and then he returned and held out his hand.

"C'mon. Let's get you upstairs. I've got permission to take you both and Remy inside. If they need anything else from us, they know where to find us."

Getting out of the chair proved challenging, even with Joe's assis-tance. I had to scoot to the edge and take a few shallow breaths like a woman in labor before I could steel myself to get to my feet. It wasn't so bad once I got moving but the first couple of steps were brutal.

"Why didn't you say something?"

Joe insisted on supporting my elbow as we went back into the blessed coolness of the lobby.

"I thought I was okay until I sat down for a while."

"You've got nothing to prove here, you know. Everyone knows you can pin an alligator."

"I know." I felt foolish now, trying to hide the pain.

Joe continued thoughtfully, "I mean, it's not like you're a wounded deer and showing signs of weakness will cause the wolf pack to bring you down."

I stuck my tongue out.

"Oh wait." Joe pulled his phone out of his pocket and held it up to his ear. "What's that? It's for you. The Justice League is revoking your membership. It seems you're not Wonder Woman after all."

"Darn it," I said sadly. "See, this is what happens when you accept any help. Street cred totally ruined."

"You wish."

That last was said so close to my ear, it was practically a whisper. I shivered in spite of myself. Despite my best intentions not to look at him, I gave him the side eye.

He just smiled and arched an eyebrow back at me. "Six to one it will be all over the internet in less than an hour."

Not liking those odds, I said nothing.

Chapter Twenty-Three

TAKING THE STAIRS WAS not an option. Liz waited until we were in the elevator with the doors shut to say, "So tell him about the flash drive."

The short version of the story, which included realizing the paintings had been swapped as well as finding the drive, lasted as long as it took to reach the third floor. Joe said nothing during the ride, merely listening with narrowed eyes and a furrow creasing his brow. I began talking faster as a result, either in an attempt to finish the tale before we hit our floor or to stop the upward climb of Joe's eyebrows into his hairline—take your pick.

The elevator released us onto the third floor. Joe strode down the corridor as though heading out to make an arrest. Apparently, attitude made the man more than clothes. Gritting my teeth, I was determined to keep up.

"You've turned the drive over to the deputies, though."

The tension in his voice lay coiled like a snake, ready to strike if I fought him on turning over the evidence.

"Of course, I did." Annoyance pricked as sharp as a paper cut, as if the notion of keeping the drive to myself had never occurred to me.

"She made a copy first," Liz volunteered, and then continued on despite my glare. "We could use an expert opinion. According to Ginny, there's a little of everything in the files—evidence of the art theft, some prime swindling deals, and a strong suggestion of blackmail."

I let us all into the unit, with Remy leading the way. He headed straight for the water dish and began glugging it down. I made a beeline for the kitchen and was relieved to find Liz had purchased more ibuprofen on her grocery run. Joe came in last, shutting the door behind us, and you could see the indecision writ on his face. If I didn't know better, I'd guess he had his own devil and angel sitting on his nicely tanned shoulders right now. Curiosity about what they may or may not be wearing, made me pinch the bridge of my nose in order to redirect my focus on the matter at hand.

A wicked smile curved one side of his mouth, and I knew which supernatural being had won the argument.

"Okay, you pull up the files. Let me go grab a shirt."

"You don't have to get one on our account," Liz called after him, and he headed to the bedroom with a laugh.

"Don't. You're embarrassing him."

Liz rolled her eyes and ticked her chin back, turtle-like, on her neck as she pulled a face. "Oh please. Men love that sort of attention."

Suddenly high school didn't seem that long ago after all. "No, it makes him uncomfortable."

She was still wearing her "as if" face. "How can you tell?"

"The tips of his ears turn red and they itch." I demonstrated by touching the top of my own ear.

If I'd thought Joe had looked great in the royal blue T-shirt with the khakis, the thin black cotton button down took him into drop-dead gorgeous territory. He finished rolling his sleeves partway up his forearms as he came back into the living room, and then reached up absently to rub an ear tip.

This sent Liz into honking laughter, which she tried unsuccessfully to turn into a cough before she excused herself to fetch her laptop.

"What am I missing?" Joe asked, continuing to rub at his ear.

"Nothing." I smothered my own laugh and made a vague hand gesture to encompass everything around us. "I think the stress is getting to her."

"How about you?" He touched my arm, light enough to be supportive, but easy enough to brush off as well. "Are you okay?"

It struck me as an astonishingly fine line created just for me, and the balance he maintained for my prickly benefit took my breath away for a second. As I stood looking at him, his smile an impossible blend of boyish hope and wary concern, none of the flippant or even truthful statements that I could make were right. There was only one possible answer. "Yes."

His smile went incandescent and then slid back to normal, his hand dropping back to his side when Liz returned with her laptop.

We settled in the living room, me with an ice pack wedged behind my back, and the three of us crowded on the couch so we could look at the computer. Remy lay nearby, chewing noisily on one of his toys.

Liz pulled up the files on both her tablet and laptop, which helped as we began going through the different folders. I caught everyone up to speed on what I'd found in the files I'd examined, and then together we went through the remainder. They documented several other units within the Sand Dollar that Brinkman had managed, for which he'd charged the renters a significant amount of money over the list price set by the owner. Brinkman had pocketed the extra income.

"I need a soda." Joe toed off his shoes with a little sigh of relief, tucked his socks within, and walked barefoot into the kitchen. "You want anything?"

We assured him we were good and waited for him to return.

He paused at the entrance of the living room to pop the lid and take a sip. "I wish we had a whiteboard."

"It would definitely make looking at the material a lot easier. We could spread everything out, move it around. Spot the pattern." I shifted the ice pack, which was starting to melt a bit, and winced at the fresh, cold, contact.

"I could run down to the hardware store and pick up some X board," Liz volunteered, eyes on Joe as he paced about. "The girls had a school project, and I found that worked better than poster board."

"If that hurricane is headed this way, places like that will be a madhouse." Joe stopped pacing long enough to add, "By the way, I checked with one of the residents, and he recommended closing the storm shutters on the windows up here tonight. We need to go to the building community room on the ground floor if the hurricane actually hits the island. If they don't get the dock repaired, no one is leaving by ferry anyway."

"I know. Mother has stopped sending me texts to get off the island while it's still feasible, and instead is sending links to articles on hurricane prep and survival." I blew out my breath hard enough to make my bangs flutter.

"At least you got to keep your phone. The sheriff's office won't tell me when I can have mine back." Liz's fingers twitched in imaginary texting as she spoke.

"I left mine in the unit." I shrugged. "Therefore, I couldn't have videoed the crime scene."

Liz huffed a little. "Mom sends you the survival tips. Me, I just get guilt-tripped into believing I'm going to leave my children motherless. That's the last message I got before they took my phone."

A distinctive ping emanated from my phone on the coffee table. Liz was closer; I waved her to it when she glanced my way.

"Oh, that's nice. She must have blown my phone up with texts and then called the sheriff's office. She wasn't pleased when they told her my phone had been confiscated as part of an on-going investigation. Oops. They told her about the harbor being closed too." Liz continued scrolling through the text. "Mom says here she's wired money into my bank account. I'm supposed to buy us plane tickets off the island. I guess she figures once I buy tickets on her dime, you'll be forced to accept them. By the way, it's too bad if you have to leave Remy behind. Getting out is our biggest priority."

"Give me that." I attempted to lunge for the phone, only to hiss with pain and pull up short as Liz snatched it out of reach.

Joe set his drink down on the end table and scrolled through his own phone. A slow, devilish smile spread across his lips as he paused for a moment to look at something. A few taps later, and a different alert pinged on my cell.

"What's this?" Liz frowned at my screen, still holding the phone out of my reach.

"Send the link to your mother. Tell her there's no way Ginny will leave Remy behind."

Liz did her snort-bark laugh again and began tapping away, only to giggle and hide the screen when I tried to see what she was doing.

"What are you two up to?"

Liz was still staring at the phone, her mouth dropping open slightly. "I just sent it to her. Oh. Em. Gee. Ginny, you have to see this."

She held out the phone and pressed play. Already, someone had uploaded the video of the newly engaged couple to YouTube, with the caption: "Woman and Gator Crash Marriage Proposal."

On screen, I did my best Crocodile Hunter imitation as I dove on the alligator and wrestled it to the ground, all while barking orders at everyone around me.

"Joe!" I whipped my head toward him in accusation.

He leaned in the doorway, sipping his soda.

"Hey, it will keep her off your back for a while, won't it?" His smile was pure evil.

Liz cackled like a witch. Her thumbs flew over the keypad, causing a ripple of unease in me. What was she doing? Commenting? Sending it to all of her friends and co-workers?

"Dead. Both of you are dead to me."

"Careful, someone will think you had something to do with Tim's death too." Joe snorted over his soda, but then said, "The truth is probably in these files somewhere. Who stands to lose the most here?"

"Andrea, for one." Liz tossed my phone aside and tucked her feet beside her on the couch. She ticked off the points on one hand. "She filed for divorce based on infidelity. But then Jeff gets pictures of her with someone we believe is Troy, so there goes her basis for demanding more money in the divorce."

Joe tilted his hand from side to side in the gesture for "maybe."

"Andrea certainly stood to gain the most if she knew about the hidden accounts and killed Brinkman before a nasty divorce. But that presumes she knew about the extortion schemes and didn't believe that a murder investigation would expose the crimes." He shook his head slightly. "In some ways it would have almost made more sense for Andrea to be the victim if it was about the divorce. The very fact a divorce was taking place called too much attention to Brinkman's finances."

"Put that way, Manny Ramirez is pretty vulnerable too," I pointed out. "Brinkman's divorce put his finances in the spotlight. If he put properties in Manny's name to avoid sharing anything with Andrea, Manny may well have decided to keep them for himself."

Joe slugged back the rest of his soda and two-pointed the can into recycling with a little flourish of his hand. Instead of rejoining us on the couch, he began pacing back and forth in front of the coffee table. "Again, Brinkman's death calls attention to the secret accounts and schemes. So, while Andrea and Manny both belong on the suspect board, I'm not satisfied."

He came to a halt in front of the coffee table, his brows lowering as he fixed us both with a stern stare. "We're leaving the shell game with the properties and the credit card accounts to the police. They've got the resources and the means to make a strong case. The credit card fraud crosses state lines, so the FBI will get involved anyway."

"What does that leave us, then?" Liz didn't *quite* pout.

"I can get a copy of the police report on the hit-and-run. Ginny, you follow up with Laney on the paintings."

"I can tackle Troy about Andrea." Liz didn't sound happy about it. "Find out if he set her up on Brinkman's behalf."

"Not by yourself, you're not." I sounded more like my mother than I cared to admit. "Someone around here has already killed twice. Probably spiked the wine last night as well. We stick together."

"Ginny's right," Joe said as Liz huffed and folded her arms across her chest. "We have no authority here. By all rights, I should have begged, borrowed, or stolen a lift to the mainland and gotten us all out of here before this hurricane rolls in. Your mother will never forgive me."

That's not the only thing she won't forgive him for. I cringed at the thought of Mother watching the YouTube video. A lecture about The Kiss was sure to follow. What had I been thinking anyway? I'd kissed Joe like he'd been the one popping the question. I couldn't think about this right now.

"Then why do this at all? Why are you turning a blind eye to our poking around?" Liz thrust her chin at him.

Joe shoved his hands in his pockets, his expression turning thoughtful. "Because I think Wilson's in over his head. Because we *can't* leave, and there's a killer who's becoming bolder with each strike."

He dropped his chin slightly, and a slight smile tugged at the corner of his mouth. "Which is why I think we should throw a Hurricane Edna party tomorrow night."

Chapter
Twenty-Four

BETWEEN US, WE DIVVIED up the rest of the files. Liz pointed out that the fact all the credit card applications had been placed in a woman's name strongly suggested a woman had to be involved as well, though it wasn't a given. But both Andrea and Emily seemed to be likely candidates if that was the case. I could see either woman in the role. Maybe getting cut out of the money was part of why Andrea soured so badly on her husband and found herself suddenly attracted to Manny.

"Something about that suicide case back in 2008 seems familiar. I thought as much when I read it earlier but then I dozed off." Liz pulled the laptop closer to her and began typing, frowning in concentration as she stared at the screen. "Poor girl. She was only twenty-seven. I'll keep digging."

"I can't do much more until I hear from Laney, so I'll whip up some less-than-fancy invitations and go around to the building residents. Find out how they're planning to ride out the storm."

The latest report, sent courtesy of my mother, indicated that while Hartberry Isle wasn't in the path for a direct hit, there was still plenty of punch to be worried about. Fortunately, it appeared to be a fast-moving storm, which would limit how strong it would get. Even in just the outer bands of the storm, however, we would be in for a long night. Perhaps the other residents would be happy for a distraction.

A quick dash back into Amanda's unit provided me with colored pencils and paper to make silly invitations and a couple of blank sketch pads. We might be able to tape the sheets to the wall as a kind of DIY whiteboard, if needed. I checked first to make sure the pads were empty—the last time I found one of Amanda's sketchbooks, they'd contained a set of hidden drawings.

The sketchbooks were blank, but one of them had the little ripped tabs at the top that indicated paper had been torn out. It wasn't the kind of thing Amanda did with old or abandoned sketches, and I wished Jeff Brinkman's dead body was in front of me so I could kick it a few times. Another thing to tell Laney once I caught up with her—there may be a few charcoal drawings out in the wind.

An artist, I am not. I can manage drawings a bit better than stick figures, but not by much. Still, I thought the stylized twisting cloud blowing air was effective (and easy to reproduce) as I sketched a number of invitations.

Clearly, the diplomatic course of action was to invite everyone in the building. This would also have the added benefit of making it less obvious it was a gathering of suspects. As I knocked on doors, however, only the long-term residents seemed to be at home. I stuffed a flyer in the crack of the door in the unit across from us, hoping Hairy Grumpy Man had other plans just the same.

I ran into Troy and Andrea coming out of her unit on the second floor.

I pretended not to notice the way Andrea looked like a deer pinned in headlights at my approach, and then leaned back against Troy, who took a subtle step away from her. I shoved a flyer at them.

"I'm glad I caught you! We're going to throw a hurricane party in the community room tomorrow evening. Are you going to be around?"

"A party?" Troy took the flyer with automatic politeness and held it steady while Andrea read it as well. "Isn't that a little..."

My grimace wasn't entirely an act. "In poor taste so soon after Tim's death? I kind of felt the same way, only Liz insisted. See, we were planning a cookout tonight, and we bought all this food and alcohol, which will go to waste otherwise. And if I'm being completely honest, neither one of us are happy about being trapped on the island with a big storm rolling in. So why not party like it's 1999?"

I sang the last few words, moving my hand around in a little circle, as though dancing.

Andrea snatched the flyer out of Troy's hand when he started to crumple it.

"Free food and booze. Can't beat that. How are you going to manage the cooking though? It'll be pouring down by then, so grilling is out." Though she spoke to me, Andrea watched Troy with the intensity of a cat at a mousehole.

"We'll have to cook everything upstairs and then bring it down when it's ready. My understanding is the community room has tables and a microwave, so as long as we have power, we can reheat anything that cools off too much. Do say you'll come. It will be terribly flat without you."

Troy inhaled slightly, and then the tension bled out of his shoulders on the exhale. "Sounds fun, actually. Can we bring anything?"

I beamed at him. "Oh yay! I was hoping the two of you would come. We're good on food and beverages, but it might be a good idea if you could bring flashlights or candles, just in case. And board games if you have them."

"I've got an old game of *Clue* somewhere." Troy shrugged at my lifted brows. "A gag gift. Because of the cop show, you know."

"I've got a couple of hurricane lamps," Andrea volunteered.

"Excellent. I hope we won't need them, but you never know." I smiled brightly. "I'm just going to run around distributing the rest of the flyers, but the building seems awfully quiet. Do you know where everyone is?"

"Most of the renters went back to the mainland when the first storm warnings went up. Us die-hard residents can't be run off that easily, but anyone who's still here is probably at the grocery or hardware store. We were just headed to the store ourselves. I'm surprised you didn't leave the island when you could." Troy stood before me with a nice, helpful smile on his face, but there was tension in the lines bracketing his mouth.

I didn't have to fake a shudder. "We considered it, only it didn't seem like Edna would blow this way at first, and there was Brinkman's death to contend with. Between the fire at the harbor, Tim's death, and what happened to Liz last night, we didn't even get the chance to rethink our decision to stay."

"Liz? What happened to your sister?" Troy frowned and his expression flickered before it was replaced with what seemed like genuine concern. But then again, an actor's job was to sell you on believability.

"You didn't hear? Oh, I suppose not, what with Tim's murder and all. Someone spiked Liz's drink at the bar last night and she had to be hospitalized."

"Tim was *murdered*?" Andrea screeched, at the same time Troy said, "Oh my word, is Liz okay?"

And then the two of them looked at each other. Andrea had a death grip on Troy's arm. I was much better at reading animals than people.

Was it telling that Andrea didn't ask about Liz? Or that Troy focused on Liz and not Tim's death?

"Liz is fine," I said to Troy. "She'll appreciate you asking about her, though. Thank you."

To Andrea, I said, "Wilson seems to think someone hit Tim over the head before sending him into the water. They'll know more after the autopsy, though."

Andrea went pale under her tan, giving her a slightly green complexion. "On second thought, maybe I'll just ride the storm out in my unit."

"Safety in numbers," Troy murmured, and his smile went sardonic as Andrea abruptly let go of his arm. "We'll be there."

"Oh good," I said in all honesty. "It wouldn't be the same without you."

Troy gave me a kind of blank stare before he forced a tight smile.

I waved them off and continued with my flyer distribution. If no one answered my knock, I left a flyer wedged between the door handle and the jamb of their unit. I spent twenty minutes trying to get away from a woman who, upon opening her door, shrieked, "It's the Alligator Woman!" and hauled me by the arm into her condo, where I was fussed over by what turned out to be part of the wedding proposal party. Even though most of their group was staying in another building, I invited them to join the hurricane gathering anyway. It was the only way to escape their clutches.

I was just about to turn away from a unit on the first floor, having knocked several times with no answer, when the door flew open. Emily stood glowering at me, nostrils flared, one hand clenched and the other gripping the door frame as if to block any entrance. The supremely defined tone of her tanned arm braced in the door jamb suggested yoga wasn't for wimps. Emily definitely had the upper body strength to whack both Brinkmans over the head.

"What do you want?"

"Oh. Um. Hi." I must have sounded inane, and Emily's tiny eyeroll confirmed it. Hopefully, if she noticed my assessment of her physical strength, she'd assume it was out of envy, and not that I was sizing her up as a candidate for murder.

Behind her, the unit looked as basic and devoid of personality as the one Liz and I were staying in. I realized the condo was one of the ones listed on the drive as belonging to Brinkman. The unit was already stripped bare of any personal items. Behind Emily stood a tower of boxes from several major online companies, many of which appeared to have never been opened and included enough popular appliances to start a cooking show. Several half-open cardboard boxes sat on the coffee table, along with a roll of packing tape, and a stack of luggage stood in the center of the room. Four giant boxes alone were labeled "SHOES." Since her imminent departure was impossible to ignore, I cued in on it.

Flicking my fingers in the direction of her packing, I said, "I see you were planning to leave too. As soon as we found out the storm was coming this way, Liz and I wanted to go home, but then we heard about the fire down at the harbor. And now we're stuck here."

I chose not to mention seeing her at Bennie's last night.

Emily said nothing.

Whew, tough crowd.

"Oh." I made a show of touching my lips in surprise. "It didn't occur to me, but I guess since Brinkman is dead, they won't let you stay in his unit anymore."

That got a response. Her eyes narrowed into slits, and she leaned out of the doorway toward me. "What's *that* supposed to mean?"

Shoot. I wasn't supposed to know that Brinkman owned multiple units within the development. "Nothing. I just assumed. You know. That you were living with Brinkman."

She relaxed back into her former position, though her eyes remained wary. "You know what they say about people who assume."

I made a weak noise that could be construed as a laugh and pushed a flyer toward her. "Anyway, since none of us are going anywhere, come to the hurricane party in the community room tomorrow night. Food and drinks on us, though if you'd like to bring something, you're more than welcome to do so."

She began shutting the door without taking the flyer. I was losing her.

"Andrea and Troy are coming," I blurted out. "She's bringing lamps in case the power goes out. They make a cute couple, don't you think?"

The door stopped moving. Emily fixed me with the kind of stare I'd seen just once, coming on a bobcat unaware in the forest. The small but deadly predator had fixed me with just such a look of disdain before melting back into the brush.

Like then, I held my ground. Emily looked me up and down and then reached out to pluck the flyer out of my hands. She slowly closed the door with an enigmatic smile that gave no clue as to her intentions on attending the hurricane party or not.

Drat.

There was only one unit left on the ground floor. To my surprise, Gordon opened the door when I knocked on it. I suppose I figured they'd have one of the nicer units with a view, and that I'd already left a flyer on their door. From my position at the door, I could see the perks of living on the ground floor. Instead of a balcony, the Olsens had a large patio on the other side of a large sliding glass door. In preparation for the storm, Gordon must have moved the heavy potted plants indoors, because the living room looked like a veritable greenhouse.

"Come in, come in." Gordon waved me inside. "I'm just getting ready to nail up some plywood over the glass back here. You can keep Hattie company, if you don't mind."

After a careful look over his shoulder, he added, "Hattie hates storms. She gets upset at even the notion we have to do some prep for it."

"I'd be delighted."

"I guess you heard about Timmy."

The way he phrased it made it unlikely he'd heard about my career as an alligator rodeo rider, so I stuck with a generic, "It's dreadful."

He nodded with a sigh. "We came back from the store to find the police everywhere. I don't understand it. Timmy was the first to warn you about staying away from the water out back."

I followed Gordon into a room filled with the earthy scent of the potted plants, as well as the warm sweet odor of sugar and cinnamon. The unit had a well-lived-in look, decorated with furniture that could have come from my mother's house, with a rich patina that glowed from years of wax and polish. A pile of brightly colored yarn with knitting needles sticking out of it lay on a comfortable chair upholstered in chintz, the beginnings of a beautiful scarf in the greens and blues of the sea. An upright Steinway stood against the inner wall with sheet music on the rack. Mentally, I snapped my fingers. No wonder they had a ground floor unit.

"Hattie, love," Gordon called out. "We have company."

Hattie appeared in the doorway to the kitchen, wearing potholders and a smudge of flour across one cheekbone. Her face lit up on seeing me. "Hello! Come in. You're just in time. I've got snickerdoodles coming out of the oven. The first batch is cooling now."

"She bakes when she's stressed. I'd appreciate it if you didn't bring up Tim's death. It took me over an hour to calm her down earlier." Gordon pitched his tone in a register that suggested he knew she couldn't hear him. Raising his voice, he added, "I'm just going to go out back and take care of some things. Don't mind me now."

He didn't say anything about me riding an alligator, so I decided I wouldn't either.

Gordon collected a toolbox and stepped through the sliding glass door, pulling it shut behind him. Outside, he manipulated a large sheet of plywood closer to the door, and placing a few nails in his mouth, began positioning the wood to cover the glass.

"Come in, come in." Beaming, Hattie waved me toward the kitchen. "I'm just finishing the last batch."

I entered the small kitchen and paused at the entrance to inhale the delicious scent of baking cinnamon. "Mmmm. My favorite cookies."

"Mine too." Hattie sent a delighted grin over her shoulder before turning back to roll out the cookies. "Though I swear, I don't know what that man does with my things when I'm not around. I couldn't find half my baking utensils this afternoon."

She used a tall tea glass to roll out the dough into a flat sheet, and then flipped the glass over to cut out cookies with the rim. She dropped the cut cookies onto a baking sheet and sprinkled them with a sugar and cinnamon mix. "Couldn't find my silicon baking sheets or my rolling pin. And I have no idea where the mixer is."

A stand mixer stood on the counter beside her, apparently unused. I said nothing. It would only make her feel bad.

She placed the tray of unbaked cookies in the oven and set a timer. She handed me a plate of warm cookies that practically had me drooling and ushered me back into the living room. "You take a seat out there. I'll bring some tea."

I resisted diving into the cookies until my hostess could join me. A few minutes later, Hattie came out with pot of tea. I jumped up to help her navigate her way to the coffee table, taking the tea tray from her.

"Thank you, dear. Now isn't this nice." She took her seat on the couch.

I poured tea into the kind of lovely, fragile cups I could never own, due to the risk of breakage. Outside, Gordon began hammering up the plywood, and the room became much darker as he cut out the light.

Hattie didn't seem to notice. "So lovely to have you visit. Please, help yourself."

She sat bright-eyed in anticipation as I selected a cookie and bit into it, picking up one of her own at the same time.

"Mmmm," I murmured as I bit into the cookie. "Miz Hattie, this is delish—"

A second later, brine hit my tongue, as though I'd drunk directly from the sea. Trying not to gag, still forcing a smile, I passed a hand over my mouth and spat the piece of cookie out.

There was no disguising it from Hattie, though. She choked and spat her own cookie into a napkin before grabbing a cup of tea to wash the taste out of her mouth.

"Oh, what have I done?" She wailed. Tears welled in her eyes and her lower lip quivered. "Salt. I mixed up the salt and the sugar. These are terrible!"

She put her old, wrinkled hands over her face and wept silently with small jerks of her shoulders.

My father had also gone through these mercurial changes of mood toward the end of his life. I swept up the plate of cookies and rose. "Now, now. These aren't so bad. As a matter of fact, the reason I'm here is to invite you and Gordon to a party tomorrow night in the community room. I'll just save these for the party if that's all right with you. They'll be perfect. Do you have something I can put them in?"

The tears stopped, even though their tracks still ran down her face. "Are you sure? Well, let me see. I have a tin here somewhere."

I followed her back into the kitchen and watched as she opened cupboards and banged around looking for the cookie tin, her agitation growing with every cabinet door slammed shut. "Where have I put them? I swear, that man of mine moves everything around."

We located the tins on top of the refrigerator, and I boxed up not only the cookies that had been plated, but the ones on the cooling rack as well. I couldn't do anything about the ones in the oven, though. I had the tin tucked under one arm as we returned to the living room. The light from outside was completely blocked out now.

Hattie stopped in the doorway, with one hand grasping the collar of her blouse. "It's come over so dark so fast. Is it the hurricane? Is it here yet?"

I switched on the lamp beside one of the comfortable, overstuffed chairs. The warm glow it cast did much to relieve the gloom, and I helped Hattie to her seat.

"No, that's just Gordon boarding up the glass to protect it. You will come to the party tomorrow, won't you? I'd love to hear you sing again."

Her face lit up at that, a beam of light breaking through clouds. "You heard me? Oh, that's right, we saw you at Bennie's."

"You were truly magnificent. I'd love to hear more about your career."

She was telling me about her ride-or-die friends, the singers who had hoped to get together for a reunion tour, when Gordon came through the front door carrying his toolkit.

I stood up, still holding the cookie tin. "I need to run along, but thank you for the hurricane cookies, Miz Hattie. We'll see you tomorrow night?"

I handed Gordon a flyer. "There'll be food and board games, and I'm hoping we can persuade Miz Hattie to sing for us."

Gordon gave us a pretend eyeroll. "Well, now there's no stopping her. We'll *have* to go."

Hattie preened a little, even as she made a swatting motion and said, "Oh, go on with you."

Gordon escorted me to the door.

"Actually, it might take her mind off the hurricane." He spoke quietly again, pitched out of Hattie's hearing range. "Thanks."

"The cookies were inedible," I warned at the same volume, giving the tin a little shake. "Salt."

His smile grew pained. "I'll watch her when she makes the next batch. Can't be everywhere at once. At least the storm prep is done."

I took my leave and then wandered down the corridor to check out the community room. The door was unlocked, so I stepped in and turned on the lights. A series of long tables and folding chairs ran parallel down the length of the meeting area. Near the door, a cardboard box served as a container for dry-erase markers, erasers, construction paper, crayons, coloring books, and the like. A whiteboard took up the inside wall, making me think we could have moved our detection brainstorming session down here had we known. With a little adjustment, we could rearrange the tables to form a big square, with the food down at one end next to electrical outlets and microwave if needed. As long as the power stayed on, that is.

Four windows ran along the outside wall, facing the front parking lot. The storm shutters appeared to be in place, giving the room an institution-like feel under the stark fluorescent lighting. Tim had probably closed them before meeting his untimely death. The thought sent a little frisson of unease through me and goosebumps rose on my arms.

If Tim was still alive, I'd ask him if there was a formal signup sheet for using the community room. As it was, I thought it wise to lay claim to its use tomorrow evening. I stole a couple of pieces of tape from the dispenser in the supplies box and was taping a flyer to the door when the elevator doors opened and Joe stepped out.

"Hey," I said as I fixed the flyer to the door and stepped back. "Unofficially reserving the room for tomorrow evening. Did you find out anything?"

Before he could answer, my cell phone rang. "Hang on. It's Laney."

Silently, he offered to take the cookie tin so I could handle the call. He started to open the tin, but I waved him off, grimacing and pretending to gag while I answered the phone.

Predictably, Laney was livid about the stolen artwork. I let her blow off steam, and then listened while she told me about the steps she'd taken to track down the purchases, as well as inform her friends in the art world to be on the lookout for the paintings.

"Of course, if the buyers are private collectors—and the odds are they are—there's no way of knowing. However, from that list you emailed, I'd say Gwyneth Jordan is your best bet. She's known among the New York galleries for not examining too closely the provenance of an item she wants."

"But without proof..."

Laney made a sound of disgust. "Given that her name came up in a homicide investigation, and there's the potential for art fraud, maybe the FBI can get a warrant. It's a long shot, but maybe we'll get lucky."

We ended the call with promises to keep each other posted, and I looked up from my phone to see Joe leaning against the wall waiting for me. He straightened when I pocketed the phone.

"I might as well give up those paintings as lost forever."

Joe offered his arm, and I tucked mine hand around it as we headed back to the elevator. "Don't give up just yet. Art theft falls under the purview of the feds. They have to be better at their jobs than Wilson. What's up with the cookies?"

I made a face and pulled up short. "Hattie stress-bakes, but she put salt in by mistake. I pretended I was taking them for the party. Let's empty the tin in the dumpster out back. I don't want anyone—including Remy—eating them by mistake."

The sun beat down out of a brilliant blue sky as we crossed the parking lot and headed for the wooden enclosure that contained the dumpsters. I held my breath as I opened the container. Spoiled hamburger meat warred with rotting fish for the most potent stench, and flies boiled in small black clouds with the disturbance. Plastic garbage bags had been split open, no doubt by the earlier police search, revealing wilted lettuce, congealed pasta, and liquefying cheese. It looked as though someone had tossed their entire makeup collection, resulting in a scattering of rose gold body glitter over almost everything. A cracked rolling pin rested beneath a broken baby stroller on top of the mound of trash. The dusting of gold flakes coating the bags reminded me of a teaching video I'd once seen, using glitter to demonstrate how easily viruses could be transmitted. I hastily upended the tin of cookies over the rest of the trash and slammed the metal door shut.

Waving a hand in front of my face until I'd put some space between me and the dumpster, I said, "Gah, that stink is unbelievable."

Joe snorted. "Yeah, I pity the poor devils that had to wade through it earlier today. Wilson ordered a search, which is probably why it smells so bad because they broke open the bags."

The thought made me choke back a gag. Being a vet has given me a tough stomach but not that tough. The heat radiated off the asphalt as we crossed the parking lot and headed back toward the building.

I shielded my eyes with one hand as I glanced up at the cloudless sky. "Hard to believe a hurricane is headed our way. It looks like perfect beach weather right now."

"First bands of rain should roll in tomorrow morning."

"According to my mother's latest update, yes."

"No response to the YouTube video yet?"

"No." And that worried me. Her reaction to the video was hanging over me like a maternal sword of Damocles. I wouldn't rest until she'd said her piece. It was a tossup which would bother her more, the bit about the gator riding or me and Joe kissing in public like I was dying of thirst in the desert and he was a canteen of cool water.

"I have to warn you, Liz is a bit bummed right now." Joe tipped his head toward the building. "Turns out Tricia Markham, the woman who committed suicide, used to work as a stunt double before giving it up."

I pulled up short to stare at him. "Don't tell me. She worked on *Logan's Law*."

Joe stopped beside me. "Got it in one."

I did the math in my head. "She couldn't have been much more than a teenager then. I don't like where this is going."

"It's the only real connection we've found between the files and the people living here. I know the two of you like Doherty—"

"I barely know him. As for Liz, her teenage crush may have clouded her judgment, but if he's a killer..."

"We still can't connect the dots. Mind you, Brinkman could have been blackmailing people from all over. But the odds are someone local killed him. My guess is Doherty is on that spreadsheet. We just can't prove it."

"Try looking under something like 'pretty boy'." I heard Manny call Troy that last night at the bar. We may be able to correlate payments with when Troy moved to the Sand Dollar."

My stomach clenched like a fist. The notion that Troy had done something worth being blackmailed over was sickening. No wonder Liz was upset.

As we began walking again, I remembered we'd been interrupted by Laney's call. "So, the hit-and-run. Did you find out anything?"

The breeze ruffled Joe's hair, not that it needed any excuse to look messy and untamed.

"Not much, which isn't unexpected, given the fact no arrest was ever made. Took place the summer of 1998, outside Los Angeles. Bad night, poor visibility. No street cameras. Only witness too far away to make out a license plate but described the driver as getting out of the car to check on the victim and then burning rubber to get out of there. By the time the witness reached the vic, it was clear nothing could be done."

"How horrible."

"For all concerned." Joe nodded. "Dying like that is terrible, but living with the knowledge you accidentally killed someone? That's got to weigh on you."

I nodded as well. "Yeah, I mean, every time I lose a patient, I beat myself up. I can't imagine how much worse it would be if I killed someone by running over them."

Joe took my hand briefly, giving it a squeeze before letting it go. "It's the same with law enforcement. Most of us get into our line of work because we want to make a difference. It's the failures that eat you up."

Not for the first time, I wondered if Joe was referring to a specific incident.

"Do you think Tricia Markham's suicide could be related to the hit-and-run? Like you said, filled with remorse, that sort of thing? L.A. in the late nineties—*Logan's Law* was filming then."

Joe spread his hands wide in a mini shrug. "I don't see how. If Tricia was the driver and she committed suicide, then who is left to blackmail?"

I conceded with a sigh. He had a point.

He opened the door to the building, and the coolness of the air-conditioned lobby was a blessed relief.

"Still, someone had to know more about the incident other than the witness. Why else is the article in the Brinkman files?" Joe kept working through the problem as we headed for the elevators. "Either there was someone else at the scene—maybe a passenger in the car—or else the driver talked. Couldn't hold it in, a secret like that. Otherwise, how could Brinkman make the connection?"

"Ugh." I rubbed my forehead. "We're no closer to solving this than before we found the files."

The elevator opened. Joe ushered me in and turned to press the button for the third floor. "Yes and no. We have a better idea of where to start looking. Heck, we have the easy part actually."

We began our ascent.

"How so?" I asked.

"Brinkman either had a line to follow with his blackmail victims in the first place or he applied leverage until he found a chink in someone's armor. We have the beginning and the end. All we need to do is tie up the middle." He leaned against the back wall of the elevator with a grin. "We've set the stage for the final scene. Now we need to gather the suspects in one place and apply pressure until someone cracks."

Chapter Twenty-Five

"You ready?" Joe asked, as he picked up the cooler containing cold sodas, beer, and ice.

"As ready as I'll ever be." I pinched off a piece of bread, rolled it around Remy's tranquilizer, and tossed it to the dog. Remy caught it with a snap and wolfed it down, not realizing it contained the chill pill.

Telling Remy to wait behind in the unit, I opened the door for Joe and followed with more items to take downstairs. We'd been cooking for the last hour, and Joe had found a cart from somewhere to load the food onto it. Keeping everything warm was going to be challenging, but for now, all the hot dishes were wrapped in tin foil. We'd also opted for cold cuts, fruit, and other items which didn't need heating, particularly since there was no guarantee we'd have power once the storm hit in earnest. Liz put the finishing touches on the burgers as we left with the cart. I'd come back for the rest of the party foodstuffs and Remy once we took this load down.

"What did you give Remy?" Joe glanced over at me as I pushed the cart toward the elevator.

"The pill? Since this past spring, Remy still gets a little freaked by loud noises." Having a gun go off in close quarters was enough to make anyone sound-sensitive, including me. "I've been counterconditioning him and he's a lot better than he was, but I'm concerned a bona fide hurricane might be too much for him to handle."

Counterconditioning a dog meant modifying behavior by creating a positive association with something that they found scary or overwhelming until they began to see the scary thing and look forward to the positive reward. For it to work, you had to be on top of it constantly and be prepared to continue the rewarding as long as the scary thing was going on. Some dogs were so overwhelmed by a stimulus—for example, thunderstorms or fireworks—that medication was needed to bring their anxiety down to a level where they could accept conditioning.

"The medication isn't going to gork him, though. Right?" Concern creased Joe's brow as he set the cooler down inside the elevator.

I bumped the cart over the jamb in the floor and he closed the doors behind us. "No, it's not a tranquilizer that will sedate him. Just a little anti-anxiety medication. Something to take the edge off."

"I want him to be sharp. You know. In case you or Liz needs backup." The look he gave me implied a warning somehow.

We began our descent to the ground floor. This didn't seem to be the right time for an explanation of how, in some cases, anti-anxiety meds could actually decrease a dog's bite inhibition—that is to say, increase the likelihood of a dog biting because the medication can sometimes cause irritability and agitation. Kind of like a mean drunk. "You're really worried about this, aren't you?"

A small sigh escaped him. "I wish you hadn't implied to Manny that you'd seen Brinkman's files. Or that you hadn't turned everything over to the police."

Anyone who knew Joe would recognize the low growl of irritation in his voice beneath the drawl.

"Not me—we—as in all of us." I ticked off the points on one hand. "First, that it wasn't just one person who knew, so there was no reason to come after me alone. Second, how else were we supposed to get him to come to the party tonight? Anyone would have half a dozen reasonable excuses not to come out during a hurricane."

Yesterday afternoon, Liz had been sullen and snappish since finding out Tricia Markham had worked on the set of *Logan's Law*.

"How am I supposed to act around him now?" Liz had asked when we discussed her findings.

"Treat him exactly as you would before," I'd suggested. "We don't have anything definitive to accuse Troy of doing. It's a link, nothing more."

"Ginny's right." Joe had lent his support, even though the lifted brow and the glance he'd cast in my direction said a lead was a lead. "All we have now is supposition. If Doherty is on Brinkman's blackmail list, he's under a code name. The death of someone who worked on the same show years after it went off the air isn't much to go on."

"Except the notice about Tricia's suicide is in the files, and that means Brinkman was likely blackmailing someone over it." Liz had glowered as though she wanted to punch someone. That anger would come in handy when we put the screws on Troy, but in the meantime, it was probably best if she didn't run into him.

Because I could sympathize with her disappointment in Troy, I'd offered to spring for dinner at Bennie's. Liz had wanted to try someplace new, but I'd wanted a shot at getting Manny to join our hurricane party.

As I'd hoped, Manny had been nothing but solicitous when he'd seen us arrive, making sure we were seated quickly at an outdoor table with an ocean view. He'd personally seen to our service, and in the blink of an eye, a plate of crispy calamari and sauce had appeared.

"He probably thinks I'm going to file a lawsuit," Liz had grumbled, though that hadn't stopped her from tucking into the food when it came.

When Manny had stopped by the table to comp our ticket, I'd invited him to the party. As expected, he'd started to say it was impossible for him to come, but I'd merely nodded and said that I imagined as the CEO of several businesses on Hilton Head, he must have a lot of properties to look out for during the coming storm.

Manny's smile had seized up in a forced rictus, and suddenly, his schedule had opened up.

Which was good for our gathering of suspects but clearly, Joe was still annoyed about the risk I'd taken. He leaned on the rear panel of the elevator, his hands tucked behind his back. "Why not paint a bullseye on your back while you're at it?'

He hefted the cooler up when the doors opened and led the way out of the elevator. I pushed the cart behind him and caught up with him at the door to the community room.

"In a few minutes, we'll be putting everyone in the hot seat," I pointed out. "Was it really so bad getting a jump start on things with Manny?"

"There's a difference between calling people out on the spot to see their reaction and showing your cards in advance of the game. You've given Manny too much time to think about a response or tell someone else who may be involved. He could have shifted assets by now, or even gotten off the island. Or word may have spread to the other people on the blackmail list."

Crestfallen, I paused while reaching for the knob to open the community room. "I didn't think of that."

"I know." He lifted one shoulder in a resigned shrug. "You were thinking like an amateur sleuth and not law enforcement. The feds won't be pleased if he pops off to some place without extradition."

Belatedly, I recalled how I might have tipped off Emily as well with my observation about her living in one of Brinkman's condos. There was no point in wincing. "He'll have to get off the island first."

"There is that." Joe sounded unexpectedly calm for someone trapped on a small island with a murderer and an incoming hurricane. He caught me staring at him. "What?"

"Nothing, you just..." I took a deep breath. "You seem to be okay with all this. Unusually so."

"If by 'all this', you mean you and me on the same side for once—working together instead of against each other—yeah. I'm okay with this." He flicked me a mock-stern glance. "You putting yourself in unnecessary danger, not so much. But then again, you *are* Wonder Woman."

"Nope, I thought we settled that already." I rubbed the small of my back, which still ached a little. "Besides, I'm not sure I want to be Wonder Woman. She ended up alone. It's hard being up there on that pedestal by yourself."

"Peggy Carter, then." His smile said he knew quite well he'd tapped into my love of fandom. "No nonsense, tough-as-nails, and not above shooting Steve Rogers when he pissed her off."

My laugh trailed off as I remembered how that movie ended. "She wound up alone as well."

"Oh, maybe at first." The way he stared at me made me think we were no longer talking about movies. "But in the end, he came back for her."

I might have rolled my eyes, but a reluctant smile tugged at my lips when I opened the door to the community room. To my surprise, the room wasn't empty. Troy stood by the windows, looking out where the wind whipped the bushes against the glass. Andrea was in the act of placing a covered tray of cookies on the table where we'd stacked the paper plates, cups, and plastic cutlery earlier.

"Hello." Troy turned from the blustery scene; his hands shoved in his pockets. "One of these storm shutters has failed to latch properly. I suppose there was no one to check it after Tim's death."

Frowning, Joe hefted the cooler onto the table and said, "You're right. We should try to shut it before the weather gets any worse."

As if to punctuate his point, a hard rattle of rain knocked against the panes.

Earlier this morning, during my walk with Remy, I'd embraced the changing weather. The sky had dawned dull and gray, with leaden clouds hanging low over the horizon. Damp, gusty wind had kissed my skin and warned of storms to come. Moisture beaded on Remy's coat during our walk; the air had been heavy with the suggestion of rain. Waves had rolled in to crash on the shore in greater fury than I'd ever seen. It had been exhilarating. I'd loved every minute of it, preferring the stormy seas and skies to the relentless sun beating down in the days before. In the intervening hours, however, something had changed with the falling barometer. What had seemed romantic now felt menacing, like discovering a favorite stuffed toy was a flesh-and-blood bear.

One that might not be content with prowling around the building, scratching at the doors, looking for a way in.

Joe sized up the room, measuring what? Exits, potential weapons, my proximity to Andrea? I couldn't tell. His gaze met mine, and then with a slight smile, he turned to Troy.

"I'm Joe Donegan, by the way. Friend of Ginny's. Mind showing me how the storm shutters work?"

Troy shot a despairing glance at the windows, clearly not wanting to go outdoors with the heavy rain coming down. Behind him, blackened branches clawed at the glass. Waiting almost a beat too long, he finally said, "Troy Doherty. Yeah, I'll give you a hand."

As they walked to the door, Joe flashed me a subtle wink. "Doherty? As in the actor?"

Troy visibly brightened. "You've heard of me?"

The rest of their conversation was lost as they left the room. Andrea watched them leave, though it wasn't clear if it was Joe or Troy who held her interest.

Her next words clarified her target. "Friend of yours, eh? He picked a bad time to visit."

I pushed the cart over to where she stood and began unloading the food onto the table.

"I know, right? He got in the night before last. Same night as the harbor fire, so we all got stuck here." My laugh sounded tight to my own ears. "My mother has been hounding me all day to leave the island. I finally had to break down and tell her the harbor was out and there were no flights. She started sending survival tips after that and wanted to know if I'd made a will."

"Yikes." Andrea made a face, and then opened a small closet to remove some folding chairs. "I don't think it's going to be that bad. We'll probably only catch the outer bands. This party's a good idea, though. I think it would be worse waiting it out in our units, hoping the power stays on and the storm surge doesn't flood us out."

I hurried over to help her arrange the chairs around the tables. "Could that happen? The surge, I mean."

She shrugged. "We're back off the shore but not that far back. Depends on if Edna makes landfall before coming up the coast. That could downgrade her to a tropical storm, which is bad enough, but not as bad as a hurricane."

A shriek of protesting metal made me jump, and when I turned, the storm shutters had clicked into place, cutting off the eerie greenish light from outside. Andrea flipped on additional lights. The fluorescent glow from overhead was harsh and unforgiving. It brought out shadows under her eyes and accentuated jowls at her jawline. I couldn't help but wonder if the lighting was as cruel to me.

Curiosity made me ask. "Why didn't you leave?"

Another shrug, though this one didn't seem as complacent as the first. "I probably would have, if not for the harbor fire. You heard they caught the arsonists, right? It was all over the news. Bunch of teenagers on vacation with their parents. I hear there're going to be lawsuits over the fact that the dock was so badly damaged it prevented people from leaving."

"I'd hate to be their parents."

The door to the community room flew open and Joe and Troy entered almost as if they'd been carried in on a blast of wind. Their rain-soaked clothes stuck to their skin. Both Andrea and Troy watched as Joe leaned over with a laugh to run his hands through his hair, shaking the worst of the water out. Andrea's glance was speculative, with a hungry gleam to it. I don't think she even realized she'd reached up to smooth a strand of her hair as she stared.

Troy, on the other hand, radiated displeasure. If he'd been a cat, all his fur would be standing on end and he'd be licking it furiously. He grabbed a handful of paper napkins to wipe his face and glared at Joe from behind their cover. His wet shirt revealed the slightest paunch, and between getting drenched and the fluorescent lighting, the illusion that Troy's hair was as thick as ever had been destroyed. It wasn't until Joe pulled off his T-shirt to wring it out over the trash can that I recognized the naked emotion on Troy's face.

It was envy.

"I'm going upstairs for some dry clothes." Troy balled up the napkins and threw them with as much force as he could muster into the trash can.

"You're coming back, though. Right?" I had visions of my denouement falling apart. What would Poirot do? Appeal to Troy's vanity, of course. "Liz will be so disappointed if you're not here for the party."

The flattery worked. Troy's expression softened at the mention of Liz. "Of course. Wouldn't miss it for the world."

Joe chuckled, almost to himself, mischief glimmering in his eyes as he met mine. He tugged the damp and wrinkled T-shirt back over his head. "I'm running out of clothes to change into."

"I've got to take the cart back up and get the rest of the food. I'll bring back some towels." I grabbed the cart handle.

Troy pulled his dignity around him like a cloak and said, "I'll go with you—at least as far as the elevators."

That wiped the smirk off Joe's face. He opened his mouth, glanced at the table piled high with food and drink, and quickly clamped his lips shut again. I didn't need to be a detective to know he was reluctant to leave the food with Andrea unsupervised yet didn't want me getting into an elevator with Troy, either. Poor Joe. A border collie torn between two groups of wandering sheep, knowing there were wolves nearby.

Briefly raising an eyebrow at Joe, I pulled out my phone and began composing a text. Hopefully that would reassure him that if I didn't reach my destination, someone would come looking for me soon. "Great. I'll text Liz and let her know I'm on my way up. She can bring the burgers, and I'll get something dry for Joe and bring Remy."

Andrea broke off watching Joe to throw in her comment with the slightest curl of her lip. "You're bringing the food thief to the party?"

Half a dozen snippy comebacks came to mind, but I settled for a fake laugh. "True, it's a risk, but one I'm willing to take."

Once inside the lift, Troy faced the elevator doors, studying the lit panel as the numbers changed as though there might be a quiz later. "Joe seems like a nice guy."

"He is. We've known each other since high school."

We ran out of time to say more, and Troy got off on the second floor. He gave me a little wave as the doors closed, and I tapped my foot impatiently until the doors opened on the third floor. Joe's concern for our safety had infected me. Even pushing the cart, I was at the door to 1302 in seconds. Liz waited on the other side with a platter of cooked meat. Remy, for once, wasn't leaping like a loon, but instead sat with a fixed stare at the plate Liz held.

"No burgers for you." I petted Remy's disappointed head and pushed past them both to head into the main bedroom, where Joe had slept again the night before, leaving Liz and me to share a bed.

"I thought you were champing at the bit to go downstairs." Liz raised her voice to call after me. "Isn't that why you texted in the first place? So, I'd be ready when you got here?"

"Put the food on the cart," I yelled back as I grabbed the first T-shirt I could find out of Joe's bag. He'd just have to put up with damp jeans. "I texted because Troy got in the elevator with me, and Joe didn't want to leave Andrea alone with the food in case she tampered with it."

"Well, this is going to be a fun party."

I let Liz drag the cart behind her while I leashed Remy and kept his focus directed on me. Given the aroma of cooked meat made my own stomach growl, that was no mean task.

"I'm not sure I want to do this," Liz said suddenly, just as the elevator spilled us out into the lobby.

She chewed at a lower lip, not moving, one hand still on the cart. Remy would have charged forward, but I quickly put him in a sit/stay.

"I get that. No, really, I do. But Joe seems to think my hints about the files might stir up more trouble than we bargained for, and he definitely thinks neither of us should be alone right now." I fixed her with a sharp look. "Besides, he nearly blew it by showing off his abs in front of Andrea. I thought Troy was going to turn into a leprechaun, he was so green with envy. I had to use you as bait to persuade Troy to return to the party after he changed clothes."

As I'd hoped, this triggered a laugh.

"I'd have liked to have seen that—and not just because Joe has some mighty fine abs." She shot me a sly glance. "What does Mom have to say about the unique public display of affection the two of you shared with the world?"

Now I was the one whose ear tips reddened and itched with embarrassment. I rubbed one before speaking. "Precious little. She's been too busy telling me what steps I need to take to ensure everyone's safety during the storm. I suspect her resounding silence on the subject is supposed to convey her disapproval—for now."

Liz's laugh turned into a snort. "Are going to try again with Joe? Given that you insisted I share a bed with you last night, I'm not sure."

You and me both.

I quashed the thought before it could take root. "Maybe."

"Which means you haven't discussed it yet." She gave me an all-knowing look and began dragging the cart behind her toward the community room. "I'm pretty sure swapping spit while perched on an alligator is a declaration of intent, you know."

Remy followed the cart like rats chasing after the Pied Piper, his eyes half-closed with an expression of doggy bliss on his face as he followed the scent. I hurried to keep up.

"Okay, first of all, ewww. Not an image I want stuck in my brain."

"And second of all?"

We'd reached the door to the community room.

"Second of all, maybe it was just a heat of the moment thing."

Liz placed her hand on my arm when I would have opened the door. "You owe it to both of you to figure out what exactly it is. You're sending him mixed messages. Joe deserves better than that. You deserve better than that."

Her small, perfectly manicured hand rested on my freckled forearm. I knew she was right, and yet I also knew that everyone I'd ever been involved with had left me behind.

But in the end, he came back for her.

Joe's words echoed in my head.

"You're right. I need to sort it out. Probably once we get back home," I told Liz as I opened the door. "But right now, it's showtime."

Chapter Twenty-Six

WHEN WE ENTERED THE community room, it felt as if the curtain had lifted on the last act of the play. All the actors were on stage. Andrea had positioned herself as the pinnacle of a pyramid with Joe and Troy as the base. Troy now wore a white cotton shirt with thin blue stripes, untucked from his pants, in a move no doubt meant to disguise his slight middle-aged spread. I tossed Joe a dry T-shirt and watched as he efficiently peeled off the damp one to replace it. Andrea's attention during this process was more appreciative than I liked.

Manny and Emily stood side by side near the food table, with body language so stiff and unyielding that their determination to not ac-knowledge each other only broadcasted that they were more than mere acquaintances. Manny wore a Hawaiian print shirt and gray, long, board shorts. By contrast, Emily was dressed to go clubbing, with the heels and short skirt to match, which struck me as idiotic during an impending hurricane.

At one of the long tables, Hattie sat in a pretty, pink pantsuit straight out of the seventies and Gordon, dressed for a day on the golf course, leaned down with a hand on her shoulder to say something in her ear that made her laugh. Interesting that it was just the long-term residents. I suspected the ladies from the wedding proposal had gath-ered with their friends instead, and I hadn't really expected anyone else to show up. Which was just as well, since I really didn't want to talk about the alligator incident again.

All eyes looked up at me and Liz when we came through the door. Hazel, brown, blue—each with varying degrees of curiosity and welcome. Apparently, I was the director of this little production.

"Let's get this party started," I announced, waving a hand toward Liz as she pulled the cart over to the food table. "Get it while it's hot."

Food and drink worked its magic. Gordon set up a boom box that would run on batteries if we lost power and tuned it to the oldies station. "So we can get bulletins if we need them. It also has a karaoke option for later."

"Complicated" by Avril Lavigne came on the radio, taking me straight back to high school. I recalled with perfect clarity riding in Joe's pickup truck to Bishop's Lake, holding hands beneath the dashboard. Joe looked up at the song and met my gaze from across the room with a rueful smile.

The music in the background helped drown out the increasing noise from the storm outside. Joe circulated among the crowd, introducing himself with that deceptively lazy charm that worked its magic on everyone, including Emily, who laughed and put a hand on his arm at something he said. Remy stayed pressed close to my leg, his concern over the weather warring with his desire to steal food. In the end, he settled himself at my feet, all the better to catch something if it was dropped, and yet still in comforting contact with my legs. In deference to his anxiety, I pinched off pieces of hot dog and gave him one every time the shutters rattled.

"What's up with your poor boy?" Hattie asked, when Remy refused to leave my side.

"I'm afraid he doesn't like storms."

Her expression flickered for a moment, and I regretted mentioning the weather. She spoke softly, as though sharing a secret. "Neither do I."

Remy, as if sensing a kindred spirit regarding the weather, went over to her and laid his big head in her lap. She looked down at him with a tiny smile and petted his head.

But then Gordon handed her a plate of food, and she looked up at him with a beaming smile. I called Remy back before he snagged anything off her plate.

Everyone else seemed to ease into good humor, despite the howl of the storm outside. The freely flowing booze certainly helped. Tempted as I was to knock back a few mojitos, I resisted in order to keep a clear head. But how to proceed? I felt like a student facing my first surgery, scalpel clutched in gloved hands, hesitating over how to make the first cut. Too much pressure and you risk slicing through tissues you wish to preserve. Too little and you won't make it through the skin.

Sooner or later, you just have to make the incision.

I lifted my voice above the hubbub of general conversation. "Troy, Liz tells me that one of the streaming channels has started showing *Logan's Law* again. Do actors get any sort of residual when that happens? Seems unfair if they don't."

Troy slid into the spotlight as his preferred place and gave us a short treatise on how royalties worked for reruns, DVDS, and streaming of old shows—the primary characters often got a percentage, but not the secondary ones. He went on to add, "Back before streaming, it was critical to film enough episodes to hit the syndication market. That usually meant somewhere between eighty to a hundred episodes, so that a station could run twenty weeks of weekday showings without a repeat. A show could do really well in syndication, even if it wasn't successful in its first run."

"Like *Star Trek*." I nodded, remembering a time when you could turn on the television almost any afternoon and find the sci-fi show playing somewhere.

Troy nodded, steepling his fingers in an unconscious imitation of one of *Star Trek's* main characters. "Exactly. Since a season was usually about twenty-odd episodes, you needed at least three to four seasons to hit the syndication jackpot."

"You're lucky if you get eight or nine episodes a season now." Manny's contribution was unexpected. "Do we even call them seasons anymore? There's no rhyme or reason to it."

"True." Troy took a sip of his drink. "The flexibility allows actors to take parts in multiple projects at the same time, however. In the past, if you signed up for a series, you had to turn down better offers unless you could break your contract."

"Like that dude who wanted to play Bond," Andrea chimed in. "I mean, he got to play the part eventually, but that was years later."

Time to deepen the incision.

"So, with renewed interest in *Logan's Law*, do you think there will be a reunion show?" I casually helped myself to some more chips to go with my burger.

Right on cue, Liz piped up, "Oh, that would be fun, wouldn't it?"

She rattled off the names of the various actors on the show, listing what projects they were working on now and the likelihood of such a thing coming together. "Of course, you'd have to account for the whereabouts of some characters. Alec Beechwood—the guy who played the crusty old Captain of the department—he'd have long been retired, right? Maybe Logan is Captain now, but neither crusty nor old. Oh, I know, your adoptive daughter Jessica could be a lawyer and she needs your help on a case."

"I don't think there are any plans for a reunion, but if there were, you could write it." Troy chuckled lightly, looking relaxed with one arm over the back of his seat.

"It would be kind of cool, though." Andrea poked Troy's shoulder. "Seriously, Liz is right. You should contact the studio about doing a reunion episode."

"Or even a movie," Joe added, with a tip of his beer bottle in Troy's direction.

"Oh, a movie would be perfect. Even better if you could get everyone to come back, if only for a cameo." Liz ran on, happily expanding her theme. "Of course, not everyone would be available. But I'm sure most people could be talked into returning for a special production."

"Not everyone from the show is still in the business. Sarah Carter, who played Jessica, retired from acting. I think she's a schoolteacher now." Troy's shrug was eloquent.

"But we wouldn't need her to play grown-up Jessica, though she probably could if she wanted to. She had a stunt double, right? The same girl that played one of older kids on the show. What was her name?" Liz frowned as though trying to dredge up the name before snapping her fingers. "I've got it. Tricia. Tricia Markham."

The way Troy froze at hearing Tricia's name sent a sharp stab of disappointment through my gut. I hadn't wanted to think the worst of him, but when he met my gaze over the table, I knew our suspicions were true. He broke eye contact, looking down at the drink in his hands, as though he couldn't bear to face me.

"No, Tricia's not available." Though I spoke quietly, all eyes seemed to turn toward me.

As if following stage directions, the lights flickered, and moments later, there was a loud crack as something heavy hit the side of the building. Hattie jumped with a squeak to grab Gordon's arm, and

Remy pressed hard against my knees, lowering his head into my lap. I gave him a sliver of hot dog on autopilot.

Taking advantage of nature's setup, I dropped my bombshell. "Tricia Markham committed suicide in 2008."

Troy flinched as though I'd hit him and looked up. I stroked Remy's ears, maintaining eye contact with Troy while I added, "Such a sad tale. *Logan's Law* was supposed to be her big break, but everything fell apart after the series ended."

"That's right." Liz's voice had an edge to it now, a knife hidden in a velvet sheath. Her eyes gaze should have burned a hole through Troy where he sat. "I remember. She developed an eating disorder, didn't she? And then got into drugs."

"It's a tough business." After an initial abortive movement, Troy tore his gaze from mine to sit very still, staring at his drink as though it held the secrets of the universe. "There's a lot of pressure on actors to look a certain way and most of us will do anything to achieve the standard."

"That's true of singers, too." Hattie's rich voice seemed to come out of nowhere, and all eyes turned toward her. "And there's so much temptation. Bathtubs full of champagne. Lines on the table. Play with the big boys or risk being thought square. Too square and the next gig doesn't go to you."

Gordon rested his big hand on her shoulder, and she stopped speaking as though the plug had been pulled on her power. Emily's gaze flicked from Hattie to Troy, and a small, vicious smile curved her lips. Joe watched with the deceptive laziness of a lion tracking a herd of gazelles moving into range. He met my stare and nodded ever-so-slightly.

I hated this. Normally I'd do anything to avoid confrontation, to be the one soothing ruffled feathers and keeping the peace. I had to do the exact opposite now. I couldn't risk taking the pressure off Troy. Turning back to him, I said, "Tricia didn't have anyone standing up for her, did she? No one to look out for her interests. She couldn't have been much more than what, eighteen? Nineteen?"

"It's not unusual for older actors to portray teenagers on television. That show set in Beverly Hills? One of the actresses that played a high school student was nearly thirty at the time." The lighting picked out the shine of perspiration gathering at Troy's temples.

"But not in this case. Tricia was only twenty-seven when she died. Ten years after *Logan's Law* began filming. So, she was only seventeen when the show first aired." Liz cocked her head at Troy. "How did she get past the producers on that one?"

"She lied."

Andrea reached for Troy's arm, but he pulled it away as if her touch was acid to his skin.

"She lied about her age, okay? She had a fake ID from Kansas, showing her to be a legal adult. And that's what everyone on the set thought she was. Joked about it too—about her fresh face and how she could pass for a teenager." Troy's face grew redder with every word, and by the time he was finished, a vein throbbed on side of his neck.

"Why would she lie about being older?" Andrea spoke directly to me, clearly confused. "I'd think most actresses would want to hide their true age."

Joe leaned forward to rest his elbows on the table. "There are strict labor laws involving child actors. How much time they're allowed to work. What kinds of scenes they can perform. Allowances for education, percentages to be paid to parents or guardians. Moral laws, too."

Joe's casual addition to the conversation made Troy twitch as though pinched, and then he drained his cup in one swallow. One of the storm shutters bucked and fought against its restraints, banging against the glass. Edna was here in full force, and she wanted in the building.

"Moral laws?" Emily's mocking laugh grated like the scrape of branches against the shutters outside. "You mean because she was underage. What's it called when you sleep with a minor? Statutory rape. Why Troy, you sly dog, you."

"She was almost eighteen. That's legal in California." Predictably, he went on the defensive. "She said she was twenty-one. We believed her. We all believed her."

"And yet you're not denying you slept with her." Emily delivered her stinging rejoinder so rapidly I half expected Troy's head to snap back with the force of it. "I bet the producers would have *loved* that if it had come out."

Troy balled up his plastic cup and threw it down on the table. "What's the point in denying it? There's no one left to whom it matters anymore."

"You mean, there's no one who cares enough about your nonexistent career for you to keep silent any longer." Emily seemed to be taking an inordinate amount of pleasure in seeing Troy squirm.

"I broke it off as soon as I found out the truth." Ignoring Emily, Troy pinned me with a hard stare. "You can believe me or not, I don't care."

"You're right, there isn't anyone to file charges anymore, even if the statute of limitations hadn't run out." Liz's research had paid off, but I needed to hear Troy say it out loud. "But that's not why you paid Brinkman to keep quiet, is it?"

Troy opened his mouth as if to trumpet his innocence, but something in my face seemed to change his mind. He sighed, deflating with the exhale, folding in on himself like a collapsing balloon. "No. I recently auditioned for a role on another show featuring minors. Jeff threatened to go big with Tricia's history unless I paid him. It's a plum part, a chance for a comeback. I couldn't let him torpedo my shot at the role."

I nodded. It fit with the rumors of a new production Liz had found and the contenders for the lead character. Even a hint of past impropriety could be enough for Troy to lose the part.

"He had you over a barrel, didn't he?" The fire in Liz's voice was banked now, but it still glowed with residual heat. "Is that why you let him take compromising photos of you and Andrea together?"

"What? No!" Shock cracked Troy's smooth baritone and he gaped at Liz.

Andrea inhaled sharply as all the color leached from her face. "What are you talking about?"

"Isn't it obvious?" Emily managed to sound cool and mocking despite the sudden spate of rain against the windows making us all jump. "She found Jeff's files."

I glanced at Joe, who gave me the tiniest of nods. We'd agreed earlier that with him being both out of his jurisdiction and the unfamiliar face, it was best if I took the lead on the questioning. The patient was on the table and I was elbows deep in guts. I couldn't bail on the surgery now.

"Jeff had a file on me?" Andrea forced her words between stiff lips, staring at me in frank horror.

I couldn't help the automatic grimace. "Yes. Someone was quite good with a telephoto lens, and you'd neglected to close the blinds."

She wheeled on Troy with a snarl. "Photos of the two of us together? And you knew about it?"

He held his hands up in a gesture of peace. "I swear I knew nothing about it. Andy, you know me. I wouldn't do anything like that."

"I know you'd do anything to get back on camera again." Andrea folded her arms protectively across her chest and glared at Troy. It was probably just as well the cutlery was plastic, otherwise we might have another murder on our hands.

Gordon stood with quiet determination. "Come, Hattie. I think we should be going back to our condo now."

Hattie jerked her arm out from beneath his grip, her eyes snapping with excitement. "Oh pish, this is just getting interesting. I'm not going anywhere."

He tried again to get her to come with him, but she shook her head and crossed her arms, hunching her shoulders as she hunkered down in her seat. With a sigh, he sat back down.

Emily, however, seemed to take this as her cue to leave. "Well, this has been illuminating, but I think I've had enough fun for one evening. I've still got packing to do."

"That's funny. It looked to me like you'd never finished unpacking when I was at your condo yesterday." Turning my attention on Emily was a pleasure. "As a matter of fact, your unit could pass for a major retail outlet. How did you pay for all those flat screen televisions, Emily? Or is it Carol Watkins? Perhaps we should call you Marilyn Rogers?"

Everyone turned to gape at Emily, who had gone rigid when I rattled off a few of the names on the credit card applications. "I don't know what you're talking about."

Two bright pink spots appeared on her cheeks. Darn it, she even blushed prettily.

"I'm talking about credit card fraud. All the purchases present in your condo. How many air fryers does one person need?" I did a quick mental inventory of what I'd seen. "Let's not forget about the boxes of shoes, either."

"No, indeed." Liz's smile looked feral in the garish light. "There are a lot of high-end clothing stores here on the island. I know because Ginny and I went shopping the other day. You really should have stuck to online purchases, Emily. No video of your presence that way. I guess you couldn't resist though. Those Louis Vuitton heels *are* gorgeous on you, and you have the legs to go with them. Still, overdressed for the party, my dear."

Liz flicked her fingers in the direction of Emily's shoes, shiny black pumps with a needle-like heel. I'd thought them impractical, but it had never occurred to me how much they might cost. Good on Liz for spotting that, even though it was risky to assume Emily had gotten them on the island.

I should have known when it came to shopping, my sister knew what she was talking about. Emily's face underwent a strange transformation, blanching out and then turning a sickly green. She worked her mouth several times as she struggled to respond, but before she could speak, Manny shot her a cutting glance and said, "You just couldn't stay out of the stores, could you?"

He then maligned both her intelligence and species, calling her a stupid female dog. Which I found ironic, as most female dogs I know are quite smart indeed.

"Shut up." Emily turned on him, stabbing a finger in his direction. "You shut up."

My grin came easily as I turned toward him. "I don't know, Manny. Buying shoes with stolen identities can't be as dumb as using those same cards to buy prints from my own website in an effort to pass them off as the real deal. Shipping them to properties you own? Even dumber."

It was positively delightful to turn the flames up under his own seat.

"You did what?" Emily screeched, finally losing all appearance of beauty as her rage spewed forth. "Are you kidding me? You used my cards to buy those paintings?"

"Not your cards, sweetheart." Manny got up in her face, and out of the corner of my eye, I saw Joe poised to intervene if he took it any further. "Cards you stole, remember? And it wasn't me, anyway. That was your boyfriend's idea."

"For the last time, he wasn't my boyfriend!" Emily's perfectly manicured nails looked like claws as she curled her fingers in frustration toward his face.

Not to be outdone, Andrea leaped in. "You were sleeping with him!"

"And you were sleeping with Troy, all the while pretending to be the injured party here. Besides, do you think I wanted him? Ew, as if." Emily's dismissive tone was too real to be faked. The blow to her pride was too great, and she seemed compelled to explain herself. "He found out about the identity theft and held it over me. I had no choice. If he and Manny hadn't gotten so greedy, none of this would have been an issue. They couldn't resist trying to steal the paintings. I told them it was too risky, but would they listen? No."

"You keep me out of this." Manny lurched to his feet to yell at Emily. "I had nothing to do with the art theft. He used me as much as he used you. I didn't even know he'd put all those properties in my name."

"And yet, now that he's dead, you're sitting pretty with the lot, aren't you?" Emily got to her feet as well. "Don't play the innocent with me. Jeff dying works out just fine for you, doesn't it?"

"What properties?" Andrea leaned forward to place her hands on the table. "What are you talking about?"

"Nothing to worry your head about because you won't see a dime of it." Emily spoke with malicious relish. Jerking her thumb at Manny, she added, "Everything's in his name."

"What 'everything' are you talking about? If Jeff died with property, then it's mine legally." Andrea pushed to her feet, looking to start a fight.

"Only if he obtained it legally in the first place." The archness in Liz's voice grated like nails on a blackboard, and Andrea's reaction didn't surprise me.

She turned on Liz, nostrils flaring. "You stay out of this. It doesn't concern you."

"Really?" Liz lifted her head like a bull who'd just seen a red flag waving. "Getting drugged at Bennie's and nearly dying as a result doesn't concern me?"

"What?" Andrea reared back momentarily, and then parried again. "Well, if you hadn't been so drunk that night, maybe you'd have paid more attention to what was in your glass. It's your own fault someone spiked them."

"Now see here—" Liz began.

I felt like the man spinning plates in the circus, the one who runs from pole to pole to keep the plates revolving, knowing that sooner or later, they'd all start to fall. I looked to Joe for guidance, but he sat with the patient expression of someone waiting for a mistake to occur. He caught my glance with a slight smile and small shake of his head.

I was to let it play out.

Liz and Andrea might have gone as far as to start pulling hair, only Edna had other ideas. With a bang that sounded like a shotgun had gone off in the room, the wonky shutter blew open and began slamming back and forth against the window. With each crash, Hattie let out a little gasp of fear.

She wasn't the only one. Remy whined and pawed at my leg, causing me to yelp when his claws dug into my skin.

Unfortunately, I couldn't stop to reassure him. I was committed now. Standing up along with the others, I said, "We should move back from the window. Joe, isn't that shutter the one that wouldn't stay latched earlier?"

Troy answered for him. "Yes. I don't see any point in trying to fix it, though. Certainly not in this weather. I'm calling it a night."

"Same here." Gordon agreed readily. "I think we've all had enough for one night."

"I'm with you." Emily distanced herself from Manny and shot us dead with a baleful look.

I was losing control of the scene and we still hadn't proven anything.

At that moment, the lights went out. The room was plunged into a watery gloom, with the rain lashing against the glass. On the radio, a sad flute began playing an accompaniment to the wailing wind. Celine Dion sang that eerie ballad about someone dead and gone who haunted her. It made gooseflesh stand up on my arms. Remy tipped his nose toward the ceiling and uttered a quiet, woeful howl.

"No."

It began as a single word, but rapidly became a chain of noes, each rising in pitch and duration until it turned into a single wail. By the shifting light cast from the window, I could make out Hattie's silhouette as she stood with her hands pressed to her ears.

"Make it stop. Make her stop. Make her stop singing!"

Someone fumbled beside me, reaching across the table. A feeble glow came on from one of the small lanterns Andrea had brought with her.

"I have more," she said, placing the first one in the center of the table. "Hopefully the batteries are stronger."

"Gordie! Make it stop!" Distress wrecked Hattie's voice in a way time had not, splintering it into shards of glass.

"I've got it, my love." Gordon's deep voice rumbled out of the darkness, and the music suddenly switched off.

With Liz's help, Andrea found the rest of the lanterns and turned them on.

One by one, soft yellow glows illuminated the room.

But Hattie remained agitated.

"You heard her." She turned into Gordon's arms and trembled. "Every night in my dreams."

"We should go." Gordon's gaze met mine over Hattie's head, and he tried to steer her toward the door.

"No!" She pushed him away. "The rain. The rain's coming down too hard. We can't see. We should have stayed at the club."

"Uh-oh." Troy's voice was soft beside me. "I think she's having a meltdown."

I wanted to stop it. To wrap my arms around her and soothe her into silence. But I couldn't. *The play's the thing, wherein I'll catch the conscience of the king.*

"That song on the radio. You couldn't get away from it. Stations played it again and again, all summer long."

Hattie paused to sing a few bars, her voice somehow magically transformed into a higher, lighter pitch. It was as though Gordon had never turned the radio off. She ended the lyric with a strangled gasp.

"Raining so hard. Driving down."

She raised her clenched fist and plunged it down repeatedly, as though stabbing something.

"Hattie, love. Let's go." Gordon stepped forward to take her arm again, but she drew back, slapping at his hand.

"No. You leave me be. I'm not going. I'm staying here. I'm safe here." She hugged her arms to herself and rocked back and forth. The shutter slammed against the glass again, and Hattie screamed.

"No! Stop the car!" Hattie threw her hands up over her face. "I didn't see her! I didn't see her."

She broke down into sobs. Gordon gently folded her into his arms. "We know, honey. We know."

"I want to go home. We can go home, can't we, Gordie?" Hattie sounded like a small child, and my heart wept along with her.

"Yes, let's go home, my love." Gordon helped her to her feet.

Instead of moving with him, she clutched at his shirt. "You won't let him take our home, will you? Where would we go?"

A nauseating sense of satisfaction and dread sent my stomach into freefall as soon as the last pieces of the puzzle clicked into place. Brinkman's insatiable need for money and his acquisition of properties. The night at the bar and the likelihood of Tim failing to recognize the danger in the sleeping bear he undoubtedly poked. Hattie's inability to find things in her kitchen and the layer of glitter coating the trash. I wanted to be wrong, but I knew I was right.

I had to clear my throat before I could make the words come out. "You'd do anything to protect Miz Hattie, isn't that right?"

Gordon met my gaze with a fierceness that made me shrink back. He stood, tall and proud, a warrior shielding his own. "That's my job."

I nodded in understanding. "Of course, it is. Miz Hattie needs looking after, and there's no one better at it than you."

His arm tightened around her shoulders. She continued to hide her face against his chest, her sobs trailing away into muffled gasps.

I spoke slowly, as though my words were drowned in molasses, and I had to force each one out. I didn't want to say them, but there was no other way. "I don't know how—maybe Miz Hattie let something slip—but Brinkman found out about the hit-and-run in 2008."

Someone in the room gasped, but I didn't take my eyes off Gordon long enough to figure out who it was.

My voice cracked with strain as I continued. "It ruined her, didn't it? That's why Miz Hattie refused all offers to do a reunion tour. Why she never made it on her own as a solo artist. She was haunted by that night. She thought she didn't deserve success."

Out of the corner of my eye, I saw Andrea open her mouth to speak, but Troy's quick grip of her arm stopped her.

"You've got nothing. You're just fishing." Running full tilt into the coldness of Gordon's eyes was like hitting a brick wall.

"I don't think so." I hated myself for continuing to speak but it was compulsion beyond my control. "Brinkman bled you dry, didn't he? When the police look into your financials, I bet they'll find regular payments that match what Brinkman listed in his private accounts. And after there was no more money to be had, he insisted you turn over your condo to him. Right?"

Gordon didn't respond, but he froze with the wary stiffness of a rabbit hoping not to be noticed by a dog. I was on the right track.

"Of course, he did." I nodded to myself, as though Gordon had confirmed my statement. "But you showed him. A quick bash on the head and problem solved. Right? Only it didn't stop there."

I had the attention of everyone in the room. A tree limb could have crashed through the window and no one would have noticed.

"I think I could have let it go if it *had* stopped there." I let my gaze pass round the room, resting lightly on each of Brinkman's victims. "Jeff Brinkman was a horrible man who tortured each of you in his own way. Many would see his death as justifiable, and I'm not sure I would argue that."

I leveled my gaze on Gordon again. "But it didn't end there. The other night at Bennie's. You were holding Hattie's purse. Does she have a prescription for sleeping pills? How much do you want to bet her prescription matches the drug found in my wine glass that night? The police have a sample. All they need is a drug to match it against."

Gordon tightened his lips as though they held back words that would defend his actions. Any sympathy I might have had for him was crushed under the weight of his silence.

"I might have even been able to overlook *that*," I said, conscious of Liz's indignant bridling at my words out of the corner of my eye. "Only then Tim died. Where does it end, Gordon?"

Still, there were no cracks in his armor. Time to bring out the big guns. "It was a smart move on your part, hiding the murder weapon in a place the police have already searched. But how much do you want to bet that there is some evidence still present on the rolling pin you tossed in the dumpster?"

The utter look of shock on Gordon's face told me I'd nailed it.

"You must have thought you had no other choice. You were on a fixed income and Brinkman stole it all. He tracked it, Gordon. Every penny you gave him." I kept my voice matter of fact, no hint of accusation.

Gordon's hunted gaze traveled slowly around the room, looking for support and finding only our horrified expressions. I could tell the moment he gave up. His shoulders slumped and he seemed to cave in on himself, the years coming to the surface and revealing his true age.

"We had nothing left but the condo." Gordon rubbed Hattie's shoulders as he spoke. "He didn't care that it was our home. That it was a safe, familiar place to her. He didn't care."

"He deserved what he got." The bitterness in Troy's voice was like a poisonous gas leaching out of the shadows, tainting everything in its presence.

"Maybe." I almost agreed with Troy, if only murder hadn't become Gordon's way of solving problems. "But then Gordon had to cover his tracks. He spiked the wine at the bar. Liz almost died."

Gordon shook his head slowly, like a big bear baffled by captivity. "I didn't know Hattie's sleeping pills were so strong. I just wanted you to stop asking so many questions."

I could almost overlook the attack meant for me, but there was more. "What about Tim? How can you justify killing him as well?"

"He was starting up with the same nonsense!" Gordon's voice went hoarse with an unexpected geyser of rage. "Telling me the condo's sale had to go through, that he expected the payments to continue. I couldn't let him do that to us. To her."

He placed a large hand over his face and began to cry. "I just wanted to take care of Hattie."

Chapter Twenty-Seven

"That's the last of the luggage." I shut the back of the Subaru. "We're ready to go just as soon as Joe gets back with Remy. It's a long drive. I wish we could have started sooner."

It was the final day of our trip. Hurricane Edna had blown out a few days before, and though there were broken branches and storm detritus scattered about the complex, the sun shone down from a nearly cloudless blue sky. It was back to business as usual for the island, including the tourist trade.

Liz, dressed to reintegrate back into her soccer-mom life, dropped her movie-star sunglasses over her eyes. "I know you would have preferred leaving before dawn—seriously, you must have gotten that trait from Dad—but I for one am glad the first ferry doesn't run before nine. Just be glad the harbor is open again. What are you going to do with the key to 1302?"

"I'll take it when you're ready." Andrea shielded her eyes with one hand. "I decided to apply for the manager position. The development was desperate enough to say yes."

"Don't sell yourself short." Whatever animosity Liz had held for Andrea had dissipated in the aftermath of the storm. "You'll do great."

"I can hardly do worse than my former husband." Andrea laughed nervously and gave a helpless shrug.

"Well I, for one, feel better knowing you'll be in charge. What with me being an absentee owner." I gave her a reassuring smile. "I trust you to look out for my interests when I'm not here."

"It's the least I can do, given all the trouble Jeff caused for you." She tipped her head to one side. "Were you able to recover the paintings?"

I waggled a hand from side to side. "Yes and no. Yes, we found the buyers, but one of them is contesting our right to the painting. We'll prove provenance, of course, but they're threatening to take us to court."

"A decent lawyer will tell them to cut their losses and not throw good money after bad." Liz waved off the potential lawsuit as if it were nothing more than a bothersome mosquito.

"I'm sorry, just the same." Andrea lifted a hand to stop me from replying. "I know, I know. Not my fault. But I was married to him after all."

She shook her head. "I knew he was less-than-honest. Heck, I didn't trust him as far as I could throw him. But I had no idea he was so—horrible—in his quest for money."

"At least Emily and Manny got their comeuppances." Liz practically beamed at me. "When you laid everything out for Deputy Wilson, it was so satisfying to see those two arrested for their crimes."

"No small thanks to you." I gave Liz the credit she deserved. "Your suggestion to check the video footage at the expensive shops gave them the evidence they needed to nail Emily for the credit card fraud. She rolled over on Manny with everything she knew about Brinkman's various schemes in order to cut herself a deal."

It had been satisfying to see the law come for both Manny and Emily, even if I'd only heard about it after the fact. What hurt was knowing that the police had come for Gordon, too. A sigh escaped me. "I hated having to call Wilson out that night to arrest Gordon, but I was honestly afraid for his mental health—and Hattie's well-being—once it was clear there was no way out for him."

"You made the right call." Andrea gave me a tight smile. "It had to be done. He was determined to take out anyone who he deemed was a threat to Hattie. Where would it have stopped?"

I ached for them just the same. The love the two of them shared had seemed so perfect; something to aspire to. Had it been toxic all along? Or had Gordon's actions been born out of desperation from a man who saw his ability to take care of the woman he loved fail with his increasing age and lack of power? I didn't know. I'd never know.

"I still don't understand how you connected the rolling pin to Gordon, or how you knew he'd put it in the dumpster after the police had already searched it." Andrea pushed a hand through her hair with a frown and a slight shake of her head.

"After Tim's murder, I was in Hattie's kitchen while she was baking. She was using a glass to roll out and cut cookies and complaining how her utensils had gone missing. I didn't think much of it at the time." I was a terrible cook and only a moderately successful baker and had been known to make do with whatever I had on hand. Besides, there had been the accident with the salt, and Hattie had overlooked the mixer sitting right in front of her. "When I went out to the dumpster, I happened to notice the rolling pin. But most of the dumpster—including the bags the police had opened during their search—was covered with body glitter. The rolling pin was shoved beneath a stroller, but neither one had glitter on it. Someone had to have dumped the makeup after the police search, and the rolling pin came along after that."

No doubt, the police would interview the residents and determine the timeline for when the glitter appeared.

"What's going to happen to Hattie?" Liz caught her lower lip in her teeth in concern.

For once, Liz was thinking about someone other than herself, and I wanted to hug her. I might have done so, only the Reese family weren't huggers.

"Well, I made a few phone calls." Andrea grimaced even as her face reddened. She practically dug her toe into the ground with embarrassment. "You know those friends of hers? The singers who wanted to do a reunion tour? They never understood why Hattie refused to join them. Anyway, her friend, Alma Elliot, did pretty well for herself as a vocalist, and she's offered to let Hattie live with her. She's in a position to give Hattie the care she needs."

"Oh, that's such good news. That's so wonderful of you. I'm so glad you thought to do that." A weight I hadn't even realized I carried slid off my shoulders. When I looked at Andrea, I saw a woman determined not to be defined by the mistakes of her past. Someone I could call a friend.

"What about Troy?" Liz asked, in a slightly subdued manner.

Andrea lifted both hands in an exaggerated shrug. "He's talking about selling his condo. He got the part on the television show, so he's not going to be here much anyway. I told him not to be an idiot—keep the unit as a rental property. That way it can bring in an income and he has a fallback plan if the show never makes it past the pilot stage."

My feelings for Troy were mixed. Yes, Tricia had lied about her age, but a man in his thirties would have been better off not chasing after a girl who could pass for a teenager. At the same time, it was no skin off my nose if Troy wanted to live at the Sand Dollar. "Tell him there's no need to move on my account. It's not like I'll be here all that much either."

Andrea nodded briskly once, acknowledging my stance.

From the direction of the beach, Remy and Joe came into sight. Spying us by the car, Remy began tugging on the leash, and I watched as Joe got his attention and asked him to walk quietly beside him. Remy looked up at him with his mouth open and tongue out in an expression that would be called a grin on a human. He pranced happily alongside Joe as they crossed the street and entered the parking lot.

"Hooo-ie." Andrea let out a low whistle. "That's one good-looking man."

While I mentally agreed with her, the acknowledgment came with a sharp burst of annoyance, followed by a trickle of doubt. Was I really considering opening my life—and heart—back up to potential hurt simply because of a physical attraction? My track record with relationships, including this one, hadn't been very good.

As though aware we were all staring, Joe lifted a hand in greeting and continued his approach. Surely, we had more in common than old, if potent, memories? There were the dogs, for one. Our young dogs enjoyed playing together, and it was no hardship to hang about the pool in the evenings watching them romp and swim. I liked the fact we could sit in each other's company without feeling the need to fill the space with empty words, and that we enjoyed the same books and movies. Joe had reintroduced me to the joys of long trail rides in the woods, and I liked exploring new hiking paths with him. We'd both realized that city life wasn't for us and respected the fact each other's jobs could pull us away at a moment's notice, placing heavy demands on our mental health as well.

Was that enough to rekindle a relationship?

An unfamiliar emotion washed over me, and it took me a second to realize I missed Greenbrier. I wanted to sip tea on my balcony overlooking the valley and watch the sun rise. I longed to see the horses again, to have Ming wind his way between my legs, and to see Remy's joy on reuniting with Toad. I wanted to catch up with old friends and hear about Lucinda the cow's latest escapade. To exchange burning sand and the tang of salt air for green mountains and the smell of honeysuckle. Heck, I even wanted to see my mother again.

Most of all, I wanted to move forward with my plans to build my own clinic and yes, see where this budding thing with Joe went.

"There you are," I said as Joe and Remy joined us. Remy swung his body from side to side, curling himself around me with little "whoo-whoos" of joy. I could have been talking to either him or Joe. Or both of them. "Let's go home."

The End

M.K. Dean lives with her family on a small farm in North Carolina, along with assorted dogs, cats, and various livestock.

She likes putting her characters in hot water to see how strong they are. Like tea bags, only sexier.

Under the name McKenna Dean, she has penned several books in the award-winning Redclaw Origins and Redclaw Security series. If you like your mysteries with a paranormal flair, check out McKenna Dean's books as well!

If you enjoyed this story, please consider leaving a review on the platform of your choice. Reviews help with visibility, and therefore sales. Likewise, be sure to recommend it to your friends. Every recommendation means more than you could know.

If you want to follow M.K. Dean on social media, be sure to check out her linktree account: https://linktr.ee/McKenna_Dean. All important links are there, including how to sign up for her newsletter, follow her blog, or find out when the next Ginny Reese book is coming out!

Ginny Reese Mysteries:

As a house-call veterinarian, Dr. Ginny Reese has seen her fair share of the weird and wacky. Having returned to her hometown to take care of her ailing father, it was up to her to make ends meet in any way she could. Little did she know that making house-calls would put her in the path of murder--and give her the resources to make a difference in her small Southern community.

With her boisterous German Shepherd at her side, a mother you love to hate, and the return of her ex-boyfriend as the new sheriff in town, Ginny has her hands full--especially as the bodies start to pile up!

An Embarrassment of Itches: https://www.amazon.com/gp/product/B099QVRT7J

It's the start of a rough day when house-call veterinarian Ginny Reese discovers the body of a wealthy client floating facedown in her swimming pool. Things get worse when the new sheriff turns out to be Ginny's ex and she becomes the number one suspect in her client's murder!

It's up to Ginny and her trusty German Shepherd, Remington, to find the real killer before her old boyfriend arrests her for murder.

The Dog Days of Murder: https://www.ama-
zon.com/dp/B09V5MQFK5

The fur flies when a smoking hot newcomer scoops up the veterinary practice Ginny Reese was negotiating to buy. When Ginny finds the body of the new vet shortly after the woman had a confrontation with Ginny's mother, Julia Reese becomes the number one suspect in the murder.

It's up to Ginny and her trusty German Shepherd, Remington, to find the real killer before her mother goes down for murder.

A Corpse in the Condo: https://www.amazon.com/gp/prod-
uct/B0C26DPBB7

Vacations are supposed to be fun, but when house-call veterinarian Ginny Reese tries to combine checking out an inherited property with reconciling with her prickly sister, things quickly get out of hand. First there's a dead body in the condo. Second, a fortune in artwork is missing. Now with access to the mainland cut off and a hurricane blowing in, it's up to Ginny and her friends to solve the crime before the evidence gets washed away.

Made in United States
Orlando, FL
19 December 2023

41144541R00163